Whispers of the She-Wolf
Pauline Walters

Cover by Yosbe – https://www.instagram.com/yosbedesign/

Editing by:

- Callie – https://www.instagram.com/cjeditingservices/

- Elle – https://www.instagram.com/lavendellebooks/

- Elaine – https://www.instagram.com/elaines.proofreading.editing/

- Emma – https://www.instagram.com/emmasbookpage/?hl=en

Edition 2025

Contents

For the ones who were told to be quiet, to look down, and to
stay on their path.
Slay, queens, slay.

This book contains dark themes.

Death, violence, blood, gore, murders, mention of rape, mention of SA, mention of paedophilia, captivity, mention of mental and physical torture, biting, swearing, assault, abduction.

Reader discretion is strongly advised; your mental health matters.

Part 1

CHAPTER I

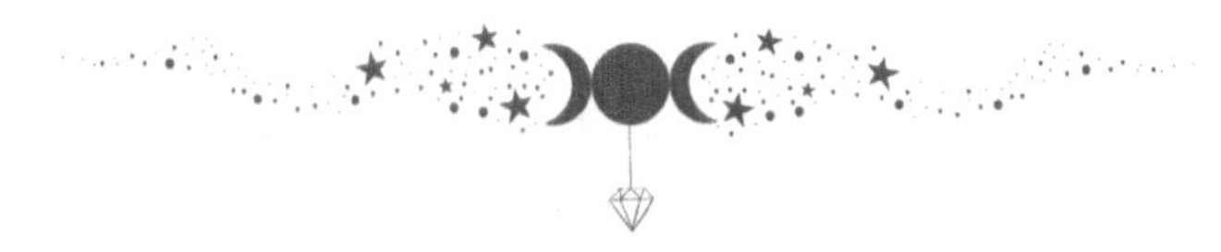

ANGELINE SNAPPED OUT OF her daydream, yanked back to reality by her shrieking siblings. She shivered and glanced at her younger sisters and brothers, who screamed joyously as the falling rain drenched their fancy clothes. The redhead giggled at the sight, but remained in her corner of the garden under the oak tree's protection. She missed innocence, missed playing in the cool rain.

Sometimes, Angeline liked nothing more than moping about her life. What she was seeing was that *she* could not run in the rain, because if she did, she would receive one of those disappointed looks her father, Duke Louis Delacour, was an expert at. It was known he was becoming grumpy with his oldest daughter—or at least the one with a beating heart—who was still unmarried, with no prospects. Not a single prospect, at the tragic age of twenty years old.

Among the many reasons he blamed his daughter for being unmarried, he considered her immaturity at the top of the list. Hence, the forbidden dance in the rain.

She used to do that a lot.

Angeline disagreed and thought she was au contraire, quite mature. Not only was she the smartest of the Delacour ladies, all centuries included, but she also had an extensive knowledge of magic and a history of magic. As she tried to remind her father, unlike many ladies she knew, she could converse with any man, either a millennial creature or a werewolf from the wildest pack on Earth. That should count for something, shouldn't it?

No, it didn't. Her previous prospects had told Louis his daughter had too many grand ideas.

So, immature? Really? No, Monsieur.

She *wanted* to get married, just not to the first idiot who presented himself to her, assuring her the world was flat. There's only so much stupidity a lady can take, after all. She had always known she would have to get married one day and wouldn't have a choice in the groom, but she had hoped at least to have a few to pick from.

Angeline sighed and put down her paintbrush. Dark clouds floated overhead, and rain beat powerfully on the ground, with wind coming from the south. She knew she had to protect her work. Gathering her few possessions with haste, she nodded at Markan, her favorite security guard, whom Louis had allocated to her safety. The bulky vampire advanced toward her, holding an umbrella to help the young lady stay dry on the way to the castle.

As far as bodyguards went, Angeline appreciated Markan. He knew how to give her space, which was rare in the castle. Unlike most men she knew, he did not have questionable thoughts about her. Even though he kept calling her "Princess" despite her telling him she was just a Lady.

The young woman walked back toward the west wing, her side of the castle. She had managed years ago to convince her parents to give her some space. They had grudgingly agreed to it after she told them she could feel one too many thoughts coming from their minds, including forbidden desires a young lady should not know of.

Angeline took a deep breath while accelerating her pace. She always regretted her decision to tell her parents about her gift. Well, *part* of her gifts.

Her Spirit-Gifts—empathy and telepathy—were not something to be messed with, she knew that now. It was more than a gift; it was a curse that could make your life harder if you were not careful.

At seven years old, her empathy activated. What was considered simple intuition became more. She could perceive people's feelings, knowing who to avoid, who to trust, and who was lying. For three years, like a little shadow, she barely left her father's side, nodding her head toward him whenever she could feel that Louis's interlocutor was hiding something. As a reward, she received one of his rare smiles.

As a little girl, she enjoyed this; she cherished those moments stolen with her father. Her presence during important meetings allowed parties to come to a peaceful agreement without bloodshed, and Angeline was proud of her contribution.

At ten years old, her telepathic gift—or curse—began. That was when everything changed. Her magic exploded, dominating her. Unwanted thoughts reached her young brain, actual words, images, and sounds. The influx of thoughts perpetually hurt her, resulting in headaches she had never known before, like daggers in her skull.

She wished she were dead.

At the sight of their daughter in pain, her parents showed a slight panic, asking what was happening. A young Angeline made a single mistake.

"I hear voices." She cried, holding her head between two hands, digging into her flesh with her nails, and rocking back and forth on the bed.

Louis's first thought? "What is this again? Those damn witches and their weird child."

Isabeau's first thought? "As long as we can still use her."

She felt their fear. She heard the word "telepath," and their reaction to the simple word was nowhere close to the comfort she needed. The fear of her gift evolving into something they would have no control over. Being an empath was fine, but being a telepath? She knew she should shut up, and shut up fast, before her family learned the truth.

She understood that when you live for a millennium, like her parents, you have many secrets—including some you wish nobody ever learned.

So, she lied. She became an expert at it. The lie she had been living for the past ten years ate her up sometimes, but Louis and Isabeau's reaction was not enough for the demanding child. She kept the full extent of her gift quiet, but they were her parents, weren't they? Who else could she trust with such heavy information?

She resented her parents for their reaction; the souvenir of their fear and panic would almost make her laugh if it did not make her so morose. Worst of all, she began doubting their genuine love for her. She already knew her family was different. After all, one does not cherish one-hundred-something children all the same; only the perfect children, the useful ones, were adored.

After that day, every time her magic evolved, she turned it off. She didn't say a word. She took it all alone, learning as she went and putting her faith into the few people she could trust.

There was one thing you learn when growing up among vampires: you do not want them to know you can hear their thoughts.

Angeline despised herself for these thoughts. She hated that she resented her parents for not standing by her when she needed them the most. She abhorred even more that she could hear all of her past suitors' disgusting thoughts, especially Paul, the most obsessed.

He terrified her, and she did her best to avoid him, making a point to never be alone with him. It sometimes ruined her day, as she had to play hide-and-seek in her home. She knew Louis was close to forcing her to marry Paul, and it was only thanks to her empathic fake gift that she had convinced her father to wait a bit longer. Knowing the right words to say could sometimes be quite useful, and she was the master at it.

Angeline stepped into her bedroom and the hair on her arms raised; she hid a smile while bowing her head and turned toward Markan.

"You can leave now. Jack is here."

CHAPTER 2

THE PALE VAMPIRE GLANCED at her. His dark eyes were lifeless, but she was sure he was ready to argue. His sole mission in life was to protect her. Markan had recently started this job and was probably just getting used to her. The creak of the heavy door interrupted him. It opened to reveal Angeline's favorite person in the world, her brother, Jack the Pirate.

The young woman laughed heartily and jumped onto Jack's neck, enjoying his positive energy wrapping around her. Of all the vampires she knew, Jack was the only one who never lied to her. As a telepath, she appreciated it. Her brother was one of the few to know about her talent and had been keeping the heavy secret. He was more than happy to do something against Louis's knowledge, but secretly wished to be present the day their father would learn the truth.

Everything she knew about intimate relations was from Jack and his dirty memories. The pirate enjoyed sharing a bit too much with whoever wanted to hear about what he called his *'body count.'* As one of Louis's Daughters, it was out of the question for Angeline to know anything before her wedding night, which she found hypocritical, knowing what would be expected from her on the day.

Angeline could still remember what she saw in some of her older sister's memories, a mix of surprise and shame. For many of them, there was also pain. Jack had guaranteed her it would not last, and if she needed, he would teach her future husband to please her. Angeline had almost choked on her breath and ran away from her crazy brother.

After that day, she took to wearing an amethyst pendant, hanging on a silver chain around her neck. It allowed her to control her gift a tad more, only picking up the thoughts she wanted to hear. The stone was a gift from the witch Nanabrok, blessed with her powerful Earth magic—the healing magic.

She adored Jack with all her might, but he was indeed a notorious nymphomaniac and was fine with it. He loved everything: men, women, men and women together. The kinkier, the better. Outsiders could wonder how Louis was leaving Jack to stay with his children, but she knew why, because she had read it in his mind. Louis only tolerated Jack because he provided his family with all the riches one could hope for. Piracy was a well-paid activity, even in the 21st century. Angeline could not complain about his presence, as he was her best friend, who drowned her in gifts of stolen silk and diamonds.

She pulled Jack into her bedroom and closed the door in Markan's face before he could protest.

"New bodyguard?" Jack asked, his head still turned toward the space where Markan had been standing. Jack's eyes sparkled with his usual lust.

Angeline sighed and gave him a slight tap on the arm. "Yes, and you must not break his heart like the last one. I like this one. He's giving me space, and he doesn't talk."

Jack chuckled and caught an apple from the fruit basket in Angeline's room. With his mouth full, he asked, "So... what's new?"

"Do you want good news or bad news?"

"Please start with the good."

"Well, I have finished a new dress. It's gorgeous and will fit perfectly with this sapphire necklace you promised me *months* ago." Angeline smirked.

Her brother pulled the most gorgeous necklace she had ever seen out of his coat.

She gasped. "Jack!" Her fingers brushed against the sparkling stone. "It's even better than I imagined."

"Only the best for the most beautiful woman on Earth."

Angeline rolled her eyes and turned, showing her neck. She removed her protective pendant with graceful fingers before wrapping it around her wrist.

The dark-haired vampire placed the expensive necklace around her frail neck and whistled. "Damn, it *does* look good."

"I know." Angeline stepped toward her mirror to admire her new prize. She didn't care about how her brother could bring back all those wonders. Vampires had to steal sometimes—or every time.

She felt the turmoil in Jack's brain before he spoke, and turned to him with curiosity. Out of respect, she waited for him to speak. Thanks to her pendant, she could usually not hear him unless she called to the stone. The pendant did not interrupt the gift of empathy, but the gift never disturbed her, especially when her only company was Jack. The vampire placed a hand on his chin, as if he were deep in his thoughts.

"Jack?"

He sighed. "Louis told me earlier that we will celebrate a wedding soon. I'm guessing that's your bad news?"

Her shoulders fell, and life drained from her face.

"I don't know what to do, Jack," she whispered. "I can't marry Paul." She barely said his name, but knew her brother could hear her anyway. "We are *not* celebrating anything".

"That's what I told our father. I made it clear that I would not support it and that I was ready to go to the extent of burning Germany to the ground. Nobody would miss them anyway."

Angeline felt a slight hope rising inside her. "You did? Well, what did he say?"

Jack moved his hand, as if to clean the nasty thoughts flying around him. "He knows I'm serious about it, but... it seems he is more scared of Paul than my pirates."

Angeline held back a chuckle. She didn't need to hear his thoughts to know what he was thinking. She could feel his arrogance and pride leaking all over his brain. He held 'his' pirates in high regard. They had all been converted to vampirism by him, picked with caution according to precise criteria, and as a result, treated him like a king.

She paced around the room. "Paul has been threatening him, only so lightly that it doesn't feel like an actual threat. He has this entire plan in his mind, ready to jump to action at the first sight of weakness from Father." Her lower lip trembled.

"Oh, sister, come here."

She threw herself into Jack's embrace. There were not many men from whom she could appreciate this kind of touch.

Jack stepped back to lower his blue eyes onto her.

"I do not want you to stress about this, or to make harsh decisions. Whatever happens, I've got your back. The entire crew of Pirates of the Caribbean has your back."

Angeline giggled between two sniffles and let her brother continue.

"Here's what we'll do, my darling," he whispered so quietly she had to lean in to hear him, enjoying the soft nickname. Jack was the only one who called her that. Her parents had long ago stopped showing affection to their children, especially her.

"If Louis is making a plan you do not enjoy, I will take you away with me." To Angeline's surprise, he continued, "I do not fear our father, and he knows better than to follow us into my territory. He won't stand a chance there. You do not owe this family anything. You can live perfectly on your own; you can pick the family you want. And your magic, My Love—*my God*—your magic. It's amazing, it's powerful—"

"It's not—"

"It *is*. I talked to Nanabrok, I talked to Misa. They both said that you are going to grow even more once you give yourself to a man. You may even be able to protect yourself. Now, how good would *that* be?"

"We don't know that... no virgin ever..."

"Ever survived, yes, I'm well aware. But here you are, twenty years old and nowhere close to danger. Nobody knows how your magic will develop, but I bet you it will be absolutely terrific."

Angeline threw him a hopeful look, wishing it could be true.

"I promise you, sister, everything is gonna be fine."

Angeline laughed and wiped the last of her tears, already regretting showing her childish, self-conscious side, but her brother had a way of breaking down her defenses.

The witch he spoke about, Nanabrok, was one of the oldest witches on Earth. She had been the wise leader of the French Coven for the past seven hundred years and had become an excellent friend. She explained to the young Delacour many times, from a very young age, what her magic was and where it came from.

"Your power," Nanabrok would say, "comes from the Spirits of the Magical World themselves, a gift that makes you unique."

Angeline always felt a surge of pride at that idea.

Unfortunately, it also meant she was what the witches called, the dreaded name of "Magical Virgin". She despised this appellation for obvious reasons. She hated even more that magical virgins could hurt no one, or the magic would turn against them.

What a stupid plot hole.

Her mind drifted back to when she was a little girl, pestering the old witch to explain to her, again and again, all that she knew about her magic. The white-haired, old hag would then bend down over the eager young brat, whispering tales of magic and hope, making sure the parents of the little one could not hear her.

"Magical Virgins are rare, Angeline," she'd say, her voice soft but intense. "So rare, they're precious. And so precious, they're desired. But such desire comes at a cost. Most don't live long."

Which is why there were not many of them in the world. There was one. The Spirits seemed quite prudent in allowing one to be born, as their magic was so powerful that it could throw off the balance of the world.

When Angeline was born, and a powerful magic was placed inside her body, Nanabrok knew a choice had to be made. All previous solutions to protect a Magical Virgin had failed over the past centuries.

When previous witches tried to hide them, they were still found.

Others tried to raise those girls as one of their own, but it didn't end well.

When Nanabrok saw Angeline's birth in one of her dreams, she tried something new. She placed the adorable baby under the protection of one of the most fearsome vampires in the world, Louis Delacour. She had been at war against the vampires for over 400 years. As a show of peace, she offered them a beautiful newborn with big blue eyes—a little girl.

The vampires were surprised at first, but Isabeau—Louis's wife—only needed one look at the baby girl to know she wanted the baby to be hers. They had hundreds of children, all adopted, as vampires could not procreate.

So, what was one more?

The only thing Nanabrok mentioned to them was that Angeline would probably show some magic later in life, but she didn't tell them anything about the Magical Virgin business.

"The less they know, the better," Nanabrok murmured to herself, and the young girl, once she could understand her, determined to see this one live past fifteen. And she did.

But then, thought Angeline, *it's easy not to get hurt when you grow up in a golden cage.*

Nanabrok's plan was good. Angeline was protected, away from anyone who could want to hurt her, with nobody questioning why she would be hidden in a golden cage. This was how Delacour's daughters were raised.

The young woman pouted while pulling harder on Jack's arm, forcing him to keep up with her. She knew her friend

Misa, from the werewolf pack, had just given birth to a new baby boy. She thought two days of waiting was polite enough, and now she wanted to visit her furry friends. She and her brother headed for the stables, to Jack's disagreement. He offered to carry her in his arms or on his shoulders, but Angeline frowned and declared that was not ladylike.

See Father? How mature am I?

The redhead went straight for the energetic mustang in the biggest stable. Tempete-Storm, her favorite horse. She had not been original in naming him, but after meeting him there was no other name that would suit this *'demon of a horse'*, as her father had called him. Louis had been furious that his new acquisition had shown nothing but rebellion against the vampire and was close to breaking his neck when a thirteen year old Angeline stepped up and asked for a chance to tame the beast.

Which she did. It was easy to tame animals when you could hear them, talk to them, and understand their grievances against you.

She laughed when she glanced at her brother, who was getting confused with the lead of his four-legged partner. A few minutes later, Tempete galloped through the forest with Angeline on his back. She laughed out loud. Riding was one of the best sensations she knew, and trusting her favorite horse with her safety was so natural that she didn't even try to control him.

Behind her, Jack pestered his horse. He was not an expert horseman. She gave him the kindest horse, Mirana, but even this horse could not deal with the unnatural, dead being on her back.

Poor Jack, she thought.

Not only had Angeline forced him to accompany her to the wolves instead of him sneaking around with one of their new maids, but now she knew she would hear complaints about his hurt bottom for the rest of the day.

As Angeline and her complaining escort galloped toward the pack's home, the warm summer breeze carried scents of pine from the forest, almost covering the musky smell of the horses. The pack's territory was a short ride from Delacour's castle, which was why they had been busy with multiple wars over the centuries against the Delacour home. Rumors were that the wolves were here before a mortal Louis arrived. Louis, of course, disagreed and insisted—to whoever asked—that he and Isabeau were on the gorgeous land way before the damn beasts.

When Angeline was young, she could only glimpse the wolves from afar. Her parents were strict about keeping her away from them, whispering, "They're dangerous, Angeline. Unpredictable. They could eat you!"

The peace between vampires and witches was stable, but as for werewolves, it rested on such a thin layer of ice that she was not allowed to meet them alone. A single bite, and that would bring them into a new war.

The possibility of harmony between all species only became an option when Quentin took his place as the new Alpha, succeeding his demon of a father, according to Louis. The young Alpha was determined to reach trust between vampires, werewolves, and witches, but especially with his closest neighbors, the Delacours. Louis was wary of watching his back on the full moon, so they agreed to peace, thanks to Angeline's empathy. She assured her father of Quentin's willingness.

This accord was so successful that nearly every European nation followed in their steps, allowing the most flourishing magical kingdoms in every corner of the Old Continent.

The Alpha of the French Pack, Quentin, was a typical countryside Frenchman; he was abrupt-looking, with fair skin and a permanently grumpy expression. He was quite wide for his height and an outstanding leader to his pack.

He had found his wife, his mate, nineteen years ago in a werewolf tribe in Africa. Unlike him, Misa was the tallest woman Angeline had ever seen. Her skin was of the darkest color, and she proudly showed a shaved head.

During the third Peace Anniversary gathering, Angeline had her first real memory of the Alpha's mate—the Luna. The night was humid, as it always was during summer, and the sky was bursting with fireworks. Angeline was a clumsy ten-year-old little girl in a fluffy lace dress. She had a perpetual frown on her forehead due to the cacophony in her young mind, which had just awakened. Amidst the explosions of light and sound, Angeline looked up and saw Misa smiling—her sharp white teeth reflecting the bright colors of the fireworks. Misa didn't dare talk to her.

Angeline knew it was because of her parents watching her every move, but the following day, they met again. She slipped away from her maids and guards to sneak to her favorite place on earth, the waterfalls. The sun was too strong. It was the middle of summer, and Angeline hated the heat, especially with those gowns her mother forced her to wear. The young girl enjoyed dipping her feet in the freshwater, thinking about how her parents reacted to the simple mention of 'voices.' If only they knew all that she could hear, they would either use her till her death, or they would make her disappear.

Angeline bit her lips, still unsure about the whole thing, but Nanabrok always said the most important thing with any magic was to follow your instincts. Her instinct was to yell at her to shut the fuck up in front of her parents, but Angeline was a good girl. She was serious about her studies, always respected the rules—even the stupid ones—and didn't like lying.

She felt Misa's presence before she saw her—a gentle, calm feeling, as if the woman knew how to approach the young girl. Angeline turned, surprised to find Misa standing nearby, her towering figure draped in a simple white dress. Without a word, Misa approached and sat beside her on the rocks, keeping her gaze soft, and the sound of her mind as gentle as a river. She was one of the most beautiful women Angeline had ever met, and she was surrounded daily by the mystical beauty of vampires.

Are you all right, little one? Misa's voice didn't break the silence; it filled her mind, resonating like a lullaby.

Angeline gasped, scared, but instantly quieted down when she heard the peaceful flow of thoughts of the werewolf.

Everything is going to be fine, little one. Misa's thoughts were the most peaceful hum Angeline had heard in weeks.

It made her want to cry. Angeline took a deep breath. *I am scared.* She answered in her mind, but realized Misa could not hear her.

"I know," she said out loud.

At the surprised fish face Angeline showed, Misa laughed.

"You can hear or make people hear," she says. "Don't be afraid. With time, your magic will be a new hope for many of us."

"What... Do you mean by that?"

"You will see. When the time is right, you will know."

Misa held her hand and caught Angeline's frail hands in hers. "Do not let anyone dictate how to deal with it. It's yours, nobody else's. And you have friends, friends who do not fear what you may hear."

Angeline bit her lips. "Father and Mother, they don't like it anymore. I can't tell them," she whispered.

"I know." Misa chuckled. "I don't think they would have let you out of the house if they knew all those amazing things you can do. Your parents think they protect you, but you are meant to walk paths they don't understand yet." She took a break. "At the next full moon, come with us. We won't hurt you. I think you need to see what freedom means to understand how to use your magic in the future."

And she had been right. After that day, Angeline found herself returning to Misa's pack. Sneaking out became her ritual under the full moon's glow, where Misa and Quentin welcomed her as one of their own.

It was on one of those nights that she quickly met the spirit she would come to cherish above all others: her twin wolf. A sleek, playful creature, a bunch of fluffy white fur, who was always getting her into trouble. Her She-Wolf.

CHAPTER 3

T HE EVENING AIR IN the stables was filled with the earthy smell of hay and the comforting sound of horses quietly chewing. Angeline took a deep breath, savoring the peace as she ran her fingers along Tempete's gorgeous black coat. She fed him an apple she had stolen from the kitchen. Angeline used to braid his hair with pretty pink bows, but the horse begged her to stop through their mental link after a few days. She enjoyed the quiet of the horse's thoughts, minding their business, eating sweets, and the adrenaline still running through the black mustang.

A swirl of anxious thoughts broke through her calm, and she turned to face Jack.

He had been unusually quiet all the way back from the pack, right after checking his mobile phone. She was not allowed to own one at the castle. As expected, Quentin and Misa's little boy was as cute as possible. Now she was a godmother to two baby wolves, and she was not sure how Louis would react to the news—he had quite a strong opinion about her being too close with werewolves despite the peace between the two species.

Raising an eyebrow at Jack, she patiently waited for him to talk.

Jack smiled, but a tension remained in his eyes. "Damn, you're good. I was barely figuring out how to talk to you."

"Since when do you have trouble talking to me?" The red-head retorted, giving a last caress to the horse before heading toward the stable doors, knowing her brother would follow.

"I... have to go away for a little while... again." His words were hesitant—unusual for Jack—and he grimaced.

Angeline rotated on her feet to face him, tense. "But you said—"

"I know what I said, but Father seems to think I could help with... some trouble we heard from Italy." His hand shook, holding his damn phone. She hated how those things kept people away from good, old-fashioned communication.

She narrowed her eyes and crossed her arms. "How? There are no pirates in Italy." Angeline rolled her eyes and stormed off in a huff. She was being selfish, but it was only because she was terrified.

"Angeline, come on!" He ran after her.

"You know Father is getting serious about Paul," she said. "I told you, you *can't* leave me now. He will sneak a wedding on me!"

"He won't, and even if he does"—Jack caught up with her and took her hands in his—"then it won't be before at least two or three months, which will give us plenty of time to decide what color you want to paint your room at your new house in the Caribbean." He flashed her a reassuring grin.

Angeline took a deep breath, blinking away tears. "I don't want to be this way, Jack," she muttered. "I feel so weak and useless."

All the rides and the strength she had gained at her friend's place faded, and Angeline felt like the useless little girl she was, with magic that could not protect her or the people she loved.

Jack's expression softened, and he cupped her face in his hands. "Of all the things in this world, Love, you are the least useless. I am going to Italy, just to check out the situation with some old friends of mine, and I'll come back. If Louis doesn't change his mind, we will leave together. I won't leave you behind, ever."

Angeline could only nod, hoping in her heart that Jack would keep this promise.

After watching him drive away in one of the many cars her father owned, she stood at the top of the stone steps for too long.

She didn't have time to think more about his departure. It was almost dinner time, and she knew her absence or tardiness would not be tolerated. She had to say goodbye for now. The thought of him going away still hurt, but she knew he would never leave her if he didn't have a good reason. She regretted not asking him about the Italian trouble he had to check out. It was unusual for Louis to ask anything from Jack except to retrieve diamonds and money. Her father had always considered his son to be too unpredictable, immature. The fact Jack was ruling over an entire ocean with his pirates was barely talked about.

Angeline shook her shoulders, not wanting to think more of it, and hurried inside the manor. She had to get rid of the horse smell on her. The last thing she needed was another disgusted face from her father, which was her fate at least once a week, depending on what she did wrong. She almost reached the entrance of her wing, but could not help but gasp at who she spotted walking toward the dining room.

Angeline straightened her shoulders, kept her eyes cold, and acknowledged her father's guest with a simple nod.

"Uncles. What a surprise." Indeed, a surprise it was.

Leonard and Lucius were far from her favorite beings. Louis's blood brothers had been made vampires around the same time as Louis, who could not resist having his brothers by his side for eternity. According to most of the vampire Lords she had met in her short life, this was the worst decision Louis had made.

The resemblance to her father was uncanny; it was as if they were triplets. Leonard's smirk flickered across his face as he extended a hand, while Lucius's lingering, appraising look sent a chill down her spine. She focused on her amethyst pendant, blocking the thought she knew would come her way.

I'm your niece, you freak.

Angeline hated them. Not as much as she hated Paul, but she despised them, nevertheless. She gave a smile that was nowhere near nice, her lips in a thin line. She sighed mentally and offered her hand.

The touch of Leonard's lips against her warm skin sent tremors along her body, and not in a nice way. While Louis had *tried* sometimes to be '*nice*', her uncles had done nothing over the centuries besides bring pain. She had known that since she was a little girl. Her senses were overwhelmed by their sick minds. When she started hearing their thoughts, she made a point to avoid them.

"Angeline," Leonard said, "gorgeous as ever."

She nodded and muttered something about getting ready for dinner.

"See you at the dinner," Lucius called.

Angeline didn't bother answering. She was relieved to spot Markan waiting by her bedroom, with furrowed brows. He kept an eye on the two men who still stood at the wing's entrance.

"My uncles," she whispered to Markan. He hadn't been around long enough to know of them. "Avoid them if you can, and make sure to never leave my siblings alone with them."

Markan was not an idiot. A look of surprise flashed on his face, he nodded and opened the door.

The dinner is going to be fun.

CHAPTER 4

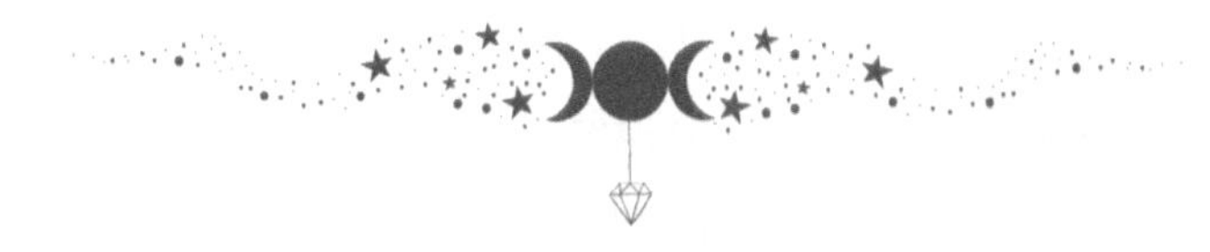

THE DINNER WAS 'FUN' indeed. It was two days later, and Angeline paced along the corridor, her mind buzzing. She was still processing the information from the disastrous family meal. Thankfully, her father had other concerns than his daughter, for once.

At dinner, her arrogant uncles bragged about their troublesome adventures, thinking themselves immortal. Well, they technically were, but they should not be so bold.

Louis shushed them, but not fast enough. Angeline saw their deranged minds and the atrocities they had committed in the last few months. She cut off the telepathic link as fast as possible, rubbing her pendant with insistence.

What she doesn't know can't hurt her, right?

The only thing she knew was that they hurt someone they maybe, probably, should not have, and now the one they hurt was going around Europe slaughtering everyone involved. The two brothers, as per usual, had run straight to their big brother for protection, hiding in the name of the Delacour and haunting her family's castle. Angeline guessed this was where her brother was sent, and she couldn't stop the fear from gnawing at her.

Blinded by the stunning gold shine, she picked up the pace as she walked down the long, glorious main wing corridor bathed in the morning light. She had convinced Markan to stay with her siblings instead of accompanying her, and she enjoyed a brief moment of pseudo freedom, longing to escape to the falls.

As she walked, she felt the tension rise around the grand entrance, and her interest piqued. That's what you get when growing up in this house. As a Delacour, you become too curious for your own good. Instead of sneaking through one of the side doors, she went straight to the commotion.

The immense wooden door leading to the hall opened in a blast, and Isabeau appeared. A worried expression crossed her beautiful face for one split second. The view of her almost-distressed mother was something Angeline didn't see often, save for the dinner with the three Delacour men, when Louis had assured protection to his imbecilic brothers. Besides the rare occasion, Isabeau was never, ever, stressed about anything. Her existence as a vampire since the Middle Ages, and her 1000-year relationship with the most powerful man of France, bolstered her sense of superiority. Being a gorgeous, rich bloodsucker didn't help her arrogant behavior.

Smiling, she sped to Angeline before her curious daughter could reach the door and see what was happening further down the hall. Her tight blonde hair, pulled into a bun, didn't move an inch.

"Angel," Isabeau said in her soft, high-pitched voice, "you should go back to your room for a while". Her worried hazelnut eyes, now devoid of a pupil—a weird vampire thing—stared straight into Angeline's.

"Why?" Angeline was looking forward to her daily run to the falls.

She could not go yesterday because of Paul. He decided it would be the right time to visit her while his old friends, her uncles, were here. It was unsurprising that those three were friends, if you ask Angeline. With Jack away, she didn't want to take any risks. The wolf inside her had been whining and begging her all day and all night to get out to run, and it was starting to pester her.

"We have an uninvited guest," Isabeau said, by way of explanation.

Isabeau was not the best mother, but at least she tried to spend time with her children, unlike Louis. Well, let's say she was spending time with the children she appreciated. It's too bad Angeline was not one of them anymore, but at least the vampire tolerated her daughter, unlike Louis, who wanted to send her off to any potential rich husband.

Angeline pouted, but noticed Isabeau's distress. The golden branches of her magic reached out to touch the vampire's mind.

It didn't take long for the gorgeous blonde to guess what her adoptive daughter was doing. Isabeau's eyes widened. She might not be aware of the full extent of the girl's power, but she still knew the redhead could detect lies.

"A dangerous man," Isabeau said. "He requested a word with your uncles."

Angeline stopped her branches, intrigued. She was so bored; she could use some gossip.

"Why don't we send them away?" Angeline asked, shrugging.

She knew Isabeau felt the same about her uncles; they were more of a pain in the neck and had been for thousands of years.

Isabeau sighed and walked toward the young woman, slipping an arm under hers. With a delicate but firm push, she sent Angeline in the other direction. "Because you know your father. He promised Lucius and Leonard they could stay safe here. Brotherly love and all." Isabeau rolled her eyes.

Louis was also a pain in *her* neck with his brotherly devotion. Those two idiots, as she called them, were constantly getting into trouble. If only her mother knew what Angeline knew, she might have convinced her husband to kill them.

She smiled at Angeline, patted her hand, and added, "Don't you worry about it, just please, don't go out today. It's not safe.
"

Angeline leaped, escaping Isa's clutch. "No way!" She whined. "I want to go outside." She was not proud of her reaction, but couldn't bear staying indoors for another day with the sun shining. She had hidden from her uncles and Paul enough already.

"It's not safe when Paul is around either," Angeline said, "but you don't tell me to hide then."

Isabeau's eyes narrowed, her nostrils flaring, and for one second, Angeline regretted her protests.

"The man outside the castle right now is a threat, one that is better to avoid," Isabeau snapped.

Despite their differences, she never talked this way to the one she considered her born daughter. "I am asking you to stay inside for your safety. He could not go through the magic barrier Nana had done for us. We are fortunate. As for Paul, he is a rich, handsome gentleman. He is not stupid. Give him a chance."

Angeline held back a scoff, wishing she could tell her mum how much of a gentleman Paul was. But then, goodbye freedom; the Delacour will never let a telepath out of their grasp. Freedom was an unreachable, dreamy goal that made Angeline hope for a better future.

"Fine, then." Angeline sighed.

She turned and walked back to her side of the castle, but a sneaky smile played on her lips.

The wolf inside of her was already jumping with excitement.

Ten minutes later, her white paws were covered with mud and leaves. She didn't care about soiling her ermine fur. As her wolf took over, the smell of the forest filled her nose, a combination of wet dirt, teeming life on the ground, and the breathtaking scent of trees following her around.

A tree was in her way. She took off, stretching her back legs, prancing over the trunk, and yapping when she landed in a huge mud pool. She would get in trouble for going out, and she knew it. The forests and the falls she was aiming for were at the opposite end of the grand entrance, where everyone was busy dealing with whatever problems her uncles had brought back home.

They would never know she left. Despite her mother's worries, she would remain safe.

Unlike Angeline, her wolf was a relaxed beast, with no issues or overthinking. She often wondered how that could be possible, but after talking to her werewolf friends, they felt the same with their wolves. Quentin told her that her wolf was being everything she wanted to be deep inside—a carefree, wild animal.

Recollecting her morning encounter with her mother, the said carefree animal sensed she would soon get in trouble.

This entity inside her always landed her in trouble, even on nights of the full moon when she joined the French Pack. When she was close to fifteen years old, it was the worst. Her She-Wolf pushed Angeline to hang out with various male wolves, all twice her size, and she would try to mate with them.

This attitude from her wolf had been a shame for Angeline, but to her relief, the pack seemed to think it was hilarious and completely natural. Angeline was going through puberty at the time, and so was her wolf—except that her wolf was a horny beast.

She was lost in her thoughts when she reached her destination. As usual, the towering falls were a sight for her eyes. The water in the pool was turquoise, and she loved the moss-covered rocks. Summers were scorching in this part of France. All she wanted was to rest on the cool and lush grass.

She walked to the edge of the pool and shifted into her human shape. Unlike an actual werewolf, she did not endure excruciating pain while transforming. Her Spirit-Gift allowed her to change smoothly, which she was not complaining about. The people who saw her shift before told her she had waves of golden glitter run through her body when she transformed. She could see those flying sparkles around her at night with the wolves. The children from the pack would jump around her joyfully, trying to catch the sparkles to Angeline's great pleasure.

She stood up and stretched her whole body, hands to the sky, taking in the sun's rays on her bare skin. Angeline cautiously descended the rocks and dipped her foot in the water to test it. Goose bumps moved along her legs, making her shiver. Her nipples hardened, and her breath quickened.

Angeline plunged her hand into the water and spread water on her skin. She dropped the chilly water on her legs and stared into her reflection in the water. With her average height and hourglass figure, she knew many men desired her. She had big, round, and blue eyes. She was cute.

She took a deep breath and immersed herself in the blue water. One more breath, and she was fully embraced in the cold, freezing her mind for one second. Her long hair floated around her, and she swam toward the swirl at the bottom of the falls. She raised her head and admired the powerful but quiet flow of falling water. This was so relaxing, she did not regret disobeying Isabeau.

Well, at least not yet, she thought, pouting at the idea of the trouble she might get in.

Trying to follow her wolf singing to her '*whocareswho-careswhocares*', she reached the falls and lifted her body as much as she could, giggling under the rush of the powerful water against her breasts.

The birds stopped singing.

Something was wrong.

"Please don't stop for me, Pet."

She gasped and turned toward the strange voice.

CHAPTER 5

A MAN STOOD A few meters from her. An irregular scar curved down one side of his face, pulling at his smirk in a way that made it both menacing and mocking. Not that he needed a scar to look like the scariest man Angeline had ever seen. He took one step forward.

Angeline's breath caught. The cool water rippled around her as she instinctively moved backward, her movements slow. She was desperate to increase the space between them. Not that it would make a difference.

Maybe she should have stayed inside. Maybe she should not have sneaked away from Markan. So many maybes, so little time.

Catching his gaze fixed on her bare breasts, she instinctively crossed her arms over them and plunged herself into the water. Her cheeks burned despite the cold environment. She hoped the shallow depth would at least hide some of her nudity, but the rocks behind her blocked her from running away.

"You are on Louis Delacour's land. You should leave," Angeline said in a crisp voice, wishing she didn't sound so broken.

Sometimes her father's name was enough to scare off troublesome vampires. *Sometimes.*

The man didn't flinch. His quiet emerald eyes shone like two jewels in the middle of his ravaged face. Vampire's eyes were always a bit terrifying, but his were on another level, as if from another world, another time. He knelt on the shore, not minding the wet moss, and kept a predatory gaze on her as if he were a cat ready to pounce.

"I know, Pet," he murmured, his voice low and unsettlingly smooth. "But I'm a bit upset, you see, so I was looking for some fun while this damn Louis came to his senses. Looks like the Spirits granted me my wish."

Angeline stiffened as his burning eyes roamed over her face. Her arms tightened across her chest.

"I doubt our Spirits would allow you to hurt random young ladies." How dare he talk about her gods? A flicker of doubt crossed her mind; maybe he was the 'uninvited guest' Isabeau was talking about. If he was, she was in even bigger trouble than she thought.

"Are you the man who is looking for Lucius and Leonard?" she asked abruptly.

There was no point beating around the bush now, was there?

At the angry—or hungry?—look he gave her, she knew she was in trouble. The man moved toward her, offering her his hand. His eyes were cold, and his lips were closed. She sank further into the water, maneuvering to the other side of the pool.

He sighed and got up, prepared to jump in, but someone landed on him.

Angeline's breath hitched. An immense relief invaded her when she saw her loyal bodyguard, Markan, locked in a brutal fight with the stranger.

"Run, Princess!"

Without hesitation, she swam frantically toward the rocks. She knew her plan: reach the edge, shift, and run. Angeline could say bye-bye to her She-Wolf being incognito, but this was a life and death situation. She will improvise a new lie.

She reached the edge, pulled herself onto the damp grass, and slipped on the wet ground. Her hopes were shattered when a flying head landed right under her nose. *Markan.* He frowned at her from death.

Angeline stared at the severed head, and a shriek tore from her throat, but she had no time to grieve. Her pulse pounded with fury as the stranger loomed behind her. Her body trembled as she twisted around. The intruder stood right over her. Her teeth chattered from the cold, and she tried to hide her breasts from the man's heavy look. Her bottom was still in the wet grass.

Under his gaze, she was powerless.

"Princess?" The man scoffed, analysing her from head to toe. "Now, I have a better idea."

Angeline had no interest in knowing what this idea of his was. She seized the opportunity and tried to read his mind. Her breath stopped.

There was only darkness in there. And silence. In any other circumstances, she would have enjoyed it.

Why can't I reach his thoughts?

Knowing how people would react in a given situation was her only strength, the only skill that allowed her to escape an unwanted situation. This had never happened before.

She tried to escape one last time, hoping surprise would give her an advantage. Golden magic took over, transforming her into a wolf. She ran away from the man, her white paws slapping against the ground. Her fear and her She-Wolf fear moved her at an unexpected speed.

It was not enough.

The vampire caught up and pinned her to the ground. Her wolf whimpered, and she shapeshifted back into her human form from terror, her sparkles flying around them. She fought against the much stronger man and scratched at the vampire.

It was pointless, and she knew it. He held her on the ground, pinning her hands above her head and pushing his body between her naked legs. She felt the same familiar fear as when she spent her days hiding from her father's guest. The terror took over the very little reason she had, and she tried to move away, but his body was like stone. He barely moved despite her legs thrashing around his body.

Her wolf whined, begging her to get them out of there. His smell took over all of her senses.

He smelled different. Not a vampire, more like a wolf? But not?

What kind of weirdo is that?

Apparently, her smell made him curious, too. He moved his nose to her breasts, to her neck, and reached behind her ears, where he took a large sniff. *This is a wolf's nose.*

"You smell like an angel," he whispered, his words so close to her ear that it triggered an involuntary shudder.

Goose bumps formed over her body, and a fiery sensation awakened between her legs. The man's visage was so close to hers that she could smell his minty, enticing breath.

"You're lucky I like my women to consent," he said in a sharp breath. His entire iris looked like fresh blood. She knew the color too well and what it meant—carnal hunger. His hands on her wrist allowed a flow of thoughts to reach her, intense, dark, but not as clear as usual; as if something was wrong within this man's soul.

A movement in the dense brush at the edge of the forest gave her a glimpse of hope, but it disappeared when the stranger smiled sarcastically.

Her captor spoke without looking away. "Nice of you to finally join us."

He pulled her to her feet. She struggled to stand, her legs trembling, arms restrained behind her back as the man held her frail body close. With so much more skin contact, she could perceive something new in him, something she knew way too well. Desire.

Great, that's just great.

She turned to look at the newcomer, but didn't know what to think.

"Who is he?" Angeline whispered.

"My brother," her captor said.

Really? The one holding her had amber hair and green eyes. Despite his height, he was not impressive. Scary, but not that impressive. His shirt had seen better days, and he wore it with basic black jeans and leather boots, which her father would never wear. The other one was something else entirely. The kind of man who made you think twice before annoying him. Platinum hair pulled back in a bun, grey eyes the color of a cloudy sky, and a giant stature confined to perfection in a grey costume.

Her thoughts scattered when the new man hurried toward them, observing her with calm, grey eyes. He addressed his brother.

"Maros," the newcomer said. "Busy?"

Crimson eyes came back to their jewel shades, and he answered with a laugh. "This cutie is a princess, one of Louis's daughters. And she is a wolf too. Not a very efficient one, though," he added, with laughter in his voice.

Angeline's blood boiled. Yes, she was quite small compared to werewolves, but still!

"There's no need to be rude!" She was ready to kick him in the balls when the second brother stopped her.

"Princess... your name? I am Manus the First, and this is my little brother, Lutumaros. Excuse him—he fell on the wrong side of the litter."

"Call me Maros," the other one interjected.

Angeline wiggled. She couldn't care less about their names, but Maros held her firmer and brought her body closer to his than necessary, placing his second hand on her lower back.

"Stop wriggling, Pet. This is getting quite nice," he murmured. His thoughts showed his enjoyment amid the dark clouds of his mind, and she could feel his pleasure in the situation.

Angeline gave him a dark look, sighed, and focused on her pendant; she didn't need to read more into him.

"Lady Angeline," she whispered at the big brother, her breath quickening and her eyelids closing when Maros traced a trail with his nose all over her neck. "And I'm not a princess."

Manus appeared undisturbed by his brother's attitude and continued the conversation as if nothing was happening. He offered his jacket to Angeline, who used this occasion to push away the sniffer and cover her naked body. Maros's burning gaze was all over her again.

"If you don't mind, you will be our leverage," Manus said. "There are two men we want very much dead who are hiding in your father's castle right now. Your uncles, I believe?"

"I *do* mind—"

Manus interrupted her.

Vampires. You would think that after centuries, they would have learned manners.

"The magical barrier around your home is impressive," he said with a curious look on his face. "Even our witch of a sister could not get through."

Angeline pursed her lips, hoping he would not ask more questions, as she was the worst liar. The barrier around the palace was unbreakable because it was made using her blood. Magical Virgin's blood would make any spell a hundred times stronger.

Her silence didn't stop Manus from continuing his little speech. She was to be exchanged for Lucius and Leonard, as Manus believed Louis wouldn't hesitate to save one of his children.

I am so going to be grounded for this.

If her father took the deal, there was no guessing what the man could do. After all, he had only two brothers but over a hundred children. Angeline was not one of the favorites. Yes, her parents had an actual list; she read it in their minds and noticed she was close to the bottom.

She thought about how her father might punish her. Certainly, by forbidding her to visit her werewolf friends.

Stuck in her thoughts, she missed the exchange between the brothers. She snapped to attention. Manus's speedy departure created a wind that made her shiver. She widened her eyes and realized she was, once again, alone with the pervert. Angeline pouted and stepped back to avoid his smell, which her wolf was quite excited about, now free of all previous fear.

Naughty, naughty She-Wolf! He doesn't even smell that good!

Her twin was the most annoying beast when it came to male wolves.

His eyes browsed her from head to toe, always wearing a sarcastic smile on his damaged lips. Like many vampires she knew, he stood tall and arrogant, aware of his immortality. There was something else about him or his brother, something she didn't feel before. She tightened the grey jacket around her body; her features were too small to fit the fancy piece of fabric. She was swimming in it, but at least she had something on.

"So... how do you do it?" he asked, breaking the silence.

Angeline's lips parted as she looked at him, wondering what he was talking about.

"Your wolf?" he pressed.

She answered with silence, searching for an answer that would not sound like a lie, without telling him the truth. She took too long to talk, and Maros moved closer, catching one of her wet curls around his finger.

Angeline shivered.

He spoke in a low voice. "I can shift when I want to, but it takes time, pain, and struggle. You shifted into a wolf as if it were nothing. I'm almost jealous."

He let go of her curl and tucked her hair behind her ear. Her wide eyes met his. Their sanguine color returned. She stared at the scar that ran from his eyebrow to his lips, cutting through his iris. Angeline couldn't understand how a vampire or werewolf could have scars. It wasn't supposed to be possible. She had never encountered a vampire-wolf hybrid before. The only hybrid she knew was Misa, who was a Werewitch.

What was he? Werevamp? Vampwolf?

His finger glided across her face, tracing her cheekbones before brushing her lips.

"Please... stop," she murmured, her heart racing like a hummingbird. She knew he could hear it, which made it worse.

A ringtone resonated in the silent forest, interrupting his touch.

Maros took a smartphone out of his pocket. While answering, he used his second free arm to keep hold of her, placing his arm around her waist. She nearly laughed—as if she could escape him anyway.

Manus spoke on the other side of the line. "Bring the girl."

Without saying anything else, Maros hung up and put his phone back in his pocket.

"Daddy is ready to make the exchange," Maros smiled.

CHAPTER 6

2 weeks later

A LIGHT BREEZE BRUSHED over her face, stirring her from the blurry dream she was floating in. Angeline opened her eyes, still half asleep, and tightened her arms around her pillow, burying her head in the silk's comfort. Maybe if she hid there long enough, her mind would stop replaying *those* dreams.

Ever since her encounter with the First, she had funny dreams filled with images that would make her nymphomaniac brother blush. Or maybe not. What was for her the edge of excitement, Maros's fingers on her cheek, was an everyday occurrence for Jack. Those dreams did not help the state she had been in since their problematic meeting.

Angeline grumbled and moved onto her back, arms stretching above her head, savoring the fresh wind blowing through her open bedroom windows. Morning was the only time she could enjoy the cool air before heading into the heat. Her thoughts migrated to the exchange of her care-less-so-much-in-trouble-now self against her uncles.

Maros had thrown her over his shoulder, which was uncomfortable and humiliating, and sped to the Grand Entrance with her screaming her disagreement. Even more humiliating was the way he slapped her bottom before running and chuckled despite her protests.

At least he didn't do it again once they reached the entrance and the magic border. Everyone was there, standing straight in a line. Louis, his jaw tightening and fists clenched, Isabeau, her lips in a thin line, and Jack, who had barely made it to the Italian border before being called back. His face displayed a funny mix of anger and laughter. Two massive travel trunks were sitting just outside the portal, with Manus resting nonchalantly on one of them. He had one leg draped over the other and a satisfying smile on his face while his eyes remained unreadable.

Angeline later learned that, as she had thought, her damn father almost didn't agree to the exchange. It was heartbreaking—even if she had predicted it—heartbreaking enough that she shed a few tears once she was alone. She wondered what parental love could mean for others.

She didn't complain about Isabeau, who was an average mother. At least she cared a bit. Louis didn't. It was a known fact that he only had children for the sake of his one true love, Isabeau. His children were more of a means to display whatever he needed to show off. With Jack's presence, he had no choice but to agree to the exchange.

Thankfully, it went as smoothly as one could hope. Louis expressed his disappointment to Manus about how the First Family handled their request. He told the scary blonde that his family was not welcome in France anymore and that there would be repercussions, to which Manus ripped off the head of another guard who had the misfortune to be present that day.

Even Isabeau could not hold back a tiny eye roll at her lover's words, as if forbidding something to this family would make a difference.

Maros let Angeline go, but before she could finally return to the safety behind the magical barrier, he pulled her toward him. His right hand rested at the small of her back, and he bent his head over her. Her heart rushed when his fingers lightly caressed her cheek. She sure hoped she was the only one who heard his last whispered words.

"See you later."

Angeline still reflected on those words, even if there was nothing to think about. He was forbidden to set foot in France, back in the USA, she believed his family lived in Chicago, and he was now annoying someone else. Besides, she was told not to leave the grounds for the next three months, which was infuriating.

Quentin and Misa disapproved of Louis's decision, and both parties had ignored each other since then, the werewolves not wanting to attract attention to Angeline's shifting gift. She sneaked into her friend's mind, which she would never have allowed herself to do in normal times, and heard all the *lovely* things Quentin thought about her father.

To Quentin's defense, his pack and the French vampire had been at war for centuries. He loved finding flaws in the immortal, blood sucking creatures.

She agreed with him, but was too much of a coward to go against her father. After all, there was no use getting in even more trouble, was there?

Angeline sighed. She could only go to the falls twice a week now, despite the hammering heat of this summer, and under the chaperonage of not only her grumpy old maid, Rose, but also her new bodyguard. Angeline's breath caught when she thought about poor Markan's fate. She really liked him. The new guard her father had allocated her, Baldur, did not talk much and refused any rapprochement with her.

Having those two breathing down her neck meant she could not shift at all. It was better for everyone to ignore this whole wolf thing going on for her. Maros had not said a thing about it in front of her parents, which she was thankful for, even though he had no way of knowing it was a secret.

Angeline grabbed her pillow and covered her face with it to muffle her screams. So many things could have gone wrong.

It would have been much easier if her parents had known every intricate detail of her magic, but Angeline had spent too many hours listening to her father's opinion about 'those beasts'.

She always wondered what would happen when she married and turned into a vampire, either on the wedding night or some years later. Would that break her wolf? Or vice versa? Angeline did not want to think about it; she had asked Nanabrok, but the old witch's answer was, as usual, enigmatic: "Trust the Spirits".

Helpful. Both she and Misa were big fans of whispered clues.

Delacour's children were not given a choice in the matter of vampirism. They could wait, unless they wanted to stay eternally youthful, but in the end, they would be converted to vampirism. Some of her sisters were even turned on their wedding night, because their dear husband enjoyed their fresh faces and bodies.

Ew. Angeline had heard so many disgusting things; no wonder she didn't trust men.

Her heart raced, much to her fury, as she thought about what she had found at the falls six days after her encounter with Maros. She had to be sneaky and hide it from Baldur, who was gentleman enough not to look at a swimming lady, and Rose, who thankfully was too blind and aged to care about the princess's whereabouts.

Angeline moved her legs over to the side of the bed and reached for her locked drawer, where she hid her diary. The young girl took her green leather book in her hands, and with a scant breath, opened it to the last page. There it was. A drawing of her. Half her face was in the shape of a wolf—her wolf.

The artist could only be Maros. She was unsure if he liked to draw, but it *must* be him. The drawing was lovely and accurate, even if she had a naughty look in the picture. Angeline was sure she didn't display such a look during their meeting.

The second thing she found was a shiny bracelet with a little diamond wolf that fit perfectly around her tiny wrist. When she saw the gifts, she convinced Rose it was time to return home, before the First jumped on her again.

Who knows if he was hiding in the shadows?

She sure wished all the legends and the fiction books she read about vampires were true, but unfortunately, there was no safe space from them—unless magic was used.

Daylight? Isabeau's favorite holidays were in Spain, lying on a beach under the scorching sun.

A stake in the heart? That hurt, sure, but the best way to kill a vampire was either to rip out their heart—easier said than done—or cut off their head.

Garlic? Nope. Angeline tried adding more garlic to her food, but undesirable suitors kept coming at her.

Holy water? Nope, the only gods were the Spirits, and they were far from being holy.

As for Maros, so long for the banishment from France. The vampire was probably used to doing whatever he wanted. Since then, she dreamed of him, to her shame. Of his hands on her body, either as a woman or as a wolf. It happened too often. She woke up in sweat, panting, and with a new, fiery, unknown sensation between her legs.

Angeline sighed, rubbing her temples. The last thing she needed was to have her mind and body betray her. She needed to stay focused and forget the feelings creeping up on her. She had been fine—perfectly fine, in fact—hating men and living her boring, quiet, golden cage life.

She had better get up and clear her mind of all those naughty thoughts. She blamed Maros for this change, but she also blamed Jack and his open thoughts of debauchery that were impossible to ignore.

She used to laugh them off, pretending to cover her ears, as if this simple gesture would block out the flow of images he so carelessly projected. Now, though? She wasn't laughing anymore. She was intrigued. Whenever she was intrigued by something, it got her in trouble.

Her fingers brushed against the delicate bracelet as she tucked it back into her diary. The smart thing would have been to throw it away, to burn every reminder of her connection to Maros. But no. She decided to keep it, like some damning proof of her demise. *Stupid.*

She loved the bracelet but hadn't been brave enough to wear it, convinced Maros was watching her somehow. If he saw her with it, she'd be doomed. The only comfort was that he probably didn't want to kill her if he was offering her expensive gifts.

Unless he was a weirdo. Which he was.

With a frustrated groan, which was not at all lady-like, she jumped out of bed, ready for another day of Louis's disappointment and anger.

Her father's frown had become a permanent fixture since the rumors about her and Maros had spread. At least Jack had decided to stay longer before setting off on a new pirate adventure. She could use him as a chaperone whenever she needed him.

It was a known fact that Jack was not the best at chaperoning. He was notorious for disappearing at the first opportunity, usually with one of the maids or one of the stable boys, depending on his mood. Angeline could not complain about it, as it gave her freedom and time to spend alone, which was well deserved.

Officially, though, he stayed because he hoped Maros would swing by. Typical. As soon as he returned from his impromptu Italian travels, Jack confessed that it was why he had to leave on the infamous day, sent by Louis to get a sense from the First Family about their slaughtering holidays in Europe.

Angeline wandered to her wardrobe, an imposing piece of furniture that housed nearly two hundred dresses—yes, she had counted during a particularly boring punishment. After scrolling through the silk, velvet, and lace, she settled on one of her favorites: a sky-blue summer dress. The soft fabric flowed like water around her legs, and delicate white off-the-shoulder sleeves framed her shoulders. The corset was comfortable for once; it held her waist just enough to give the illusion of an actual tool of torture, but without the awful pinch of one.

Hopefully, the view of the fake corset would make Louis warmer to her. He loved his daughters wearing corsets, as ladies were apparently supposed to, but Angeline hated them. Angeline liked to breathe, run, and bend over without feeling like she was about to snap in half. She loved this particular dress; it was one of her best creations.

Dressed and mentally prepared for the new day, she went to the dining room to eat breakfast. To her relief, Baldur was nowhere to be seen. He didn't talk much, but he had many thoughts about the whole 'dead previous bodyguard' thing.

She let her thoughts wander... to Maros... *again.*

Jack found the situation with Maros quite hilarious. Once his initial state of worry passed, he did not take it seriously. He and Maros met hundreds of years ago, while he was actively pirating in the Caribbean, and the foolish pirate had decided it would be a smart idea to board a ship occupied by the entire First Family.

As a mortal child raised by vampires, it didn't take him long to know the deep mess he was in.

As a man raised by Louis Delacour, he saw the opportunity to anger his adoptive father by convincing Maros to convert him into a vampire.

His crew didn't survive, such was the price for immortality by the hand—the fangs—of the First. Later on, it was not one, but two of the redoubtable family who ended up having passionate intercourse with him.

He didn't say who the second one was, though. Angeline tried hard not to read his mind. The scenes he showed her with Maros had already been blowing on her increasing fire; she didn't need to see more. He was quite the boaster, asking her what she thought about Maros, which was why she blamed him for her dreams of the First's hands on her body.

She was thankful for Jack, though, because he spent time with her while she was grounded. He continued to do this daily, rather than going back to pirating.

Angeline was relieved to find the breakfast table empty. The buffet showed dozens of breads and pastries to pick from. She hurriedly wrapped some cake in a serviette, eager to find a hiding spot and avoid encountering her family.

Jack appeared out of nowhere and jumped on her. She nearly dropped her favorite chocolate cake on the floor.

"Jack!" She screamed. Nothing was more important than chocolate, especially now.

"How is my favorite, and naughtiest, sister?"

Angeline glared at him and whispered fiercely, "I am *not* naughty."

She looked around, worried someone would hear him.

Rumors were already spreading through the Kingdom of France following her damn encounter with Maros, who had quite the sulfurous reputation with the ladies. The fact that he brought her back naked, or close to it, on his shoulders after having spent some time alone with her was the best gossip of the month.

That made Louis even more furious at her, and he was then joined by Isabeau, who, when choices needed to be made, would always stick by her husband instead of her children.

In their world, nothing was more important than a lady's reputation. Angeline's reputation was sinking as fast as the Titanic, and the few sparse prospects who showed interest in her were gone. Except Paul.

CHAPTER 7

T HEY WENT TO THE morning room, her favorite place
in the castle. Their laughter and chatter stopped when
someone in the sunlit, round room interrupted her happiness.
Louis. Her ultimate goal of the morning, avoiding her father,
had failed.

The millennial vampire stood as if he were waiting for her,
wearing a serious look. His arms were crossed, and he stood
stiffly. It didn't give Angeline the best vibe.

His grey hair was tidily coiffed, the same way he had styled it
for 184 years. He went to the hairdresser's one day and decided
it was the best hairstyle that ever existed. His eyes were a hazel
shade of brown. As a mortal, he was an average-looking man.
Unlike many vampires, Louis died late in life, aged forty-five
years. To be fair, it was already quite an achievement for the
Middle Ages. His first act as a vampire was to slaughter Isabeau's family and steal her away after her father refused to
support their union. Her parents' version was that Isabeau was
in love and happy to be taken away by her lover. She told the
story to her children often.

The authentic version, the one Angeline read through her mother's mind, was darker. Angeline chose to ignore it for her own sanity.

Jack's body tensed up at her side, and even the warm light in the room could not stop the cold from falling between them.

Louis, towering and elegant, paced before a small wooden table, his expression as cold and calculating as ever.

"I've accepted the proposal from Paul," Louis declared, his voice cutting through the silence like a blade. "You are to marry him at the next full moon, next month."

Angeline stood still as her father's words echoed through the room. Her heart sank, her blood froze in her veins, and she swore she could feel her heart ready to crack in two. Of all the men she could marry, Paul was the worst. Her thoughts raced, panic rising. She knew this was coming, but she thought she had time.

She looked at her brother, hoping for an ally.

Jack didn't disappoint. His fists clenched; his voice was raw with anger as he faced their father. "You can't do this, Louis! I told you, you will not let my sister marry this man! This isn't just some alliance—it's her life, and you're putting her in danger."

He growled at his father, showing his fangs, which she had never seen him do. It was not easy to make Jack furious. She could sense a furor in her brother that she didn't know he was capable of.

She still could not say a word, but tears pricked at her eyes. She felt the heavy weight of betrayal once again. How many times did she tell her father? She told Louis what she could feel from Paul's mind, hiding that she could hear and see—images with colors—but she made it clear that it did not entice her to be his wife. She tried to make him understand that they should not trust Paul.

That her father could do something so cruel to her was beyond her comprehension. She did not deserve it; she just made one mistake. Forcing her to marry was too big a punishment.

Their arguments were muffled. Jack hated Paul, mostly because Angeline shared everything she could hear in Paul's mind.

Handsome and typically Germanic looking, Paul was a 500-something-year-old vampire at the head of his country now. Tall, blond hair and ice-blue eyes. If his thoughts were not a disaster, Angeline could have maybe fallen for him. The beauty on the outside was a bluff for the terrible ugliness he had inside.

He met Angeline when she was eleven years old, when her father's only goal in life was to finalize peace in Europe and to forge powerful alliances. France and Germany's vampires always fought, each supporting their own country according to any mortal wars happening at the time. Angeline met him for the first time at the wedding of one of her big sisters, Catherine, who was off to get married to one of Paul's friends. It was Angeline's first wedding, and the entire day gave her a heavy headache and doubt. This was not what a wedding looked like in her mind. This was also the day she wondered about any kind of truths from Isabeau's wedding.

She came back to reality when she heard Jack's words. "She doesn't even love him!"

The comment almost made her laugh. It was not as if any of the Delacour children had married for love. Jack had run away from a forced wedding and became a pirate. Now that it was her turn, Angeline found the idea of fleeing quite enticing.

Louis turned slowly, his cold hazel eyes narrowing on his son. "Love has never been the cornerstone of our survival, Jack. You know that better than anyone." His tone was calm, almost too calm. "This marriage is not about emotions. It's about ensuring the strength of this family. Paul has waited long enough for the girl."

The girl. That's all she was.

Angeline's chest tightened. She wanted to shout, but her voice was trapped beneath her body. She had always known her opinion did not matter, but this... this was too much. She knew she would not survive Paul. There was no saying what he would do once he grew tired of her.

Her mind reviewed options one by one, analyzing and de-cluttering thoughts from both vampires. She took in the waves of their brains, but she was also trying to make a good damn decision for her future.

Angeline was not a decision maker; she had never been. She had always listened to her parents. Her magic was the only thing that kept her apart, that woke her up, and screamed at her to follow her instincts. She wanted to protect her magic and her She-Wolf from her parents. Any decisions she made were based on this. Paul was known for killing werewolves. Who knew what his reaction would be if he learned his wife was a beast?

Talking about freedom was different from making a move. She realized that now. Her dreams might quickly become nightmares if she and Jack were not prudent enough. Not only Louis, but most likely Paul, would come after her, hunting her and her brother until the end. But a little voice inside of her, the damn She-Wolf, was there, whining, pushing her around, whispering her wishes of freedom and running under the moonlight. Her wolf was not thinking about repercussions, so Angeline had to be the one to do it.

Jack's voice rose, interrupting her internal debate. "Strength? By selling her off like some shiny diamond?" He stepped closer to Louis. "How does this make us stronger? What's so damn important about Paul? His country is shit, the First killed half his people. He has no control or alliances over any witches or werewolves, but we do."

This was all true, thought Angeline, nodding her head involuntarily.

The Kingdom of France was much stronger, especially with the ongoing alliance with the redoubtable French Coven led by Nanabrok, and the French Pack, the most feared werewolves of Europe. She turned her attention to Louis, curious about the argument he could come back with.

Louis sighed, as if annoyed he had to explain his reasons to the principal concerned. Angeline reached his mind for a split second and saw that he missed the good old times when his daughters respected him. That made her scoff.

"It's not just about Paul," the old vampire said, "it's about Europe as a whole. You've seen how tensions have been rising since the First Family's attack. Europe is on the brink of war against the First, but also against each other. People are trying to decide who they want to follow. Their country? Or do they want to swear allegiance to the First and avoid the slaughter? This marriage will forge alliances that can help us avoid conflict between the most powerful nations, or at the very least, prepare us for what is to come. If France and Germany are allies, others will follow us, all against the First."

Angeline could hardly breathe. War? Which war? She hadn't realized it was this bad. She'd been kept out of politics for a few years. Her father was tired of listening to her advice and strategies. Angeline loved strategies. She wished she could be free to use her amazing brain as much as she wanted, but men, especially vampires, didn't like it when women took an interest in their war plans—especially when it was a good plan.

Jack shook his head, incredulous. "A war against the First Family? Yeah, right. That sounds like a good plan. We're supposed to sacrifice her freedom and future for the sake of politics? Paul should be grateful that we didn't kill him. He has nobody left. No friends, no witches, and let's not talk about wolves."

Louis stepped closer to his son, his presence commanding, but Jack only smirked. He had never been impressed with his father, even as a young boy. In a fight, despite his younger age, Jack would win without a doubt. Rumors were that if you were converted by one of the First, you had greater strength.

"You speak of sacrifice?" Louis said. "Do you forget the lives we've already lost?"

Jack rolled his eyes. He could not care less about the lives the First Family went after. As far as he and Angeline knew, they were not that big a loss for the community, but the vampires of Europe liked to think they were better than everyone else.

Louis did not stop speaking despite the mocking looks his children exchanged. "The First Family's attack left us vulnerable. They came in, did their deed, and left without any sort of punishment. We can't afford to appear weak, not now. This marriage will solidify our alliances and prevent further bloodshed. Paul has been watching my every move for decades, waiting for a weakness. He found one now, thanks to your old friends."

Louis's gaze flickered to Angeline, and the weight of his next words crushed her. "Her feelings are inconsequential. The Delacours must stand strong."

Angeline bit her lip, fighting back the anger and despair that threatened to overwhelm her. Was this truly her destiny? To be a pawn in their never-ending game of power? She had imagined something more for herself—choices, freedom. Her father knew how selfless she was, and he knew she would bend to his will if needed. She read that in his mind, already certain of his victory over her, which made her sick.

Jack was still arguing, his voice loud and impassioned, but Angeline could barely hear him over the thudding of her heart. Her thoughts spiraled as Louis's words replayed in her mind: *Her feelings are inconsequential.* This was not even about her feelings; it was about her spending the rest of her immortal life raped and tortured by her husband. Bringing her potential children into this? Never! There was also no saying how her magic would react once linked to a man. What if it made Paul stronger?

Louis's voice rang out again, sharp and clear. This was the final argument. "This is for the good of the family, Jack. If Angeline's marriage can secure peace, then that is what will happen. End of discussion. You will thank me when we beat the First Family next time they come here. If they dare."

Angeline's throat tightened, her body rigid as she held back a snort. Inside, a storm was brewing—her decision was made. She placed her hand on her brother's arm, her fingers shaking despite the calm she tried to project in front of their father.

"Jack," she murmured. "It's okay. Our father is right."

Jack's attention snapped to her, his wide eyes showing disbelief. He tried to talk, but Angeline cut him off by reaching into his mind, pushing into his mind.

Trust me, it is time.

Her voice echoed in his thoughts, a soft yet firm command. Jack blinked, calming down as he took in the message. The tension in his shoulders relaxed, and he gave a slow, reluctant nod.

They had talked about it for a while after all. Angeline's dreams of freedom took over all common sense, and her fear of getting into a forced marriage to Paul grew bigger every day. An escape was necessary. She knew it, and so did Jack. She was ready. Ready to leave behind the world of forced alliances, manipulation, and lies. Ready to be Queen of the Caribbeans, or as Jack said, 'Queen of the Mojitos on the beach,' which was fine with her.

Not that she knew what a mojito was.

Louis, sensing his victory, stepped forward, the faintest trace of a smile touching his lips. His pale face, always stoic, glowed with satisfaction. "Good," he said, his tone cold. Before he could finish, the door burst open with a loud thud. Impressively, the sudden interruption made everyone jump. One could not easily scare two vampires and a telepath.

A breathless, sweaty housekeeper stumbled in, his eyes wide with urgency. "Lord Louis!" he gasped, clutching a folded letter. "We've just received a message."

Louis took the letter that was destined for him from the man. It was yellowed and worn, stained with patches of crimson that screamed of blood. He unfolded it with care, scanning the lines quickly, eyes moving back and forth as his frown deepened.

"What is it, Father?" Angeline asked, excited that an outside event had come to stop this terrible conversation and knowing very well that curiosity was one of her biggest faults. Tension radiated from Louis as his eyes darted over the letter, jumping from line to line as fast as he could. She refrained from spying on his mind to read the words.

Louis took a moment to answer, his fingers tightening around the paper. His voice, when it came, was grave. "This … this is big."

"And?" Angeline's patience was running thin as he hesitated to answer.

She stared at her father, trying to keep her telepathy in check, but it was hard. She glanced at Jack, who shrugged. The pirate had no idea what was going on.

"Our werewolf allies in Ukraine were attacked," Louis said.

He stopped when Jack gave him a look, warning him not to go further.

Angeline's heart skipped a beat. She had many good friends among the Ukrainian pack, including the six-month-old little boy for whom she was the godmother. The color drained from her face as memories flashed through her mind.

Andrei, the Alpha of the pack, proposed to her years ago, but Louis refused on her behalf, declaring that no daughter of his would marry 'a beast.' She had been devastated at the time, but fate intervened, and Andrei found his mate shortly after. Angeline accepted it as fate, and when their child was born, she proudly took on the role of godmother for the adorable baby boy. She tried very hard not to think about what her life would have been like as Luna of a strong pack, held in the arms of the Alpha, smothered under his caresses.

Louis visibly held back his emotions, and she refrained from entering his mind with her golden branches. She had avoided reading him as much as she could since the Maros incident—what she found there had been enough to scare her.

"I'm sorry, my darling..." Louis's voice was soft now, almost kind, as if he knew what she felt.

Angeline took a deep breath, bracing herself. Louis hadn't called her a nice name since she was ten years old.

"This letter says... none of them survived."

Angeline wailed.

His words landed like a hammer, and the sound bursting from her chest was inhumane. Angeline's tears streamed down her face, blurring her vision. Jack's strong arm wrapped around her shoulders as he helped her sit, taking care of his sensitive little sister as he always did.

Everything around her was a blur—Louis's voice, the housekeeper's hurried footsteps, Jack murmuring reassurances in her ear. She heard Louis barking orders to his staff, his voice commanding and urgent. "We need to take action now," he snapped.

She felt his mind shifting from sorrow to strategy. Typical of him.

"There is a lot to do," Louis came back and spoke to Jack. "Contact everyone we know. I want to ensure we start taking the necessary precautions."

Jack grunted but left the room after giving his sister one last hug.

Angeline, drowning in her emotions, lost control of her gift. Minds opened to her without permission, their thoughts invading and mixing with her own. Louis's thoughts were a swirl of names, strategies, alliances, and somewhere in the mix, she caught a single word that made her blood run cold.

Russians.

"The Russians?" she asked, her voice thick with anger. Her hands clenched into fists, and her heart pounded with fury. "It was the Russians, wasn't it?"

Louis turned to her, his eyes narrowing, and she knew by his expression that she was correct. For months, there had been rumors of a rogue Russian Alpha, a madman, planning to use some of the darkest magic existing to become stronger. She had begged Louis and the other vampire lords to act against him, to do something before it was too late, before he worked on the spell. No one had listened. Now, the situation was worse than before. The Alpha had begun.

"We should have done something!" She blamed her father, her voice shaking with anger. "I *told* you this was serious!" She felt like a little girl when the tears exploded in her eyes, and her lips trembled. This was why they didn't trust her, because she was just a little girl with a funny, magical gift.

Her father's eyes widened, taken aback by her outburst, but then his eyes darkened with suspicion.

"How did you know it was the Russians?" her father asked, folding the letter as fast as he could.

Angeline froze, her mind racing. She had made a mistake. She hadn't meant to reveal how much she knew.

Taking a breath, she forced herself to think fast.

"I'm smart, remember?" she retorted, her voice thin but steady. Her heart was beating fast, and an old vampire like Louis could probably feel her blood flow speeding up. Even if he couldn't, she thought her eyes would give her away; they always widened when she was lying. However, Louis seemed to accept her answer.

"We'll handle this," he added.

With a sharp bark, he issued more commands to his house-keeper and stormed out of the room, leaving Angeline to wallow in grief.

CHAPTER 8

ANGELINE TOOK A DEEP breath when she realized she was alone in grief, witnessing the various maids and staff running around, whispering to each other, unperturbed by the conversation they had just witnessed. Angeline used the moment to leave. She didn't want to be around anyone. Thoughts from those around her swirled in her mind, and she could feel the headache coming. Without control of her gift, she rubbed the amethyst with her thumb, begging her mind to close to the horrors rushing through her entourage's minds.

She needed to have a clear mind for what was now a necessity—her escape.

Angeline didn't *want* to be selfish, but she needed to be. Hopefully, all the Lords of Europe would stop being lazy cowards and start doing something to stop the Alpha. Louis was busy contacting all of his friends and allies across the continent. They would need all hands on deck, meaning that Angeline could probably plan her escape with almost no inconvenience.

Her heart sped up at the thought of her godson and the gruesome death the little boy must have suffered. Tears pricked her eyes again. While sobbing, she remembered her conversation with Nanabrok a few weeks prior.

If the old witch and Angeline were correct, the Alpha should be able to create wolves with a bite. This was not supposed to be possible; being a werewolf was a gift from the Spirits. They heard rumors about the Alpha planning a shadow spell to obtain the bite, and it seemed like the spell had worked.

Angeline tried intervening before the spell was done, but the vampires ignored her. When she heard about a gulag deep in Russian land being attacked, she begged her father again, but neither she nor Nanabrok were taken seriously. And now? There was no way to tell how long it would take the Alpha to create a fully fledged army. Who knew which kind of monster he was creating? There was a reason shadow magic was forbidden.

She knew Louis would try to plan a meeting with the Lords at their castle in a few days. The full moon, her wedding, was in fifteen days. The Alpha could only create werewolves on a full moon, so it makes sense to attack him before that, right? She hoped not only that the Lords would decide fast, but that they would leave for war before the dreaded wedding.

Her thoughts ran wild. She could finally run away. She would have to be cautious and act like a good girl if she didn't want to be caught. While all the men and most women would be at war, she would escape Isabeau's watch—easy enough—and freedom would be hers. She was even ready to play the part and enthusiastically create her wedding dress, which should be enough to convince her parents how excited she was about the damn wedding. She didn't want to think about the second option, where they would celebrate the wedding before going to war.

She wouldn't hesitate to ask for help from the witches and the wolves, pushing them to ask for a quick intervention against the Alpha. Then, when they were at war, she would make her move.

Angeline ran to the labyrinth in the garden, glad nobody was paying her any attention. The frenzy was all over the castle, and gossip was spreading like jam on toast.

She slowed her pace when she reached the rose arch at the labyrinth's entrance and made her way through the maze. That was one of her favorite spots, a little slice of heaven, consisting of a garden of statues that were stolen by the Delacours over the years, and surrounded by her favorite trees: lilac trees.

The sight of the purple flowers lightened her spirits, and she felt the usual calm sensation running through her body when she placed her hand on the trunk of one. Through her magic and her little knowledge of Earth magic, she could feel every living being on Earth. Trees were alive and breathing.

Angeline knew he was there before she saw him. She took a deep breath and turned to see Paul and his disgusting, victorious smile. She sighed and, without a word, returned to the main path. Experience had taught her she was better off not being alone with this man.

"You look lovely today, Angeline," he said while joining the young woman in her vivid walk.

"Thank you," she murmured, but continued to walk as fast as she could. It was important to reach a crowded place.

In her mind, she screamed for her brother, pushing her branches to their full extent, trying to reach Jack. Her gift had become stronger with the years, and she knew she could get to him from quite a distance now, as she understood exactly how his mind worked.

Touch from an icy hand on her arm interrupted her screaming thoughts, and she stopped walking to protest. Paul held her so tightly that she knew she would be marked, her fair skin not letting anything go by without looking the ugliest purple black color.

"I am talking to you, little whore." His words cut like ice. She didn't know what 'whore' meant, but that didn't sound like something nice. She had heard that word before from Jack's mouth.

"Let me go, Paul, or do you want me to show my bruises to my father?"

The man laughed loudly, the most unpleasant sound.

"Your father is so desperate for you to be married, and for a powerful alliance, especially with this Russian guy, that he will do as I say. Too sad for those beasts of Ukraine, isn't it? Well, as I always say, a good werewolf is a dead werewolf."

He said the last words in a raspy murmur while pulling Angeline closer. Both his hands moved over her body, and she hated it. Even if the situation was similar, it felt nothing like her time with Maros. Cold sweat and sharp breath invaded her, and this familiar feeling of fear she always had when alone with him took over. Her wolf was angry and whining, and her inability to protect herself was a pain.

Angeline kicked hard, even if it made the situation worse. She threw the first punch at Paul's face. He acted surprised and came back at her in anger, his left hand surrounding her thin throat while his right hand ripped out her corset.

She kicked again, but the air left her body, and she desperately tried to move the hand away from her throat. Clawing nails and kicking feet landed with no impact on Paul; instead, thin red streaks opened across her own arms, while his skin mended under the power of vampire blood.

Damn Magical Virgin business!

She felt her body lift from the floor, but her senses were fading. The hand was still holding her airway, and she felt like the veins on her face were going to explode. She used her last strength to call for help.

JACK JACK JACK!

Paul threw her on the floor, his body immediately following her, her lungs still begging for air. She could feel the breeze on her naked breasts; her corset had been ripped off, and the man was now kissing her nude body, moving his free hand along, closer to her inner thighs.

Tears streamed down Angeline's cheeks as the dry fingers reached her, penetrating her, causing her to scream out loud with the last remaining strength she had. The screams were silenced by a harder pressure on her throat. Everything finally faded, and the trees above her disappeared from her vision while darkness took over.

Part 2

CHAPTER 9

T HE SCREECHING SOUND OF the bell woke her from a blurry dream of screams and snow, endless white landscapes still bright under her eyelids. Usually, she managed to get up without the help of the huge copper gong the nuns loved to use to wake up their 'guests.' Angeline inhaled deeply, attempting to return her heartbeat to a standard pace. Her mind was still trying to grasp whatever it was she had dreamed of.

Flashes of snow covered in blood reached her sleepy mind, and she remembered the mark of paws left in the fresh snow. Her paws. Her chest tightened, and before she could stop them, tears blurred her vision. She hadn't felt, heard, or argued with her She-Wolf since a few months after she arrived in this damn place. Now, there was only silence inside her; it was deafening.

Angeline angrily wiped her eyes, and she looked around her tiny room, taking in the slight ray of light coming through. The sun was barely rising, indicating the start of the day for the prisoners in this fortress. She was lucky to have a window;

it was the last gracious gesture Louis had made after he sent her away to this place of the damned, this manor of shame.

That was five years ago.

She closed her eyes and her fists, clenching on the rough fabric of her one and only blanket. Thinking about Louis was never a great way to start her day, and she knew it. When she began to think about her father, her thoughts wandered to Paul, which was a sure way to make her day even worse.

She had to learn to stop moping. That was one good thing her time here had taught her. Moping was useless in a place like this. Only survival mattered.

Angeline moved, letting her eyes wander over the ugly room where she had spent the last years. The room was on the ground floor of the convent of Lamursa, known for being the worst of all, where the vampire lords sent their daughters. Their naughty, better-get-gone daughters.

The most troublesome girls, like Angeline, were always on the ground floor. It was dark, cold, and barely held any heat in the frosty winter. Soon after her arrival, on the first night of autumn, when temperatures were low, she had tried to shift, hoping she could use the warmth of her She-Wolf to stop her shivering. She realized there was some powerful spell over the convent. When she heard the rushed steps of the nuns in the corridor, heading toward her door, she knew she needed to shift back.

Protecting her wolf was all she had left. The nuns were all witches, and she was not surprised they had tricks to detect magic. Her only magic left was her telepathy; there was no stopping that Spirit-Gift.

She shook her head, pushing away negative thoughts. Angeline grunted as she moved onto her knees, grimacing at the frozen touch of the stone beneath her. As she had done every day since arriving, she used a sharpened rock to mark her wooden bed.

Time moved so slowly. Days had become weeks, weeks had become months, and before she knew it, years had passed. She never stopped counting. She didn't want to lose track of time, even though she was sure the solitary confinement the nuns sent her to a few times had caused her to lose some days here and there. Solitary confinement visits were commonplace at the start of her 'stay.'

Once the mark was done, she got up to get ready. You didn't want to be late for breakfast, or anything else, or your life in the hellish convent would worsen. She learned this the hard way over the past few years and was smart enough not to get into trouble anymore, especially now that Louis and Paul seemed to have forgotten about her.

Good. She didn't want to think about those hours of torture she went through, thanks to her dear father's request. As for Paul, as far as she was concerned, this place was heaven compared to an eternal life with him.

She put on the ugly outfit they had to wear; it was such a change from the beautiful dresses she spent hours sewing back at the castle. The white dress was made of heavy cotton fabric.

She had to keep it white to avoid trouble with the nuns. When she heard the second bell, a sign that it was time to leave, she adjusted the leather belt they had been given. The decorative object held a spoon through a tiny hook. The only spoon you would be given for a year. If you were to lose it? That was on you to find another way to eat.

She stepped outside her room before the last ring of the bell, pulling the heavy wooden door toward her and unclenching the squeaky springs. She stood straight, not letting her eyes wander to her neighbors.

Like every morning, she knew Sister Agatha was walking down the long corridor, slowly checking their outfits. Their hair, their cleanliness, looking for a single detail to give her an excuse to hurt one of them.

In five years at the convent, Angeline had never seen a day without this sister finding some kind of fault. Angeline had been found guilty of a few things at first and was punished for it. The nun never ran short of new torture ideas. Angeline knew better than to be sent to the East Tower or the solitary cells in the basement. So she did what had to be done. She learned how to be perfect, silent, and obedient.

After a few weeks, she understood she had no choice. Escaping was impossible. She had tried—more than once—until the punishment became so harsh that she finally gave up. Her She-Wolf gave up too. Her twin left her utterly alone, and the emptiness in her heart and body was worse than anything the nuns could do to her. It was as if she had lost a limb, or her very sight.

She howled her pain at night, screaming from the pit of her belly, begging her wolf to return. It didn't happen. They could have run together once out of the borders of the convent, but Angeline didn't blame the animal. It was better this way.

Angeline felt her closest neighbor tremble, and her breathing quickened when the nun stopped in front of her. It was always better not to show fear or look too confident with Sister Agatha . Angeline had an advantage, as she knew how to adapt herself according to which thoughts the raven-haired Sister had. She was, for once, thankful the convent magic hadn't muffled her telepathic gift.

The sister stopped in front of Annabella, Angeline's immediate neighbor, from whom she could hear the muffling cries coming every night.

A cruel smile appeared on the nun's face as she examined the poor girl from head to toe, looking for any tiny fault in her appearance.

Angeline clenched her fists. Annabella had been the target of the nun since she arrived six months prior. She was the daughter of some Lord from Italy, Signore Arregazzoni, and rumors were that he made it clear to the nuns that they could teach his daughter decorum.

They all knew why they were there. Some of them just needed a small 'get back on the road' treatment and usually left after one year in hell, beaten, submitted, and ready to get on with their life—a forced wedding.

Others, like Angeline, had no foreseeable future outside of those stones.

They were called the Lost Ones. And the Lost Ones, like Annabella, who were not virgins anymore, could not expect an enjoyable life in the convent.

She knew Annabella had been faulted with a man who promised her love and thunder, but unfortunately, only thunder was left once he found another gullible lady to spend time with. She heard other girls gossiping about it, but she also spent much of her time using her telepathic gift to the best of her abilities, reaching so deeply into any of the girls' memories that she felt as if she were beside them.

The complexity of minds had no secrets from her anymore. The nuns should have thought about that before stealing her amethyst pendant. She didn't need it anymore. Grounding herself to Earth was enough to give her some control, and she found herself thankful to Nanabrok, who taught her everything about Earth magic.

Angeline focused on her thoughts, not wanting to pay attention to Annabella's struggle. You had to be strong in this place, and Angeline quickly learned that making friends would only make things harder. Not that any of the other girls wanted to be her friend. After all, she was a Lost One. Nobody knew why, but everyone was sure she must have been naughty with this First guy—none of them had any idea Paul was the culprit.

She had been tested, of course, as did everyone in there, and the nuns had confirmed to her father she was still a virgin. That didn't change Louis's decision.

Traitor. Coward.

When Sister Agatha was finally done adding some beaten fingers to poor Annabella's daily schedule, the girls made their way to the great hall where breakfast was being served. If one could call clunky, cold oatmeal breakfast.

They were assigned seats on their first day, Lost Ones mixed with the Hopeful Ones, but everyone knew there were two categories of ladies in there. No one wanted to know too many details about the Lost Ones. Most importantly, nobody wanted to attract the nuns' attention by befriending one of them.

Once the nuns left the tables to eat their breakfast, the whispering started. Mealtime at the convent followed strict rules—they could talk, but only about pre-approved topics. Of course, laughing was strictly forbidden. The allowed conversations were not that interesting, so the girls had to whisper to talk about entertaining things. Most of the time, it was about Angeline, who was used to all the gossip about her being a Delacour sent to the wrong side of the convent.

After spending five years there, she had grown used to it and gladly listened to any new rumors they started. She heard it all. Recently, with Annabella's arrival, it gave her a few days of rest until her companions decided that a random Italian Lord was not as interesting as being found naked in the arms of Maros the First.

Which, to be fair, Angeline agreed with.

If only they knew the real reason, the violation Paul subjected her to, and worst of all ... her father's reaction.

Everyone was shocked to see her, a Delacour among the Damned. The rumors started about *why*. They all knew to stay away from her as she plunged deep into the category of the Lost Ones. The nuns, who knew she was still a virgin, said nothing to correct the rumors. They allowed the whispers of her impurity to fly around unchecked. It kept the girls quiet, happy, and ensured Angeline's isolation.

Today was different, though. Something was off. She was busy chewing her disgusting breakfast, still the same tasteless mud since her first day there, when she realized something was different about today. Unlike the other days, the girls weren't whispering her name.

Nothing.

It was rare that the nuns informed the girls about the outside world. The only news they usually had was from the ones lucky enough to receive a monthly letter from their family, which Angeline was not part of. It seemed that Louis, Isabeau, and whoever she used to consider her friends had given up on her.

Regarding Louis, she was not surprised. He had tried to compel her to forget the rape, which hadn't worked. It was a relief as much as a torment. Sometimes she wished she *could* forget about it.

She expected better treatment from Nanabrok, or the French Pack, not to mention Jack. She hoped Jack couldn't possibly know about her situation. It was the only plausible explanation for why he would leave her in this inhospitable place. Jack would not care about her being 'impure.' He would go and punish Paul for what he did.

So, where was he?

Angeline raised her head from her ceramic bowl. She didn't like to think about her old life; she knew she wouldn't get back to it anytime soon.

Still chewing and swallowing with difficulty, Angeline extended the golden branches of her mind into her surroundings.

Fear.

She felt it even before she heard the words.

Instead of their usual gossip, her companions of misfortune were getting worried about a war raging outside the walls of the convent.

Her breath caught as she felt the tension in their minds. For weeks now, the nuns had allowed whispers of a war to filter in, though the details had been vague. It was hard to ignore, especially when her ex-fiancé and ex-kidnapper were contestants for it.

Indeed, Paul and Maros had declared themselves contenders for the crown—a crown forged by the Spirits of the magical world, though the Spirits had inadvertently forgotten to say *who* was to be king.

Angeline genuinely thought that the Spirits, in which she had believed all her life, wanted to see the world burned and the magical world destroyed. Gentlemen disagreed about who the king should be. The goal, given by the Spirits, was that whoever got the most votes would get the crown.

She was not sure how it worked. One would think allowing every magical creature to cast a vote would be the simplest, smartest solution, right? But no.

Instead, Paul and Maros the First were fighting about who would kill more people from the other side.

Angeline shuddered at the thought of Paul being a king. She would have no way of escaping him. It surprised her that he hadn't already convinced her father to get her out. It was Louis who had 'saved' her on that dreadful day, interrupting Paul's attack. Angeline had been punished for it, but she was ready to bet Paul hadn't. She would have heard if the leader of Germany had met his death; not even the nuns could keep that sort of gossip secret.

Maros's name resonated too strongly in the others' minds. She gripped her spoon harder, glancing at who was talking about him, thinking about him. The fear running through the ladies almost made her laugh.

If only they knew how bad Paul was compared to Maros.

Lucia was one of the Hopeful Ones and was highly respected amongst the young women as she received monthly news from her parents. Angeline opened her branches wider and took the information in.

Lucia thought Maros's army was getting close to the convent. That was terrifying, sure, but more important than his actual whereabouts... Was he coming for Angeline Delacour, his lover?

Angeline rolled her eyes. It was all about *her* and how Maros had brought her back naked to her dad, like the light skirt she was. Which, according to everyone, was why she was there.

She brought her bowl to the kitchen under the watchful eyes of the crowd: the nuns, making sure she wasn't hiding some food for later, and the curious looks of the others, trying to spot any hint of impurity, as if it would show on her face.

Angeline knew she would spend the rest of the day alone, as she usually did. There had been gossip about her knowing things she shouldn't, and that kept others away most of the time. She had been playing smart, letting out some information when needed.

Knowledge is power.

Angeline went to the garden—or what they called a garden—for fifteen minutes before her Lady's Study, and her mind wandered back to the idea of escape.

She said she would stop. The last time she tried was right after her first three months at the convent. Her plan was perfect, or so she thought, but she failed. She failed so hard. As a result, the nuns tortured her for so long that she lost her wolf.

The world outside, the world she knew, was ruled by bloodshed. This could either be her win or her downfall. The meeting of armies of vampires, wolves, and witches could quickly go wrong, but that also meant everyone was too busy for her. If only she could convince her She-Wolf to wake up. That would make things easy.

She kept hope for a long time.

A. Long. Time.

Nobody came. No Jack, no witches, and no pack. By this point, she was almost praying Maros would come. Louis had probably taken a stance and made sure to keep alliances strong by forbidding anyone to rescue her, but she didn't see how that would work. She knew the wolves would rather stand by her side a hundred times instead of by her father's. Jack even more. Hell, she should be the one to become queen; she would have many votes. Five years had passed, so why would they not come for her?

Her fifteen minutes of fresh air were almost over, and tears welled up again.

Maybe I'm still moping about myself after all.

She used her sleeves to wipe her face and rose to go to the study, but something stopped her—someone.

Annabella was there, below the stone arch. Staring. Waiting.

Angeline held back an eye roll. She didn't want any friends. Friends only made things worse in this place. They made you weak. If friends were worth her time, someone would have rescued her by now. Her kindness deep inside of her was screaming at her to pay attention to the poor, abused girl, but her brain disagreed.

"Hi," Annabella whispered, biting her lips while observing Angeline from under the longest, darkest eyelashes she had ever seen.

"Annabella." Angeline paused for five seconds, and with no reaction from her interlocutor, she added, "I'm going to the study."

"Me too!" the other girl exclaimed, as if Angeline had just offered her a ride.

Angeline could feel hope inside of the other; hope was a bad habit in the convent.

"Great," Angeline muttered.

They walked side by side. Angeline could already spot a few other girls whispering. She sighed and slowed down, making Annabella match her pace.

"Annabella," she whispered. "I know it's hard, but I can assure you, having me as a friend would only make it harder for you."

Annabella, she realized, had the most beautiful green eyes she had ever seen, even prettier than Maros's. They looked straight into her soul, already bright under the threat of tears.

Angeline caught the young girl's arm and made her move before someone saw her.

"Don't do that," Angeline ordered.

Annabella let one sniffle out. "Don't do *what*?"

"Don't make it harder for yourself than necessary. Being friends with me? Bad idea. Showing your weaknesses to everyone? Extremely bad idea. Gossip about you is already slowing down, just wait a little longer."

"I don't care about the others," Annabella retorted, her voice shaking. "But the nuns... they will not rest until they hurt me enough. My father gave them instructions."

Angeline took a deep breath. "I know. My father did the same. But the more you show your fear, the more they will enjoy hurting you. Trust me, it's a matter of balance." She paused and decided that a little lie could help. "It will get better. Soon there will be another new girl to torment, I'm sure."

That was a terrible lie, or a terrible thought, but it made Annabella laugh. Angeline thought her heart would break from hearing her perfect laugh.

After the day dragged on, as usual, Angeline finally returned to her tiny room, where she could let her mind go quiet. Isolation was both a blessing and a curse, as was her gift. It allowed her mind to rest a bit from the incessant chatter, but it also gave space for darker thoughts and bad ideas.

She was angry at herself for allowing Annabella to break down her walls, which she had so cautiously built over the years. They sat close to each other at the study; the nuns didn't notice, but others did.

Angeline knew this would not help the brunette, but she had felt her despair. Besides being sent here, Annabella had a broken heart. From what Angeline could read inside her mind, it was not a funny thing to go through.

Angeline braided her hair, struggling as it was longer than ever, and changed into her nightgown. She held her breath. Something was different. Her heart was going wild. She sat on her bed, her hands clenching the blanket. All of her senses were on high alert.

Then, the first scream echoed through the convent, followed by a loud crash at the entrance.

Her blood turned to ice.

They were here. One of the armies had arrived. She wasn't sure which one, but in either case, she was doomed.

Annabella's panicked scream from next door woke her up from her torpor—*and this is why I don't make friends.*

Before she could react, her door burst open, and two vampires stood before her. Blood dripped from their mouths. Their eyes glowed bright red. They were enjoying themselves a tad too much. The vampires hesitated when they saw her; she was the only one who did not run or scream.

They advanced, wearing wicked smiles.

Angeline froze. *This will be the end.*

CHAPTER 10

S HE STOOD HER GROUND, her back against the stone wall, refusing to let them see her fear. She knew fighting a vampire was not possible for her, as she sourly remembered from her time with Paul. For a moment, she considered using her telepathy to call for help, but who would come? An army of terrified girls and women, waving their unique wooden spoons?

Weren't the nuns supposed to be witches? Why weren't they fighting back?

A vampire stepped closer, licking his lips. "You're a pretty one. Why don't you come with us?" he hissed.

Take over.

"What?" Angeline said out loud, under the incredulous look from the vampires.

Take. Over.

A shudder went through her body, a feeling she had long forgotten. The most natural magic flowed through her veins.

Her She-Wolf.

Angeline's breath hitched, and she instinctively brought her hands to her belly, as if she could feel her fur ball back inside her.

TAKE OVER THEIR MINDS.

So, she did.

Angeline had had little success with compulsion before. She had experimented with it long ago, before being in the convent, but it ended up in a series of unhelpful—or hilarious—situations. All it did was create doubt in her parents. She had never tried again. Until now.

This was life or death.

With a sweeping motion, she unleashed her power, propelling her magic and creating a golden barrier that only she could see. There was no reason to be discreet anymore. This was war. Branches licked down her skin and flew onto the ground, ramping toward both men. Before they realized what was happening, it was too late. Every cell of their brain was gone. They belonged to her now.

Angeline smirked at the sight of the two vampires, standing now before her, motionless, their lifeless eyes showing complete surrender. The only problem was that she didn't know how long she could keep them under her control.

Do not move until I tell you to move, she ordered in their minds.

She knew they could hear her when she saw their fists clenching and their eyes filled with rage, which gave her satisfaction.

Inside of her, the She-Wolf was running in a circle, jumping, scratching. *You did it; you did it!*

Before Angeline could tell her wolf what she thought about her abandonment, Annabella's frantic voice broke through. She was crying for help somewhere down the hallway. Angeline's instincts kicked in. Annabella was just another young woman — innocent, terrified. She couldn't let her die, not like this. Angeline felt stronger than ever and ready to mind-control anyone on her way if needed, at least for a few minutes.

She darted toward the door, pushing past the vampires in an adrenaline rush. Her bare feet were silent against the cold stone as she sped down the corridor toward Annabella's screams.

Angeline rounded the corner and found the girl huddled in a corner, her dark hair tangled, her face streaked with tears.

"Angeline!" Annabella cried, reaching out for her, relief showing on her face.

It seemed Annabella had managed to escape the vampires among the incredible mess. Every door in the corridor was open. Blood splattered the ground. Screams resonated on the lower floor and through the stone stairs leading to the Hopeful floor.

"Shhh," Angeline whispered, pulling Annabella up. "We have to go. Now."

"Where?" Annabella whimpered. "They're everywhere. We can't leave."

Angeline paused. She had no idea where to go. Dark, frozen forests surrounded the convent, and she had no doubt that there were actual wolves in there. But staying here, with whatever army this was, would be worse.

"We'll head for the kitchen," Angeline decided. "It's the safest place for now, with a door leading outside. Come on."

Angeline once tried to escape through the kitchen, but she didn't make it past the high wall. Annabella did not need to know that.

As they crept through the narrow hallways, Angeline focused only on listening to her surroundings. Annabella followed, and whenever Angeline pushed her, she allowed it, observing Angeline with her big green eyes.

Once they reached the end of the corridor, she saw it. The kitchen and its large wooden door which was now closed. She could already smell the leftover pumpkin soup they had eaten earlier. She sped up and pulled on Annabella's hand, but stopped.

A figure emerged from nowhere. Tall, smelling of death, with blood on his usually impeccable costume. His blond hair was still pulled as tight as when she last saw him.

Manus.

Angeline breathed. She felt Annabella's fear taking over.

"Princess Angeline?" the old vampire asked, a hint of surprise in his voice. He sped toward the two girls, let his eyes wander longer than necessary over Annabella, then turned to Angeline. "How surprising to see you here. I'm guessing you're the 'witch' my poor friends had encountered earlier." His thin lips pulled into a slight smile.

They came from behind, boots stomping against the stone floor. The two vampires from earlier watched her, grumpy with her, but she could read their minds. They were more afraid of their leader's reaction. It was with satisfaction that she heard them fear her as well.

Good, let them fear me... I am strong! I am brave! I am haaaaaa...

Her thoughts were interrupted when one of the men picked her up and threw her over his shoulder. The second one was ready to grab Annabella, but Manus's gesture stopped him. Manus himself, with a wave of his hand, invited the brunette to walk.

Why am I being carried like a potato bag while she is shown around like a princess?

Well, she *was* the one who got the vampires in trouble.

They reached the grand entrance. Her fear overwhelmed her mind, and the dozens of terrified girls and women around did not help her control her damn gift. She could feel the lust and excitement in the vampires, and from her uncomfortable position, she could see many pairs of legs, some covered in blood and mud, and others hidden under the long nightgowns of her fellow prisoners.

Great, this is just great.

The vampire carried her only to drop her roughly on the floor. Once back on her feet, she instinctively moved away from him. His hand on her ankle had projected his dirty thoughts straight to her brain. That was not something she missed from her time outside the convent.

Yep, men? Didn't miss those.

Her heart stopped when she saw the disaster. Dead nuns were laid on the floor, broken like puppets, blood and guts spilled from their wounds. Some survivors, held by vampires and werewolves, seemed barely alive. Angeline knew witches could usually heal faster than the average mortal. The cries of snatched girls were painful to hear, especially for her tired brain, but Angeline was relieved to see that all her companions seemed alive and well.

Weirdly enough, some vampires did not even pay attention to them; others, especially the young ones, looked like they could use a snack. Angeline knew it was harder for new vampires to resist the urge of blood, especially when confronted with virgin blood. She had learned with time that young vampires were best to avoid, as her blood smelled even better than a random virgin. Should any of them drink from her, they would not be able to stop.

She was lost in her reflection when she felt it.

Goose bumps tingled over her skin. Her heart raced. Her She-Wolf howled inside of her.

Angeline knew why.

The door burst open to reveal Maros.

Angeline gasped while trying to control her She-Wolf, whose whines filled her mind.

Seriously? You leave me alone for five years and then go wild for him? We don't even like him!

He was exactly as he appeared in her memories and dreams. The shiny scars remained, and his outfit was even more pitiful, stained with blood, both fresh and old. His people moved away from his path, creating a guard of honor for the millennial monster. A few creatures swiftly moved to Maros's side, looking as if they were floating by him.

Of course, Manus was there. She was surprised he didn't brag about what he had found. With him were some of the most beautiful women Angeline had ever seen. Maros stood nonchalantly, like he owned the place, with one of his arms resting on his neighbor's shoulder—an ethereal blonde woman.

Angeline was used to vampires having a mystical beauty. Her beauty was *different*. This one had what looked like the smoothest ivory skin. Her straight, shiny blonde hair flowed to the middle of her back. She had a beautiful oval face and looked like an angel.

Angeline tried to turn her gaze away from the area, but it was too fascinating. She guessed they were the entire First Family—the first vampires. It was hard to recall the sister's name, but Angeline sure remembered her reputation, which was enough to make any vampire turn paler with fear.

Alongside her was another blonde angel, whose features were so similar that you would think they were twins. Angeline knew who she was—Blanda, the First Witch. The oldest witch alive, and the only witch still practicing the magic of druids from when France was still called Gaul.

Okay, this is bad.

Angeline desperately searched for an escape or a tiny hole to hide in. She was still a Delacour, after all. As usual, Louis made poor decisions about choosing whom to follow in the raging war. She knew her imbecile of a father supported Paul instead of Maros. Surviving this convent to end up slaughtered by her father's enemies — that would be just great.

Thank you, Father.

While Maros was speaking to one soldier, Angeline succeeded in getting closer to the wall. She pushed the other girls out of her way with no pity and was pushed back, earning an incredulous look from Annabella.

Maros stopped speaking. He lifted one dirty finger in the air, and silence fell over the room. A smile twisted onto his damaged lips. His next words froze Angeline to the bone.

"Princess Angeline."

CHAPTER II

Angeline's breath hitched as she lifted her head, only to meet his piercing green eyes. Her heart came to a standstill, and her chest tightened as he advanced toward her. His lips curved in a mocking smile, sending a shiver down her spine.

Oh no.

She pressed herself against the cool wall, but there was no point. Maros was already on her, letting his eyes wander over her body. It was like she was naked again, their skin pressed together. Her nightie wasn't helping much to keep them apart. She could hear all sorts of thoughts from her convent companions. Despite their situation, they were all sure in their tiny minds that he had come back for his lover.

How romantic.

Angeline suppressed a sigh and a roll of her eyes, but any trace of annoyance evaporated when Maros moved closer. She sucked in a sharp breath. Her gift remained as useless as ever against him, blinding her to his thoughts.

He reached for her hand, and her fingers twitched.

Without a word, without looking away, he lifted her hand to his lips. As if she were a fragile porcelain vase, he placed a kiss on her shaking, freezing fingers.

She flinched when he reached for her face, but he only tucked a loose strand of hair behind her ear. His finger slowly traced the contour of her jaw and neck, lingering at her collarbone. He hesitated to move lower, a spasm crossing his face.

The simple touch of his finger down her neck sent a shiver through Angeline's body and brought her pulse pounding to her ears.

"So, this is where you were hiding," he whispered, his thumb brushing her lower lip, pulling it.

She did not answer, unable to think about anything but his touch. Her skin was begging to finally be touched again.

After a few seconds of endless silence, Maros turned toward her initial captor.

"Bring her to my room. She is mine." He then spoke louder. "Share the other ladies. One sip of their blood is enough to satisfy you for the night. Do not kill or touch them, or I'll kill you. Clear?" He let his gaze wander over the troops, as if he were making sure nobody dared snicker at his words. Angeline guessed that having dozens of valuable hostages, 'Daughters of Europe' as they were called, could be useful.

She would not complain about that. This may save some of them.

Angeline obediently followed the vampire, wanting to get away from Maros's gaze as fast as possible, but she especially longed to flee from the gossipy minds of the crowd. Between the convent girls and the army of hundreds of magical creatures, she thought her brain would explode soon, despite her skills at controlling her gift.

A vampire named Ronan brought her to one of the rooms on the upper floor, and after a quick inspection, she guessed it was where the Mother Superior, Mother Athena, lived. Yes, that was her name. Angeline shuddered when she remembered having seen the Mother's favorite whip lying on the floor earlier, covered in blood. She was gone now, and the young woman was not sad about it. She'd had enough taste of her whip for a lifetime.

Angeline didn't resist when Ronan forced her to sit on the floor in front of the fire and tied her ankles together in front of her. The ropes bit into her fragile skin, and she winced. Where exactly did he think she would run? He caught her exasperated look, and with an air of defiance, tied up her hands.

"Is this really necessary?" she asked. "I don't see myself running away in the blizzard surrounded by hundreds of vampires and werewolves."

Well, now that my damn She-Wolf is back, maybe I will.

She stopped talking when Ronan growled at her, displaying red eyes and sharp fangs. Too bad she needed more than that to back down.

"What are you growling at?" She lifted her eyebrows. "I grew up with your kind. A mewling baby vampire cannot scare me."

The smirk on the man's face vanished, replaced by something far more dangerous. His crimson eyes glared at her, and his fangs shone under the flickering light of the fire.

"Little piece of advice, Princess," he said, his voice filled with sarcasm. He kneeled far too close to her for her taste. "Be nice to him and he might return the favor, but don't expect the same from everyone else. As far as I'm concerned, once he is done with you, I don't mind having a taste."

"Is that so?"

Angeline drew her hands and legs closer and raised her chin. In a swift movement, she propelled her magic, sending her branches toward the man without hesitation. He froze in front of her, his eyes widen.

How about you tell those exact words to Maros?

His mind was feeble. It was easy to give the instruction.

Ronan stood and walked to the door, then stopped with his hand on the handle. Every muscle in his body seemed to contract, as if he were fighting an invisible force. He turned back toward her, eyes wide, mouth pressed into a thin line, unable to speak.

"Bye, Ronan," she said.

Once the man was gone, Angeline almost regretted sending him to his probable death, or at least some probable broken bones. *Almost.*

She sure hoped his words weren't meant to be dirty. Hopefully, Maros would just feed on her. He looked paler than at their last encounter, and vampires were already pale. After all, feeding during the war was troublesome for them.

It was too bad her new gift would likely not work on Maros or any of the First Family.

Angeline sighed. Despite her brave face and her fun banter with Ronan—still not feeling fully sorry though—she was terrified of what was to come. She repositioned herself, putting her bare feet by the fire to enjoy the warmth on her skin for the first time in five years. The rug's softness made her stay on the floor quite comfortable. Besides her bound legs and hands, it was not so bad. Yet.

Look at you, Miss Optimistic.

She had been in the convent for so long that she didn't know, besides some rumors, what was going on between her family and his. If Maros was grumpy at Louis, he might make her pay for it. Not that Louis would be that upset. After all, she was a single daughter among his hundreds of other children. After five years, she had no doubt she was at the bottom of his list of favorite children.

She held her breath when her wolf jumped inside of her. Maros was coming closer. How come this damn She-Wolf could do that? Why did she shut down for so long, only to return with full strength?

Maros entered the dark room with a smile on his previously morose face. His emerald eyes wandered over her legs, and he scoffed when she tried to cover them. He removed his bloody shirt, throwing it on the floor.

Angeline tried not to look, but the man's body bore scars worse than the ones on his face. From what she had learned, they were gifts from her uncles. She turned her head away, pouting, when he kneeled to her level and caressed her arm, sending shivers through her.

"Did you spend the last five years here, Pet?" Maros asked, his expression showing genuine curiosity. "Daddy must have been furious with you. Is it because of our little adventure?"

Angeline breathed harshly as she remembered why she was here. Flashbacks of violence and Paul humiliating her came to mind.

She shook her head. "The world does not revolve around you, you know? Just do what you want. I don't care anymore."

"No?" asked Maros, his eyes turning red.

"No."

"So, I can do everything I want? You might not like it."

"I spent five years in this place. Try me."

Maros scoffed and, in a fast movement, without a word, laid her down on the rug while she let out a broken scream of surprise. She was not expecting him to actually do something. *What a boor!*

He yanked on the ropes that held her ankles together, breaking them with a groan. Angeline whimpered, and he rubbed her soft skin where the binds that left their mark. His touch was worse than anything; so soft.

Angeline decided to give him the cold shoulder. If she had learned anything, it was that men enjoyed it when women fought back. She turned her head and ignored him while he did his business. That sounded like a brilliant plan. She just had to focus on the fire.

Maros settled down between her legs. He touched her leg and torso, brushing her breast so lightly that Angeline was not sure if it was his intention. Both his hands followed the shape of her body hidden under her dress. His touch was soft and rough at the same time. The sensation gave her goose bumps and triggered an uncontrollable tremor.

Her wolf whined with excitement, to Angeline's great displeasure. Her wolf was the one who caused her all of her problems.

You shush now!

She said nothing when his hands ran over her breasts, this time firmly and with purpose. An uncontrollable whine escaped her when she felt his fingers on her sensitive nipples. She took a deep breath and looked at the man who was caressing her. His eyes reflected the fire, filled with lust. His body tensed above hers.

The rub became an intense pinch, and Angeline's breath jerked. A new sensation took over her body; this time, she didn't think it was only her wolf's fault. Confused, she tried to push him away with her tied hands, but he pinned her arms above her head. Lowering his face, he peered at her for a few seconds. He moved his hand to her cheek, brushing her so gently she wanted to cry.

Tears welled, and she closed her eyes. She had forgotten how it felt to be touched by something other than a whip, a leather belt, or a wooden bat. He released her arms from his steel hold, but she was too ashamed to open her eyes. That's when it happened.

A soft brush against her lips.

Angeline's eyes flung open to look at the vampire. He was kissing her.

She didn't say a word but opened her mouth when Maros found her lips again, this time with more intensity. One of his hands slipped under her dress and moved toward her intimacy. She whined.

Maros stopped the kiss and dove his crimson eyes into hers, which were filled with tears.

"You just have to say no, Princess, and I won't go any further," he whispered in a raspy voice. "I thought you would use your little trick on me. Poor Ronan learned his lesson, I fear."

She inhaled, holding back the tears threatening to spill. "It's not working on you..."

She—or was it her wolf?—had only one desire: for him to take his hand a tiny bit higher. Flashbacks of pain and violence came back to her in a wave, and once again, she could not help herself. Tears ran down her cheeks.

Maros sighed and removed his hand, kissing Angeline's cheek and tasting her tears. "One day you'll be ready for me, White Wolf."

CHAPTER 12

ANGELINE WOKE UP TO muffled voices, pulling her away from her dreams of paws in the fresh snow. The same freaking dream. These have been recurring images for years now, and she wished she could dream of something else. Like paws in the sand, or paws in the mud. *Anything.*

The night before was a blur. After her cry party, Maros had cut the ropes that held her limbs and carefully carried her to the only bed in the room. She managed to fall asleep after a few minutes on the same bed where Mother Athena used to lie. The cotton sheets smelled of an old patchouli candle that had burned for too long. It was much more comfortable than her previous bed, so she was not complaining.

She certainly also wasn't complaining about the vampire's presence in the bed. She had felt him join her before she fell into the arms of Morpheus. Maros slept beside her, without a word, with his hand resting on the swell of her hips, and both her She-Wolf and herself had enjoyed his presence more than they should have.

It was morning time now, and Angeline tried to keep her eyes shut, not ready to confront the world. She couldn't stifle a yawn, interrupting the voices in the room. She pouted. Seeing Maros was not how she wanted to start the day. Unfortunately, she didn't have a choice. She was presented with his sarcastic smile as soon as she opened her eyes.

"Good morning, Princess," he greeted her, arms behind his back. He wore the same bloody shirt as the day before, but the blood had dried.

She grunted and rolled her eyes, which didn't seem to discourage him.

"You should get up; we have news from Paul and his minions, including your father," Maros said emotionlessly. With a single nod, he dismissed the soldier with whom he had been talking to.

Angeline doubted Paul would trade her for anything. He could have any woman he wanted now that he was planning to be king. And really, there was only so much rejection a man could take... wasn't there? Besides, going back to Paul was the last thing she desired.

She stood up from the bed and froze upon seeing the piece of fabric Maros held in his hands.

"Knowing you, you must be tired of this ugly nun outfit," he smiled. "Here's a little something I borrowed."

She didn't answer but took the midnight-blue velvet dress the First handed her and examined it skeptically. The feel of the fabric made her smile; so soft and beautiful. She sure missed having nice things.

She glared at Maros, hoping the look on her face would let him know he was not wanted while she was getting undressed. The man scoffed and let her pass, but did not move his eyes away from her.

Angeline sighed and looked around the room to find a dark corner where she could change into her new prized possession. The best choice was a rocking chair, where she could at least hide a bit. With a provocative look, she went to the chair, made sure that at least her white bottom was covered, and took off her ugly nightgown.

"We gave your father and other daddies a choice yesterday," Maros said behind her.

"Which choice?" she asked, putting on her velvet dress.

Gosh, not being able to read his mind was so irritating. For once, she wished she could use her annoying gift, but his brain was still full of darkness; it was impossible to read.

"We told them we would happily give them back their lovely daughters, almost untouched, in exchange for them and their kingdoms to cease fighting," Maros explained.

Angeline's blood froze, and her breath quickened. She finished adjusting her dress, locking the golden lacing with her expert touch, and looked back at Maros. "What... what did they say?"

"There were a few disagreements among them." Maros smiled. "A few of your little friends still have caregivers who love them, and they have already left the premises as promised. Others like you, I'm afraid, will spend more time in our company. Virgin blood is unparalleled in terms of nutrition." His smile grew, showing all his teeth—including his fangs.

She wasn't expecting much from Louis, to be honest, but she had hoped that maybe Nanabrok would negotiate her freedom better, or even Quentin and Misa. The French Kingdom without the help of the witches and wolves? Well, they were better off going home. She hated herself when, once again, tears sprang to her eyes. Since when was she so sensitive? She thought the convent had made her an unbreakable wall.

She sat on the couch and untangled her long hair with her fingers, hoping to distract herself from her racing thoughts. What was going to happen to her and the others? Mostly, she worried about herself. They all made it clear they were not interested in a Delacour friendship—or at least not with a little whore like her. She knew what this word meant now.

Her mind went to Annabella. Angeline hadn't seen her since yesterday, when they were caught together. She was not a virgin anymore, and deep inside, Angeline hoped she was still alive. They could still feed from her, right?

Angeline pulled a knot harder than necessary, realizing how selfish she had become. She turned her head away when Maros approached her.

"Do you think you have it difficult, Princess?" He smirked, his voice filled with mockery.

Angeline didn't want to answer him; trolls were better left ignored, she had learned.

He swiftly caught her chin between his fingers, forcing her to look at him. She jumped and held her breath, knowing her eyes were probably red from crying. Angeline did not want to give him another reason to make fun of her.

Maros scoffed, released her from his grip, and made her an absurd offer.

"I'll tell you what... You have two choices here. You can stay with me as my cute little maid, my snack—and maybe more if I'm in a cuddly mood."

She opened her mouth to tell him to go to hell, but he interrupted her. "Or... you can join your little friends downstairs and have a few dozen vampires feeding on you daily."

Angeline jumped to her feet. "We might be in this hellhole, but we should still be treated with the respect our rank deserves!" She accompanied her screams with a fist slamming into the vampire's chest. His solid chest did not budge despite using all her strength.

These vampires are so annoying.

"Please. This convent is the worst place you could be sent to. The women down there don't matter to anyone outside, like yourself. Am I right?"

The truth hit her hard. She flushed with shame. On an impulse, she raised her hand and slapped Maros across the face. Angeline immediately regretted her gesture when her hand burned from the pain.

"Don't talk about what you don't know," she spat.

His eyes turned red, and Angeline knew he was holding back from hurting her. Without a word, he grabbed her and threw her over his shoulder and walked out the door.

Angeline was tired of being carried like this. She expressed her displeasure loudly as he descended a set of stairs she recognized as leading to the solitary cells. Her heart raced at the thought of being thrown into one of those cells.

He dropped her on the floor, but Angeline managed to keep her balance and stood up with a look of defiance, unconsciously readjusting her dress. A silence followed, then she heard them—both in her head and vocally. The pain, the fear, the humiliation—the feelings all came at once, raging on her, running over her skin.

She turned to find where the cries were coming from and saw most of her convent neighbors grouped in three cells. As if they didn't have enough terrible memories in there. Angeline's heart broke. They looked miserable, even more than before, which she thought was impossible. Their dresses were covered in blood, and there were multiple bite marks on their skin. Some of them were being fed on. The young women kicked their feet and hands in vague protest, but it did nothing to stop the vampires.

Her stomach turned when she realized female vampires were feeding on them, too. Angeline always had an idea of women supporting women, but she had to learn that it was not a thing with vampires or mortals. The little voice in her head screamed at her that they had to feed, but it didn't matter; she was too upset to be forgiving.

Maros touched her neck, his fingers brushing her skin, and murmured into her ear, "You can stay here with your little friends." He caught her chin between his fingers, turning her tear-filled eyes toward him. His gaze was unforgiving. Cold. "Or you can stay with me and be my little thing." He seemed so proud of himself.

She and her wolf were bursting with hate. How could he go from putting her to bed nicely to being what her brother would call an absolute asshole? *Men.*

The thought of being touched by so many men was unbearable. Her Spirit-Gift would not be able to handle it. The influx of thoughts would drive her to madness within a day, and she would not be able to bear the suffering of the other women crying in her mind.

"Say it," Maros demanded. She turned her head away to look at the others one last time.

Some of them were... angry? At her? Thoughts rushed into Angeline's mind, and she didn't appreciate what she heard.

"He didn't come here because of me, you fucktwat!" she yelled at Lucia, who was the most adamant in her mind that all of this was Angeline's fault.

The few girls gasped and started whispering while Lucia stepped back into the darkness of her cell, as if Angeline's gift could not reach her there.

Angeline held her breath. Another vampire peered at her curiously.

"I'll stay with you," she murmured.

CHAPTER 13

THE ROOM WAS SILENT except for the trickling of water as Angeline poured the last pitcher into the tub. Steam drifted up, filling the air with the faint scent of lavender from the herbs she had found among Mother Athena's collection. She had hoped to find some boiled foxglove, which was poisonous for a vampire. Unfortunately, there were none.

You would think any witch kept a stock handy, right?

Her wolf whined in agreement.

Making a bath for the oafish vampire took her way too long, and she hoped she would not have to do it daily. Being a servant was no fun. She set the empty pitcher aside and glanced over her shoulder.

Maros stood in the doorway, still wearing the same bloody clothes from the day before, watching her with that same unnerving stillness he often showed. He followed her every move. There was something predatory in his gaze, and to Angeline's fury, he made no effort to hide it.

"Are you going to watch me all night, or shall I take my leave?" she asked, her voice firm. Her body was half-turned, so he could not see her hands shaking or how she gripped the edge of the bath. She was still angry with him from earlier.

Angeline needed to forget the screams of the other women and how tragic they looked in their cells.

"Stay," he whispered.

With a resigned sigh, Angeline moved to the edge of the room, as far away from the bathtub as possible. She folded her arms over her chest and leaned against the wall.

She caught a glimpse of Annabella before Maros pushed her back into their—*his*—bedroom. The other young woman was apparently 'serving' Manus.

They barely had time to exchange a look, and she hoped the big brother was treating her new friend well. He was terrifying but seemed to be more of a gentleman than Maros. Then again, she knew through experience that sometimes the better-looking gents were the worst of all. *Like that ass, Paul.*

This prick wanted her to give him a bath. She had hoped that Athena would have had a modern bathroom as the Mother Superior of the convent, but she didn't.

Angeline had been ready to fight against the order, but she remembered where he would send her if she were being a brat. Neither the cells downstairs nor the prospect of being a buffet was enticing. She'd rather handle the First.

She refused to contemplate his scarred skin; her gaze was fixed on a point far past him. Some of his scars were as wide as two fingers, and the thought of the pain he had to endure gave her shivers. Angeline hadn't really seen a naked man before, and she and her She-Wolf tried to keep their curiosity at bay. The vampire didn't care about his audience. He stripped bare and jumped into the warm bath, exhaling as the water took him in.

She felt his attention on her and swallowed under the weight of his gaze roaming her face, her body, her stance, lingering on every part as though he were analyzing her.

"Join me, White Wolf," he finally said, his tone laced with an unheard-of tenderness.

Her eyes narrowed. "Not a chance."

Maros's lips curved into a slight smile, but he didn't insist. Instead, while letting out a chuckle, he lowered himself into the water. He leaned back against the side of the tub, his eyes never leaving her.

"You could tell me about the convent," he said. "It seems you don't want to talk about why you're here, but I would love to know what your life was like in here, away from everything you love."

"You don't even know what I love. We met for five minutes. The longest five minutes of my life, but still." Angeline paced the bedroom, her arms encircling her body as if it could protect her. She made sure to stay away from any grabbing hands.

Angeline knew he was a grabber.

A laugh answered her, but the vampire didn't push the topic.

With some of the others back with their families, she was sure that the story of her staying in Maros's care and private room had already reached every corner of the magical world. There was no way her family would have her back.

Angeline glanced at Maros, hesitating. If this boor was going to be king, she may as well make sure the convent would burn to the ground.

"What is there to tell?" she asked with ice in her voice. She turned her body toward him but kept a safe distance. "This is more of a prison than a convent, and you were right. The ones who are here are nothing to people outside. No one cares for us anymore."

Her voice trembled.

Maros observed her thoughtfully, his expression cold as if he was trying to read something she was not telling him. "I was surprised your father didn't ask to have you back. You must have been naughty."

Anger rose inside Angeline; she grabbed a cushion from the couch and threw it at Maros. Unsurprisingly, he pushed back the soft attack. Laughter filled his eyes, which crinkled at the corners.

"Naughty?" She spat. "I have been nothing short of perfect my entire life. I was not the one who should have been sent to die!"

His fingers tapped on the side of the bathtub thoughtfully, as if interpreting her words. "What about Paul?"

Angeline scoffed. Of all the topics, Paul was her least favorite. "What about him?"

"Well, he's supposed to be your fiancé. I thought you were sent here for protection, but it does not seem that you were catered for here. "

"I am *not* engaged to Paul," she said slowly. She would die a thousand times before giving herself to that dreadful man.

A flicker of something flashed in Maros's eyes, but it was gone before she could be sure what it was. He inclined his head, a slight nod of acknowledgment. The silence between them grew thicker.

"What happened in here then, my Princess?"

"I am *not* your princess. And nothing good happened here. The food is shit, the neighbors are unfriendly, the nuns are the worst—and they always find new ways to torture you."

His eyes flashed red, and he grabbed the side of the bath, clenching the ceramic. "Did they hurt you?"

Angeline looked away from his scarred hand and scoffed. "Of course, they hurt me. This is the Convent of Lamursa. We are the Lost Ones; that is what they call us. The nuns can do everything they want to us as long as we don't die." Angeline inhaled deeply. "Unless they had other instructions."

Angeline stopped pacing and crossed her arms over her chest. "Four weeks after my arrival, I accepted that this was the place I would die. All the women were brought into the back court to be given a show. There was a woman named Alice. Her father denied her, meaning they had the right to kill her if they wanted."

"The nuns are allowed to... kill the women?" He didn't seem to believe her, not that she could blame him. For whoever was not raised in this world, it was a tough truth to hear.

"Of course they can," she says. "Haven't you been alive for two thousand years, or something? You should know about these kinds of places if you're going to be king."

"I sure should."

Angeline looked at him, trying to tell if he was being sarcastic, and she continued. "A fast kill would have been merciful and easy to do. Instead, Mother Athena wanted to make an example. She ordered the nuns to tie Alice up to the big oak tree outside and left her there until she died. It took two days of screaming agony, right under my windows, for her to die. I don't think they buried her as per the Spirits' tradition.

Tears sprang to her eyes. She didn't know why she was bothering to tell him, but he asked, and the awful truths needed to break free. She was the only one left who remembered the event. All the others had been called back by their families, or they had died of various sicknesses or self-harm.

The vampire jumped out of the bath and ran to her in a blur.

She gasped as he pulled her into his warm, wet embrace. He held her close and whispered soft words in her ear. His arms firmly encircled her waist, drenching the fabric of her dress.

"Very well," he murmured at last. "You may go now."

Angeline raised her head to meet his red gaze. His lips were pressed into a thin line.

She pulled away, her gaze lingering on him for a heartbeat longer than intended. Angeline did her best not to look down, where she knew his desire would show. Without another word, she turned to leave.

Before she could go, he said, "Beauty, art, nature, music, passion, freedom..."

Angeline turned to him, tilting her head to the side.

"Those are the things you love, Princess. Imagine what I could learn with more than the 'longest five minutes of your life?'"

She chuckled and held back a sniffle, but she still took her leave. Her heartbeat raced like never before as she left Maros behind. She felt his burning gaze until the door closed behind her.

Later that day, he left her alone and asked no more of her. Thank the Spirits. Despite his kindness, she was ready to throw something at his face if he made the mistake of asking for anything.

She hovered along the corridors, hoping to see or hear Annabella, but she didn't perceive a single brain wave when walking in front of Manus's door. So, she gave up. She was surprised that Maros let her walk around freely. After all, she was a prisoner. Perhaps he was testing her, waiting for her to try escaping.

That was not an option. The convent grounds were filled with dead bodies and the vampire army. Soldiers spread out in various groups, either resting or preparing for their departure. Angeline stood on the stairs at the garden entrance. She had hoped to get some fresh air, but hesitated when she saw all the men. It screamed of trouble.

She sighed and prepared to go back to the bedroom. Experience taught her that taking a walk alone in a pretty garden was not a brilliant plan.

"Planning an escape, Princess?"

She rolled her eyes before seeing him. Maros was behind her; who knew how long he had been there? At least he had changed into clean clothes.

"Would you try to catch me if I did?" She asked.

"Of course. I love a good chase."

Angeline scoffed, walking back to their bedroom. Before she could leave, he wrapped an arm around her waist. She stiffened under his touch.

"Don't you want to take a walk?" He asked. "My men know better than to try to bite you."

She shrugged her shoulders, pouting. "I don't want them to touch me."

"Trust me. They won't." Maros raised his hand and delicately held her chin between his fingers.

"Just because you ordered it? You're not king yet." She lifted a brow, and a mocking smile tugged at her lips.

"No, Princess, because they know you're mine. I may not have marked you yet, but here you are: walking freely, wearing a pretty dress, smelling nice, and driving me insane."

Angeline stopped breathing; her face flushed with warmth. Maros pulled her against him, guiding her toward the garden she longed to visit.

"Come now," he said, "I need some time away from politics and strategies."

"I'm afraid that if you become king, you'll have to get used to those..."

"*When* I become king," the vampire retorted, making Angeline chuckle.

After a few steps of comfortable silence and under some curious looks from the soldiers, he asked her one of her dreaded questions.

"How come you didn't try to escape?"

Angeline glanced at him from the corner of her eye. "I haven't tried *yet*. You have only been here for a day."

Maros laughed, likely unafraid of her random threats.

"No, I meant to escape from here. With your amazing shifting gift, it would have been easy."

"What makes you think I *didn't* try?" She retorted. "No offense, but as a future king, you should really get a lesson on places like this."

He tilted his head to the side, genuinely curious.

"There are protective spells on this place, and similar convents," she said. "They block the magic of the women being brought in, but not for the witches." She stopped.

Angeline was not used to talking about her magic except with her trusted friends like Jack, Nanabrok, or the wolves.

Maros scoffed and subtly moved closer, rubbing her back. "Did they make your wolf go away then?"

Her breath hitched, and an old pain awakened. It was the trauma of having her twin gone. "I... tried to escape. Often—"

Maros's eyes glinted with laughter.

"—But when I knew about the protective magic around the convent, I tried to hide my She-Wolf as much as I could. My family never knew about her, and I didn't want the nuns to tell them. So, I stopped shifting, thinking I could free us alone."

Her voice trembled and tears sprang to her eyes. She jerked away from Maros, but he pulled her back, forcing her to look at him.

"Tell me, my White Wolf..."

"They always caught me. I never made it past the wall, and they punished me every time, but I could handle it. It took a few days of healing, but that didn't break me. One day, they hurt me more..." Angeline held her breath. This was one of those moments she would rather forget. "They tied me to the oak tree."

His body tensed. He pulled her closer, cradling her face. "For how long?"

"Three days... naked and whipped every day. It was freezing outside. I survived because of my She-Wolf pushing me, and because I have some... basics... of Earth magic. After three days... she was gone. She left me... she couldn't take it anymore. I screamed so much, the nuns had a moment of panic, and they brought me back in. I was thrown into the cells downstairs... but my wolf was gone. Her leaving was worse than the torture."

Angeline stopped breathing. He plunged her into a warm embrace, her face in his neck. His smell took over her senses, her wolf running in circles inside her mind. After so much torture and repression, the wolf was content.

"I'm sorry you lost her, Pet. I thought I could feel her again when I saw you. Are you sure she's gone?"

Angeline laughed and pulled back, locking her eyes with his. "This damn She-Wolf has been back since you arrived."

Maros laughed heartily and placed his lips against Angeline's, who let out a gurgled gasp. He stepped back, smirking, while Angeline stammered, still in shock from the kiss.

"I'm not sorry for this, Princess," he said, moving his hand closer to her face, brushing her burning cheek.

"Of course you're not," she whispered. "Are you ever sorry about anything?"

"Yes." His eyes flashed red. "Trust me, I am."

Angeline thought it would be smarter not to ask about what he could be sorry about.

CHAPTER 14

THE NEXT DAY, THE moment she had dreamed of for five years arrived. It was time to leave the convent. Angeline was already outside, standing on the broad stone steps leading up to the grand entrance. The iron-bound wooden doors loomed above her, heavy and uninviting. She was ready to run away.

Next time I set foot in this place, it will be to burn it.

That was a promise to herself she planned on keeping.

While looking at the old stone covered with snow and moss, Angeline was unsure how to feel. She never thought she would get out of the convent, at least not in one piece, but she was finally leaving. After all those nights of prayers, cries, and despair, it was over. She was leaving.

As a prisoner, but still.

She was also unsure how to feel about Maros. Her anger at him for the whole "be my cute little personal maid - snack- or more" hadn't lessened, but it was difficult not to melt when he listened to and comforted her. He must have been playing with her. Why else would he be so... gentle?

Angeline was still untouched, to her great surprise. It was especially surprising after the few kisses they exchanged. She knew the vampire desired her from the way he followed her moves around the room, or how he let his fingers caress her skin sometimes with a contemplative look. Not that she was complaining about it. Her feelings and her desires were different matters. He hadn't even tasted her blood, even though he must have been starving.

She lit up when she spotted a brunette she knew well—Annabella. She saw her too and descended the stairs as fast as she could, her emerald dress flying behind her, despite the icy snow covering the stairs.

Angeline gasped when Annabella's arms surrounded her.

Are we best friends now or what? Angeline thought.

Me like her! Me like her! Answered her wolf.

Shush!

Her damn wolf had been more and more present, taking over her thoughts, her actions, and her desire. She knew the wolf enjoyed Maros's wolf, and it was utterly upsetting while she was still trying to sort out her feelings.

Annabella finally ended the hug, smiling shyly. "I'm glad to see you."

After a few seconds, Angeline sighed. "Me too."

"I'm even more glad to leave this place," whispered Annabella while looking at the lines of nuns, the few left alive. It looked like they were coming with them.

"I would have rather they stayed here, to be honest," Angeline said. "Ideally, bleeding to death or being buried alive." She turned her attention back to Annabella, trying to find any sign of hurt besides the obvious fang marks on her neck.

Annabella saw her watching and quickly pulled a scarf around her neck. A new scarf, a new dress.

"It's okay; he didn't hurt me," Annabella murmured. Her cheeks turned pink.

Angeline chuckled. Annabella was trouble.

"I'm happy to hear that. I was not sure they would keep you alive because you're not a..." She cut herself off. There was no need to remind Annabella of her previous decadence.

Annabella smirked. "My blood can still feed them, I guess. Or at least him." She looked around and bent closer to Angeline. "Manus is a bit possessive, I think. He does not want others to touch me."

"You don't say," Angeline said, without hiding the sarcasm in her voice. Her curiosity rose. "Did you..." Her eyes widened. She always loved gossip, and she deserved to have a bit of fun on such a doomed day.

Annabella shook her head. "Of course not. I mean... he didn't try."

"Right." Which proved her point. Manus was more of a gentleman than Maros.

"What about y..." Annabella started. Her eyes held a new light. All traces of the sad young woman from the previous days were gone. She interrupted herself, biting her lips, looking at something over Angeline's shoulders.

Angeline didn't need to turn to know her own very annoying First was heading their way.

The sound of crunched snow behind her confirmed this, and she finally glanced to see Maros looking at her.

"Princess," he said, "This is for you." He gave her an old but warm cape that would be perfect for their upcoming travels through the forest.

"Thanks..."

She held out her hand, but Maros was already draping the cape over her shoulders. He moved her braided hair out of the way and pressed a kiss to her neck. Angeline shivered under the brush of his lips. He growled, squeezing her hips.

Angeline tried to forget about his touch, which triggered too many feelings. She whispered another thanks while closing the cape over her breast, enjoying the heavy weight and warmth it would give her for the long journey ahead.

When she raised her head, the other girls watched Annabella and her. One dive into their minds, and she knew they were still angry. They would still be blemished in their shame and pain; Angeline could not blame them. They stood in a herd, all close to each other, as if strength in numbers would make a difference in this place. Even though they didn't have someone allocated to watch them, there was no doubt they were prisoners.

"Should we join the other girls?" She asked Maros.

"You join whomever you want, Pet. As long as you don't slow us down or get eaten."

She tsked at him, but didn't move away, keeping a tight hand on Annabella to get her to stay with her. If the other girls wanted to hate them, let them. She let her attention wander to the funny army that was parading under her eyes. Vampires, wolves, and witches, all mixed, and helping each other.

Now, *that* was new. From what she experienced, they rarely enjoyed sticking together. Teamwork was not something that came easily when your species had spent centuries fighting each other. But then, if she were fighting Paul, she would also put aside any hate to focus on the big plan.

"Just one more thing, Princess."

Maros's voice interrupted her thoughts, and for one second, she worried he would find some new way of hurting or shaming her—just when he was starting to behave.

She gave him an interrogative look. Annabella tensed at her side.

"Come with me," he ordered, offering her his arm.

She rolled her eyes but still accepted the support, giving an encouraging smile to Annabella, who let go of her arm. When she saw where he was taking her, her breath faltered.

"Here are the nuns. Well, this is what's left of them," Maros said. He was talking to her, but it felt like he was talking to the entire army and prisoners, as they all stopped to observe their future king.

Angeline inhaled deeply. The last thing she wanted was to talk to the nuns. She was glad to see them covered in blood and throwing hateful looks at her. Sister Agatha was among them. She survived, but a face covered in blood and claw marks displayed her downfall.

Maros moved closer to them, leaving Angeline behind. He turned to her.

"Which one of them hurt you, my Princess?" He spoke clearly, but his voice resonated with hidden anger, ready to burst.

Angeline's heart raced, just like her She-Wolf.

"W-what... d-do you mean?" She stuttered, twisting her fingers together.

"Which one of those women dared touch my White Wolf?" His eyes were red, and his voice was cold as he waited for an answer.

The army was silent, unmoving.

It took only a split second for Angeline to decide what she wanted to see, what she wanted to hear, and who she wanted to be.

"All of them," she whispered, clenching her hands together. Unfortunately, it was true. Mother Athena did not choose the nuns for their kindness. "But especially her." She pointed at Sister Agatha.

Angeline was glad that looks could not kill, because Sister Agatha's glare would surely be her demise.

Maros moved with inhuman speed. In a blur of shadow and blood, he took care of the nuns. Heads flew. Intestines splashed. It was over so quickly.

There was only one survivor, Sister Agatha, standing in a pool of blood. Her hands shook, and her eyes were wide with terror.

Angeline could not help but be satisfied. Finally, this monster was brought to her knees.

"No, please..." Sister Agatha's voice was nothing more than a croak before Maros silenced her with his grip, tightening a hand around her neck. Her eyes bulged as he dragged her across the bloody snow toward Angeline.

Sister Agatha kicked, her movements weak and desperate, but it was a lost cause.

Maros caught Angeline's chin between his fingers. The sticky, scarlet blood stained her skin, but she didn't recoil from the touch.

"Do you want her on the tree?" He asked, gazing deep into Angeline's eyes.

"Please." That was Angeline's only answer.

He smiled, the most terrifying smile Angeline had ever seen him wear. He stole a soft kiss, lingering just long enough for her to jump, and inhaled loudly under his lips.

Angeline followed the path of blood left by the nuns, disappearing into the darkness of the convent. Sister Agatha screamed her pleas.

CHAPTER 15

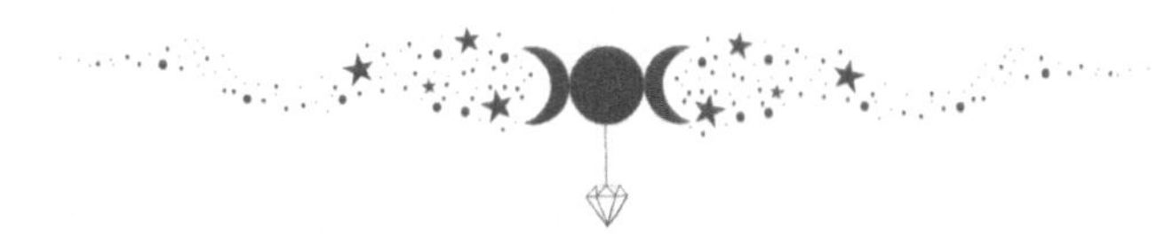

THE WIND BLEW, CARRYING a biting chill and a lingering scent from the bloodied snow where the nuns lay lifeless.

Maros returned quickly, free from Sister Agatha, whose screams resonated through the stone court. Angeline was still shocked by the previous scene, a funny blend of fear and deep satisfaction. She was raised to be kind and sweet, but now wished for more blood to be shed in her name.

It must be the She-Wolf.

Angeline didn't have time to move before Maros reached her, his lips brushing her cheek in a possessive gesture that sent a shiver down her spine. He smirked and left her standing there.

Angeline watched as he strode to the front, gathering his army with one raised hand, preparing to lead them on a gruesome journey to Ukraine. He paid no mind to the dead bodies left behind.

Angeline was pulled from her thoughts as Annabella joined her. "Looks like yours is a tad possessive too," she whispered, hiding a smile.

"He's not *mine*," Angeline retorted, glancing around to ensure no one overheard.

Who am I kidding?

Annabella's laugh rang out, light and genuine, surprising Angeline. It was the first time she'd ever heard her friend laugh so freely, and it was beautiful. She took Angeline's arm, pulling her through the snow, their capes drawn tightly. Angeline was happy to have some protection from the cold. Thankfully, the witches cleared the path of snow, and only a thin layer was left.

After an hour-long strenuous walk, Blanda joined them. She was the only one among the First that Angeline could read the thoughts of, most likely thanks to her witch side. Her peaceful yet strong mind reminded her of Misa. She knew the gorgeous blonde respected her, mostly because of her She-Wolf gift, but she was too polite to ask Angeline more about it. It was a funny thing to hear, considering the rest of her family were a bunch of arrogant boors.

"Maros told me you practice Earth magic?" The witch asked with genuine curiosity.

Angeline pouted. She didn't want everyone to know what she could do. That her She-Wolf was in the open was already a mistake. It was impossible to resist the pull of the ancient witch, her obvious kindness and care. Angeline had heard a lot about Blanda.

"I just know a few basics. The witch Nanabrok taught me," she answered, aware of Annabella's curious look.

"You could have found a worse teacher than Nanabrok. She's quite terrifying," Blanda said matter-of-factly.

Angeline laughed. "She sure is, but coming from you, that's a joke."

Blanda chuckled. "I have been... alive... for a while. My magic would be too much for modern witches to handle. I'm glad the power is spread among them."

Annabella interrupted them. "What do you mean, 'spread'?"

Angeline glanced at Blanda; it was not her story to tell.

"When the oldest witch on Earth passes away," Blanda said, "her magic goes to the next in line, who then decides how to allow others to practice. I decided centuries ago to separate the powers. To make every witch more powerful, but with less magic."

"Is it related to what they call the Elemental magic?" Annabella asked.

Blanda nodded. "I spread the magic in four distinct styles. Earth, Water, Wind, and Fire. It took one or two centuries for covens to get a good handle on those, but now, there's no debating that it was the right decision. The magic needs balance; we, witches, bring balance by using our magic in a certain way."

"So, which one do you use?"

Blanda smirked. "I practice druid magic; the Spirits allowed me to keep all four at their best. When I die, the next witch will inherit those, too."

"What if the next witch decides to mess around with what you did?" Angeline asked, frowning.

"Well, I'm not planning on dying anytime soon, but if I do, Nanabrok is next in line. I trust her decisions." The old witch pushed her sleeve up her arm, showing an impressive collection of scars that created a complex pattern. "When the Spirits are happy with you, with the way you practice magic, with the way you believe in them, they mark you, creating a new scar on your limb dedicated to your magic."

Annabella's eyes widened.

It was Angeline who explained. "The older the witch, the more marks she gets. Scarification. Right arm for Earth, left arm for Fire, right leg for Water, left leg for Air. When you're older and wiser, you can have scars marked on other limbs. Every witch practices a bit of everything. It just means they're much better at a specific element."

"But Angeline, you know Earth magic," Annabella said, "but I have seen no marks."

Angeline took a deep breath. "I know the basics. Earth magic is the 'easiest' to learn, as the earth is right there for you to use. Healing, inner strength... that's what the earth provides you. Anyone can learn as long as they believe in it. After all of this, I still believe in the Spirits, so they allow me to use Earth as I see fit, but as I'm not a witch, I don't get a mark."

Annabella pouted. "Well, I'm not a very religious person." Angeline snorted.

"People who don't belong to a magical species have trouble believing, which is perfectly understandable," Blanda said, reassuringly. She changed the topic. "We'll camp in the forest tonight."

"But it's freezing," Annabella protested, shivering.

A voice sounded behind them, low and mocking. "Guess you'll have to cuddle with my brother." It was the other sister, the blond angel of death. Her smirk flashed as she stepped forward. "Hi. I'm Carata. Don't even think about giving me a nickname."

Angeline turned, startled—she didn't even know the vampire was there. "How long have you been there?" She asked.

"Long enough to hear both your heartbeats speed up whenever my annoying brothers are mentioned." She was simply splendid, like an angel who fell on Earth to rip out your heart with a smile. Her eyes were as blue as Angeline's, but the lack of pupils gave her a terrifying, ethereal air.

Angeline and Annabella turned red as they turned away, ignoring Carata.

"I think she's here to protect us," Annabella murmured.

Angeline snorted. "Or to keep us from running."

"Why would we run away?"

Her voice had such a genuine tone that Angeline could not hide her shock.

Annabella added, "I don't know about you, but besides the biting, this is the first time in months I have been treated... well..." She swallowed.

Is Maros treating me well?

He was a pain in her neck as far as Angeline was concerned; he was cold, controlling, and always testing her boundaries. Sure, compared to the nuns, he was not that bad. He seemed to care for her, but he had a funny way of showing it. Not to mention that every time he had the occasion, he tried to grab her, smell her, and he loved to tease her.

Angeline shook her head, trying to forget their few lingering kisses. She didn't fight back that hard when it happened.

Her wolf giggled. *You mean you didn't fight at all, right?*

Annabella seemed happy with her fate. She held Angeline's arm tightly and gazed longingly at Manus.

The girl is a freaking artichoke heart, thought Angeline. Angeline hated liars and hypocrites—so, she said it out loud, too.

"You are a freaking artichoke heart. You know that, right? That's why you're here."

Annabella gasped, feigning outrage. "I am *not* an artichoke heart. If you met my Italian Lord, you would agree with me." She winked at Angeline, who scoffed, shocked by the depravity of her friend. Besides Jack, she had never met someone like this.

Angeline would not know where to start with men. She was terrified of what would come after all of this. Sure, being a prisoner under the protection of the strongest vampires was better than being a Lost One getting waterboarded or frozen whips. What about after? Was she the only one thinking about that?

She turned toward Annabella and whispered, "How do you feel about... all of this? What... What would your parents say? And anyone else?"

Angeline could already hear screams of *'traitor'* and see the punishments coming her way; she had seen the ugly side of her father. Louis was not to be trusted, and if she was to return to him, there's no saying what he would do. Her attraction to Maros was even more terrifying. When he decided to take her, would she feel as she felt with Paul? What if he became obsessed with her like he did? It had been hard to escape Paul, and she knew there would be no escape when it came to Maros.

Annabella's genuine laughter caught her by surprise, interrupting her calculations.

"My parents? The Lords? The Vampire of Europe? Why would I care?" Her eyes were bright, not with tears, but with passion.

"They sent me there, Angeline. By the Goddess, they sent you there and told everyone you were dead. So, if being nice to Manus allows me to survive this war and leave Europe as a free woman, I'll do it. Better him than the convent."

Angeline stopped abruptly in the snow, pulling on Annabella's arm and forcing her to halt.

"What did you say?" Her eyes widened, and tears gathered in them.

"What... what?"

"About me being dead?"

Annabella looked at her, lips parted. "You didn't know?" Her voice shook.

Angeline could read her mind as if it were an open book. Annabella realized that her friend may have kept hope all this time, when really, only one word from Louis, and she could have died.

Angeline shook her head. Tears trailed along her cheeks, freezing in place.

Well, that explains a lot.

She wiped her angry tears and searched for Maros in the distance, leading the army. He knew. He had to know.

She marched toward Maros but was instantly stopped by tall, powerful Carata.

Her eyes were as cold as ever, but she smiled faintly. "Sorry, darling. Maros is busy. You can solve your little trouble with him later. Stay in line."

Angeline scoffed. "No. He said I could go where I want, so I'm going to him, to slap that smug immortal face of his."

Carata chuckled and caught Angeline by the arm. "Even though I would love to see it, remember he is your future king. I will tolerate no one shaming him in front of his people."

"Well, he should have thought about that before lying to me."

"When did he lie to you?"

"When he... didn't tell me people thought I was dead."

"Did you *ask* him?" Carata asked with an infuriating calmness.

Angeline's blood boiled. "Your family is the worst when it comes to fine print."

"We know. You will talk to him later, not now. Stay in line, or I'll *make* you stay in line."

Annabella quickly caught up with both women and pulled Angeline toward her, begging her to follow.

Angeline shook, and Annabella tried to appease her with a calm touch.

"I have no value," Angeline whispered.

Annabella smiled sadly.

She knew she was right. "Louis won't let me come back into the world, that's why he didn't take me back. The witches and wolves might not even know. He must have lied to them. Asshole!" She kicked a stone, but it didn't work to release her anger.

"How did you know?" She asked Annabella.

Annabella shrugged her shoulders. "The men who picked me up to drive me to the convent. They teased me. They said I would probably stay longer than the 'Delacour girl.' So, I asked them. They said they took you there years ago. They knew I was not planning to leave soon, so they didn't care about telling me. I thought you knew. I'm sorry, Angeline." She squeezed Angeline's hand.

Angeline jumped at the images that reached her brain, streaming straight from Annabella.

"Oh, sweetie.." Angeline hugged Annabella, who didn't know how to answer.

"Ahem... I thought you were not a hugger?"

"I'm not. I'm just sorry for what they did to you." She released Annabella's hand, giving her a sorry smile.

Angeline didn't mean to pry into her memories, but her gift was out of control, surrendering to her emotions. Annabella's face became even paler than before, and she hid her face, her body shaking like a leaf.

"You know what you should do?" Angeline asked.

Annabella only shook in response.

"You should go tell Manus the drivers' names," she whispered, hoping she would do it. Angeline could compel her, but she knew she could not live with the idea of hypnotizing her closest friend, especially after what she went through.

Annabella raised her head, surprised.

"You said he was a bit possessive, didn't you?" Angeline asked. "If it were my lover who got violated, I would burn the world down."

"We are not, technically, lovers," Annabella whispered

"Not yet..."

Annabella bit her lip and glanced at the front of the line, seeming to make a decision. Her thoughts swirled as she left.

"Sorry, Bella," Angeline murmured.

She needed to be alone for the next part of her plan.

"Blanda?" Angeline said. "I really need a bathroom break."

Pee, shift, run, hide. Escape plan of the year.

They walked further away from the column of men and women trudging forward. Angeline stormed ahead, a decided scowl on her face as she scanned the forest for the perfect tree to hide behind. Blanda followed without a word, her gaze flickering between the advancing army and the young woman she was supposed to watch.

Finally, Angeline found the perfect oak tree, a towering giant with a trunk so large nobody would see her. Her boots crunched in the deep snow that surrounded the tree, and she slipped behind it, motioning for Blanda to remain on the other side. The witch didn't protest, which made Angeline almost regret her decision. Almost.

She unclasped her warm cape and handed it to Blanda for a keepsake. "To have my hands free," Angeline explained.

Without hesitation, Angeline reached for the ties of her velvet dress, and in a few excitement-filled seconds, she was out of her last layer of clothing. The rich blue fabric pooled at her feet as she stepped free of its weight. Cold bit at her skin, but soon her magic took over, surrounding her with the familiar warmth of her bouncing She-Wolf.

Her paws hit the frozen dirt with determination, claws digging into the ground as she bolted away. She was already hundreds of meters away before she heard Blanda calling her name.

Angeline's fluffy ears twitched as she caught the witch's words: "Maros!"

Damn it, Blanda!

Her She-Wolf took this as a challenge and sped up, her paws trying to beat the dense snow on her way. The white cover was so deep it slowed her down more than she thought. Her She-Wolf struggled to reach the correct speed.

It didn't take long for Maros to catch her, similar to their first meeting. He squeezed her against his body until her She-Wolf gave up and revealed her frozen skin.

"Let me go!" Angeline screamed, fighting against the stronghold of the ancient creature.

"Nope." He didn't need to fight back or move an inch; holding her back was too easy. His eyes flashed red, and his grip on her was heavier than necessary.

Raging screams erupted from Angeline, and he dared to laugh. Without hesitation, she slapped him as hard as she could. Glaring at him in defiance, her lips in a thin line, she waited for her punishment.

He picked her up from the ground, and Angeline gasped. Maros held her hands behind her and pushed her back against a tree, the hardwood scratching her fragile skin. Her legs circled his waist, his body pressing against her thighs.

She glared at him, breathing haggardly. A fire she didn't want burned within her. His lips were centimeters away from hers, and she wished for one thing. A kiss. A burning, passionate, *go to hell* kiss. Her chest rose up and down. Maros pushed closer, brushing his torso against her nipples, and Angeline let out a plaintive whine. She wished she could grind her body against him.

The wolf. It was the damn wolf again!

She closed the few centimeters separating them, pushing her lips against his, fast. With a gasp, she pulled back, her cheeks growing warm from shame.

"Oh no, my Wolf. You are not stopping so easily," Maros rasped. He moved her to sit on a dead tree lying in the forest, and laughed at the whine Angeline let out from the cold feeling on her soft bottom. Maros finally released her hands.

His hands followed the contours of her back and belly, then softly grasped her breasts. He pinched her nipples, resulting in a moan. She pulled her head back and offered her body.

He chuckled. "Do you enjoy this, my White Wolf?"

Maros squeezed her breast with the palm of his hand again, then bent his head down to give a quick bite to the pink treasure. A long shiver ran through her from the touch, and he growled against her skin. He kissed, licked, and pulled with what seemed like no intention to stop—not that her loud moans would tell him to stop.

He continued until she held his face, bringing him to her height. Maros happily followed the pull, landing his lips on her hungry ones. His tongue forced into her mouth, and he swallowed her moans. She tightened her arms around his shoulders, pulling him closer, her lower body moving in waves, trying to reach his. Maros interrupted the kiss, and with a firm push, he laid the woman on the tree, not listening to her complaints about the cold. He moved his hand around her throat, squeezing lightly, awaiting her reaction. His other hand followed her curves until he was millimeters away from her glistening lips. Maros started rubbing her, and immediately, waves of pleasure ran through her, and she must have shown an interrogative face because his next words made her whine.

"Look at this perfect little nub offered for me, my Princess. I could devour it all day."

She watched him, panting, bring his thumb to his mouth and suck on it, to better bring it back to what he just called 'little nub'.

"Do not ever run away again, my Wolf," he ordered, rubbing against this sensitive part of her body, getting an immediate answer.

"You... aaha... lied to me, by the Goddess!" She exclaimed, unable to form an actual thought while being pleased. She held on to a branch and raised her legs, bringing her knees closer to her face. She was still angry at him, but there would be time to scream and complain later.

Maros did not stop, his thumb circling with agility on her sensitive peak. She had no idea it was there and was so good to play with. She would have to discover her body later.

"I didn't lie," he said. "I omitted a detail I thought could hurt you."

"Just shut up." She let out a groan when the pressure on her nub increased.

Maros's other hand played with her nipple, which was hard as ice, and her body was begging him to keep going.

"Come for me, my Wolf." Maros's raspy voice reached her in her dreams, and without a doubt, she knew what he was talking about.

A wave rushed through her, taking her by surprise. To her despair, she screamed in pleasure, arching her back, holding onto the branch so hard that she thought it would break. Her legs shook uncontrollably while Maros moved his hand away from her lower parts to caress her face. Then, he caught her by the neck and pulled her from the tree, bringing an out-of-breath Angeline closer.

Her eyes were bright.

"This, my Wolf, was my way of saying sorry. Tonight, you and I will talk in detail about you provoking me."

Angeline whimpered.

He paused, eyes closed, as if he were controlling himself. "I have treated you well enough; you don't need to run from me. You are safe here."

Tears welled in her eyes; Maros caught the first one from falling.

"For how long?" She whispered.

He tilted his head to the side.

"My parents," she added. "My ex-fiancé. They want me dead. Not only do they want me dead, but they want me to suffer. The nuns have a list of what they are allowed to do, you know? Depending on how much trouble the girls are in."

Tears flowed down the curve of her cheeks without control. Maros wrapped his arms around her shoulders and gave her his jacket to cover her while lifting her from the tree.

"Nobody wants me," she said. "When the war is over, Louis will make sure I can't tell anyone what he did." She shook like a leaf, remembering the fear that made her run.

Maros scoffed. "No offense, Princess, but if the last few days didn't prove I want you, I'm doing something wrong."

Angeline chuckled, placing her hand on his chest. They walked back toward the army.

Maros added, "I should have told you. You're right. I was not sure who was lying to me and who was telling the truth. That's why I asked about your father and Paul yesterday. I promise you, after the war, I will make sure you're safe—no matter what happens between us. Unless you run away again." He smirked.

Angeline laughed, cuddling against him. She was thankful that the wolf side of him was warm.

"You're going to the naughty corner, though," he said.

CHAPTER 16

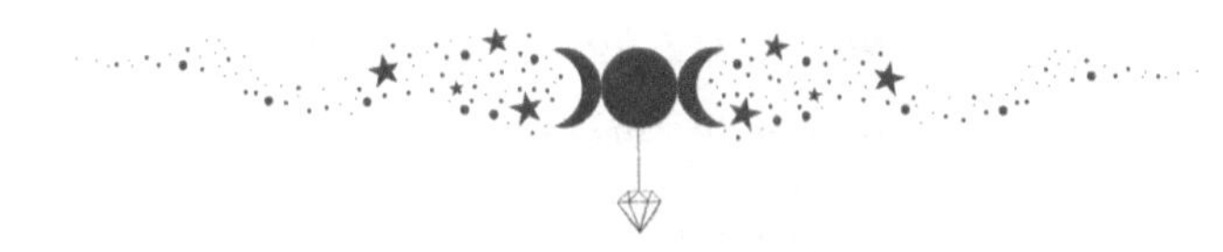

ANGELINE

HER ESCAPE PLAN, AS it turned out, was *not* the plan of the year.

Angeline pouted, sitting on a dead tree trunk and observing everyone else as they prepared the camp for the night. Her hands and feet were tightly bound with rope.

The naughty corner, that's what Maros called it before dropping her ass on the tree. Their intimate moments appeared to have been forgotten. He was the one to tie her up and seemed to enjoy the moment too much. He kissed her hands before leaving her there.

The young redhead sighed and thought back on the ultimate failure of her tentative escape. She had no regrets; it was worth trying. Her face blazed when she thought about Maros's hands on her body, the things he did to her. No other man consumed her this way.

She had heard it in others' minds, perceived it, sometimes even felt it, but all of those previous memories were nothing compared to Maros's hands on her.

Yes! Yes! Yes! The She-Wolf yapped, still excited.

Shush, you naughty girl! Angeline instructed.

The last thing she needed was to go crazy for her captor. She glanced at Annabella, who hadn't talked to her yet. Angeline would not blame her for being angry. She used her to be able to escape.

Annabella seemed to sense the heavy look as she raised her head and watched Angeline, who gave her a tentative, apologetic smile.

Annabella shook her head and approached her.

Bracing herself for what was coming, Angeline pulled her shoulders back. She deserved this.

"Hi, sneaky!" Annabella said.

"I can explain—"

"You don't need to. I am not angry, but you know, you didn't need to play me. You could have just told me your plan, and I would have happily helped you." She paused. "Or you know, you could have told me your plan, and I would have told you how bad it was."

Angeline snorted and slapped her hands against her mouth, stopping the laugh. Annabella did not contain hers, and her laugh was so damn contagious that Angeline followed her and ended up crying tears of laughter. They attracted attention, and whoever could look would never guess they were prisoners of the fearsome First vampires.

Angeline begged Annabella to stop, and jutted her head toward the few other girls who were still with them.

Annabella raised her shoulders and sat beside Angeline on the tree trunk.

"Who cares? They love gossip, let them gossip."

"I love gossip too," Angeline confessed.

"I know you do. You're a Delacour after all. So... are you sleeping with Maros tonight?" Annabella asked curiously.

"Why would you ask that?" An outraged expression answered her. "Did he say something?"

"Ahem... no... I meant, I'm sleeping in the same sleeping bag as Manus, and I thought maybe you would with Maros. I heard him say he was going to keep a close eye on you, just so you know."

Angeline sighed with relief. She worried Maros went out and bragged about their intimate time together. She turned toward her friend, who was looking at her, eyebrows raised, with questions in her eyes.

"What?" Angeline whispered.

"Did something happen in the forest?" Annabella asked, rotating her body to face her. Annabella's legs jumped.

Angeline took a deep breath and nodded, biting her lips, waiting for the other to judge her.

"How was it?" Annabella reached for Angeline's hands.

From the influx of thoughts rushing through Angeline, she knew her friend was indeed naughty. And she liked that. She had only had this safe and free feeling with Jack, and it was way more fun to share these thoughts with another woman.

She whispered, in detail, the entire scene, inked into her mind forever.

The sun set hours ago, and only a few fires were still going, trying to keep the ones not lucky enough to be immortal warm for the night. Angeline was still covered, unaccustomed to the temperatures despite her time at the convent. She was in the sleeping bag Maros loaned her, and honestly, she was disappointed he didn't join her.

Angeline had watched with an inch of jealousy as Annabella cuddled up against Manus, as if they were alone in the world.

After their earlier talk, Annabella managed to extort from Angeline her confession about how much she enjoyed her time with Maros. Annabella was smarter than she looked, and with a sad smile, she had held Angeline's hands, murmuring to her that there was no shame in enjoying pleasure. Vampires, the Lords, they enjoyed it and were absolute hypocrites about it, which Angeline vividly approved. She had heard many things.

"I'm scared to get hurt," she whimpered, "in any way."

"You haven't seen how Maros looked at you when you were not watching. I did. I will give you the same advice I gave myself when all of this started: better here than there. Better him than anyone out there that you don't desire. You may get hurt, you may get your heart broken, but it will still be better than being in your golden cage, married to a man you hate, who physically hurts you every day. Maros said he will release you; I believe him. The war won't be eternal, and the Spirits will ask for new rules to be put in place."

Angeline squinted.

Her friend added, whispering even lower, "I heard the two sisters talking about it, some kind of document, like 'promises' of some sort. Whatever the King decides to write in it, the others will have to respect it."

Angeline's mind ran a thousand miles a minute. She could already see the use of this document.

"If I had the eye of the future King like you do," Annabella said, "I would protect our sisters from everything we have been through."

Angeline nodded, reading Annabella's mind, knowing all the things they would change if they had the opportunity.

You need to be more confident.

Angeline gasped. Annabella was talking to her with her mind.

Annabella smirked. *The future King wants you so badly. Get him to help you, to help us. Make him promise.*

Angeline smiled, sneaky and cunning, and nodded, communicating silently.

Now, in the sleeping bag, freezing despite the warm duvet, doubt crept into her mind. She looked around for Maros and immediately spotted him sitting against a rock, whispering to Carata.

"Maros," Angeline whispered.

He heard her, despite her soft voice, and turned his head to look at her.

"I'm cold," she said.

He smiled, his eyes shining under the firelight, and jumped to his feet. He kissed his sister on the cheek and went to Angeline, who was smiling proudly.

"My Wolf," he said, moving into the tight bag. His firm body pressed against Angeline, who immediately felt the heat from the wolf covering her.

Angeline slipped her frozen hands under his shirt and placed them against his chest, feeling the tight muscles under her fingers. She pushed her golden branches toward Maros, wanting to know his thoughts. Five years of listening to minds without filters had allowed her to reach him more easily now.

A storm of desire and red clouds answered her, all mixed in his fascinating ancient mind. Among the many plans, notes, war maps, and counts, there it was: his intense desire and care for her.

Angeline gasped. He truly cared for her. She raised her eyes to meet his; he had this curious look on his face, as if he knew something was happening but was unsure what. Before he could ask, she grabbed his face and pulled him closer, pressing her lips to his. She was already moaning under the fire that threatened to explode between her legs.

Maros growled. In a swift motion, he placed the young woman under his hard body, pushing his groin against hers and devouring her lips.

"I am pretty sure I am supposed to punish you tonight, my Princess," he murmured, pressing his lips to her neck.

She gasped when his teeth grazed her skin. Angeline moaned softly and moved one hand onto Maros's bottom and the other behind his neck, pushing both to move him closer, inviting him to take a bite.

His fangs broke her fragile skin, and the sound of sucking was driving her insane. She never thought she would enjoy this simple act so much, but she was already shaking and holding back whines of pleasure that could wake up the entire army.

Maros stopped drinking, licked the few drops that were escaping from the bite, and stole a kiss. Angeline panted, still reveling in pleasure.

"Do you understand the lesson now?" He asked, laughter in his eyes, one of his hands brushing her face.

Angeline bit her lip and shook her head. "I think I'm going to need more than that to behave."

He chuckled, bringing his face back to her neck, but instead of biting, he kissed her. "Get on your side, back against my chest."

Angeline had no idea why, and she didn't care. She was in way too deep—and so was her wolf. They didn't care about the details. Holding back a giggle, she moved onto her side, one of her arms under her head like a pillow, while the other was placed in front of her.

A tremor ran through her body as he pressed against her. She didn't need a lesson about anatomy to know what was poking against her butt, and the idea of it created a new turmoil. She let go of every thought and closed her eyes, waiting impatiently.

She didn't have to wait long. He grazed her breast through the velvet fabric, a gesture soft and hard at the same time, and pressed his hips against her bottom. She sighed, content, and turned her head to witness the desire burning in Maros's eyes.

"Kiss me." This was a request, and the vampire knew it.

He didn't need to be begged. He caught her lips. Her neck was uncomfortable, but the fire was still burning between her legs. A moan escaped Angeline when he lifted her long dress and followed the length of her leg, moving the fabric out of the way.

She mimicked the rhythm of his hips and arched against him, moving back and forth, which seemed to be effective.

"You're going to be the death of me," he whispered, grabbing her thighs.

"You're already dead," she quipped. She caught his face and stole another kiss, pushing her tongue into his mouth and pressing her bottom against his hardened length.

Angeline gasped, but didn't stop the kiss, when his fingers reached for her intimacy. She knew she would feel pleasure again, as she did earlier, but she was afraid it would hurt as it did with Paul.

Maros stopped and searched her eyes.

"What is it, Pet?" he murmured, giving her a series of small kisses on her mouth.

Angeline took a deep breath and said, "Just... be gentle... please..."

A low growl answered while he took her mouth by force, getting another moan from her.

"You don't need to ask me. I have no interest in you not enjoying this," he joked.

She chuckled and finally relaxed in his arms.

MAROS

Slowly, Maros moved back his hand, feeling the hard nub throbbing under his fingers. Her entrance was so wet he knew he could take her, with no foreplay, and he would fit into her body perfectly. He could not hold back another growl at the thought of her tight pussy around his dick, but contained himself, pushing a finger inside of her.

He observed her reactions, took in the fear on her face; pleasure quickly replaced it. Her eyes finally closed, lips half open, while a moan filled the silence. Maros pumped in and out, slowly at first, then sped up when there was no doubt she was enjoying it. He could not help but kiss her again, pushing so hard on her lips that he knew she would have marks.

Angeline's tongue caught his, starting a ballet, while he introduced a second finger inside her drenched pussy.

She gasped and arched against him, which drove him insane. To feel her perfect ass against his cock was torture. He perfectly remembered her hourglass shape, her creamy skin, and her sizable bottom that called for him to grab it. He moved faster, fingering her hard.

When her moans grew louder, he moved her onto her back. Her eyes widened, and he covered her mouth with his hand, smirking.

"We don't want to wake up our neighbors now, do we?" he whispered, then penetrated her again.

She contorted from the intrusion, throbbing under his hand until she finally grabbed his shoulders, planting her nails in his skin. Her juice flowed along his fingers as she found her release.

"And this, my Wolf, will teach you about running away."

A breathless giggle answered him.

CHAPTER 17

ANGELINE

ANGELINE PULLED THE LACES of her boots tight. Maros loomed behind her, his scent floating through the air—rich and spiced. Her damn wolf knew instantly that he was there. She pressed her lips together and straightened up. They didn't talk after their moment of intimacy, and she was so tired that she went straight to sleep after a few minutes of warm cuddles.

But now, as she turned toward him, the memory of his hands travelling across her body sent heat to her cheeks. The vampire was indeed right there, with a smirk on his face.

She cleared her throat. "Maros. Good... morning?" Why was he not saying a thing? Was this normal?

He nodded. "My Wolf."

Relief flooded her before. *Talk about fear of abandonment.*

Before she could mutter anything else, he moved closer and pulled her toward his body. Angeline raised her eyes shyly, her body relaxing into his embrace, not minding the dried blood on his clothes.

Maros bent down and, without hesitation, his lips captured hers, soft, warm, and way too passionate for a morning kiss. She melted into him, a sigh slipping from her lips as his hands pressed into her back, not bothered by the hundreds of people watching. She moaned and moved closer, not ready to spend another day walking in the frozen forest. Kissing Maros seemed a much better idea.

A loud throat-clearing broke the moment, and Maros interrupted the kiss with a sigh.

"The army is ready," Manus announced, a cold smile on his face. By his side was Annabella, blushing and giving Angeline one of what she called her 'naughty looks.' A knowing grin spread on Annabella's face.

Maros nodded at his brother and held his arm out to Angeline, who gladly accepted. "Today we walk together, White Wolf."

Angeline tried not to look at her surroundings, which were filled with curious looks and whispers. She scoffed. "Are you scared I'm going to run away?"

"Please, as if you had a chance." He looked down on her with a smile on his damaged lips. "But if you do, I hope you're ready for more punishment."

He ignored Angeline's gargling noise of outrage and advanced, following the troops forward.

After a few minutes of blessed silence, disturbed only by the various grunts from the army, Maros said, "Blanda told me you have quite an extensive knowledge of magic."

Angeline stiffened and tried to keep a straight face, so used to staying quiet about her magic, and certainly not accustomed to being asked about magic in general.

"I know a few things. I have been blessed with the witch Nanabrok's friendship and many, many, *many*, lessons." One could not get the old witch to stop talking once she started.

Maros scoffed, but there was a light of curiosity in his eyes. "I don't know many in this world that could brag about a friendship with the damn old hag."

Angeline held back a snort and gave a light tap on his arm; it was funny because it was true. "It doesn't matter now. Nanabrok left me to rot at the convent as well."

Maros had a faraway look in his eye, as if avoiding her stare—likely out of pity. "Well, to be fair, she may have thought you were dead."

Angeline clenched her teeth. *True.* "You know what I don't know much about?" She asked.

Maros arched his brow, waiting.

"I know little about how you and your family became... this..."

"Ah..." He hummed. "You knew about Blanda and her magic, though?"

"Yes, because the history of witches is clear, reported, detailed, and kept alive. Until the 17th century, werewolves could not be bothered keeping notes on anything, and vampires,"—she smirked—"are such blatant liars. It's hard to know what is true or comes from their dreams or vivid imaginations."

"Vivid imagination?" He laughed.

"I found a book once about a theory that vampires are from another planet."

Maros laughed louder, earning a few curious glances from nearby soldiers.

"I have never heard of that one," he said. "Our parents lived peacefully in the part of France that is now Alsace. They weren't warriors—just a blacksmith and his wife. Life was simple. Until the Romans came."

Maros stayed silent for a while, looking off into the distance. "Manus, Blanda, and Carata were born already, and were... toddlers, I'm guessing. Between the ages of two and six. When the Romans arrived, they slaughtered most of the men of the village, took over... one of them raped my mum... nine months later, there I was, a little bundle of joy."

Angeline didn't interrupt him, watching intently.

"My family survived, and despite the Druids' advice and various offers of poisonous plants to get rid of me, my mum decided to keep me. Her choice meant she and my siblings were kicked out of the village. Bastards were not welcome.

"So, we all headed out to the forest. Manus was already quite the hunter, you know. He was always bringing back meat for my sisters and my mother. Blanda was only four, but she knew every edible plant. She had spent some time with the Druids, who saw potential for magic in her. Until I was a bit older, we stayed there. Then we decided to go ahead and try to find a new village, far away from our old one, where nobody would know where I came from. We ended up in Auvergne.

"The years went by. Gaul was invaded by the Romans, more and more. Every day, there were talks of them attacking us." He watched her from the corner of his eye. "Then we heard a rumor about wolves the size of a man running alongside Caesar under the moonlight."

Her breath trembled. That was a part of history she had never heard. "The Roman army had... werewolves?"

Maros nodded. "Romulus descendants. Caesar conquered all the packs of what is now Europe. And the one who raped my mother? He was one of them."

Angeline gasped and instinctively tightened her grip on his arm. "What happened?" She whispered.

Maros flashed the evilest smile she had yet to see. "He came to the wrong family. Blanda was now fifteen and overpowered all the Druids we knew. Manus had reached what was considered adulthood at the time and was an accomplished warrior. And Carata, well... she already had the gift of getting whatever she wanted."

They exchanged amused looks.

He continued. "I was all but eleven years old. I could fight too; I had more strength than anyone my age, but we never really thought about it. We were... at peace. I had no anger, no fear, no hate. Until my sperm donor found us."

A light growl came from his throat, his eyes red, filled with fury. "He came at us in his human shape, wanting—needing—for my mother to recognize him. Started blathering about how he was going to hurt her again, then how he would hurt my sisters and make all of us watch... then, when the moon rose, he shifted under our eyes." Maros chuckled darkly. "And so did I."

"Was it the first time for you?" Angeline asked.

Werewolves usually had their first shift later, when puberty hit, but 2000 years ago, kids were probably mature enough.

"It was, and without hesitation. I knew what to do, how to move, and how to kill. It was the most instinctive I had ever felt. I was smaller than him, but not that much smaller. I was faster, younger, and angrier. He didn't stand a chance. Even if I hadn't killed him, he would not have survived my sister's magic. Blanda had been working on a project for a while, wanting to make us stronger to fight back against the invaders. This was just before Gergovia."

"She made you vampires," Angeline said.

"She didn't respect a few rules from the Druids here and there, but the Spirits allowed her to do so. Manus was the first; he volunteered, of course, wanting to make sure the spell was safe for his family. When we saw it working, despite what it meant—food-wise—we all agreed to do it."

"What about your mother?"

Maros tensed. "She didn't want to... said that it was not her destiny... but Blanda made us drink her blood first to link us. Mother lived for another twelve years after that."

"So, you were vampires during Gergovia?"

"How do you think Vercingetorix won the battle?" Maros scoffed. "He didn't stand a chance against the Roman armies, so we helped. When our people started to realize what we were... they were scared of us... they threw rocks at us, the fools. Our vampiric senses were so exacerbated at the time we could not handle the rejection, so when Alesia came..."

"The Gaul lost."

"Yep. Should have thought twice before refusing our help."

Angeline smiled and moved closer. "Thank you for trusting me with this."

"It's not like it's a big secret. Blanda made a deal with the Spirits that no witch could create a new brand of vampires. Only us and a few ancient ones."

"Still. Thank you."

Maros studied her for a moment, his eyes returning to their gorgeous green shade, with a thin smile on his full lips. "I thought that if I shared something with you, you might give me something in return."

Angeline laughed, shaking her head. "You're impossible."

Maros only grinned.

CHAPTER 18

ANGELINE

A NGELINE STRUGGLED WITH HER long hair, trying to tame the jungle of dirty and messy curls that had become of her tresses. It was nearly impossible, and she knew she had lost the fight when she found a dead moth hiding between two curls.

"Ew!" She flicked the dead bug away. She released an exasperated sigh and gave up, putting her gloves back on.

It had been a week since they left the convent. They were stuck eating suspicious meals and barely washing themselves in any icy river they could find.

Compared to the army, Annabella and Angeline were doing the best due to their time spent at the convent. Bad food? Please, when you've survived on clunky porridge for years, it was a joke. Cold bath? They didn't even remember the last time they had a warm one. At the convent, there was no such thing as pleasures like hot water.

She glanced at Annabella, who sat beside her on the dead tree. She was working her way through her hair. Annabella's long, gorgeous, dark hair was an equal disaster. Angeline laughed, and Annabella gave her a surprised look.

"That's what happens when you get naughty with Manus every night," Angeline said.

Annabella groaned, but a smirk appeared on her lips. "Maybe you should try with Maros. Believe me, it's worth having a bird nest in your hair."

Angeline laughed, but her cheeks darkened. After a few seconds of blessed silence, she blurted out, "What were you doing to him last night?"

She was unsure how to bring up what she had witnessed, so she might as well get straight to the point.

Annabella raised her head, surprised. "Which part?" She asked. With mischief in her gaze, she added, "I am doing many things to him."

Angeline could not help but laugh, and she threw some snow at her friend. Annabella had shared many of her previous nights with Manus; she was not able to keep it a secret from the telepath. Angeline felt like a voyeur, but she was not used to witnessing consensual intercourse.

"You are so naughty," Angeline said.

"I'm not the one getting all cuddly with the future king every night for the past week," Annabella retorted, sticking out her tongue.

That had the merit of quieting Angeline, who hid her red face behind a curtain of hair. Maros and she had been getting closer than ever, 'cuddling' every night, which usually ended in her screaming from pleasure. That was not her favorite part of the night.

Oh no, that would be too easy.

Her favorite part was when Maros took her in his arms, burning hot thanks to his wolf's blood, and brought her face to the perfect spot on his shoulder. A spot that she now called 'her place.' She wished to do it every night for the rest of her life, which was not her initial plan. He spent most days with her, walking by her side unless he was called somewhere else. Their days were filled with conversations, laughter, and stories; the thought of a new day by his side warmed her up.

Angeline pouted and glanced at her friend. "I like cuddles. And other stuff." She giggled.

"Yeah, I heard, girl," Annabella said, rolling her eyes. She got up to sit closer. "Do you really want to know what I do to him?"

Angeline's heartbeat accelerated, and with a shriek of excitement, she listened.

Hours passed, but she could not escape her friend's secret. Warmth pooled in her stomach at the thought of it, and she wanted to try it with Maros. They had been walking for hours, the never-ending forest surrounding them at all times, and she hoped a break would come soon. As if Maros heard her silent plea, the signal came: one sharp whistle. The army stopped at once, relieved sighs coming from everyone.

While others were busy taking a well-deserved rest, Angeline smirked and walked away from the path, advancing toward the dense forest. With deliberate movements, she gave a glance at Maros. She knew he would notice. He always noticed.

Sure enough, Maros's eyes were dead set on her, his eyebrows in a frown while he watched her go deeper into the dark forest. She gave him a quick, provocative look and sped up the pace, knowing he would join her soon to ensure she was not trying something stupid like a new escape plan.

Men are so predictable, she thought, her heartbeat accelerating while she pranced through the thin layer of snow.

The trees grew denser as she left the path behind, and she counted down in her head. *Three... two... one...*

"Angeline." A sharp, familiar voice came from behind her.

She bit her lip to suppress a grin and turned to face him. "Oh no. You caught me."

He was already standing in her way, hands crossed behind his back, eyes impenetrable. Overall, Maros didn't seem that impressed.

"I guess you have to punish me again," she said, looking at him from underneath her eyelashes.

Maros laughed uncontrollably. She hated herself for loving his laugh so much.

Angeline ran toward him and pushed him against a tree trunk, enjoying how his eyes turned red.

"What's your plan, my Wolf?" He asked.

Angeline grabbed her purple hair ribbon. With deliberate slowness, she twisted her long, unruly curls into a loose pony-tail at the base of her neck. The bulge in Maros's pants showed his desire. Her plan was working—*thanks, Annabella!*

His gaze was locked on her, his jaw tight.

Slowly, she moved onto her knees, not paying attention to the wet ground. Her gaze remained locked on Maros's wide eyes, and she opened his fly, enjoying the low growl of pure desire coming from his throat. She took out his hardened cock, and gasped. They hadn't been this far yet. She had barely touched him over the pants.

Maros cupped her face, still speechless, and brushed her lips with his thumb. With his other hand, he grabbed a fistful of her hair.

With no more hesitation, Angeline gave light, wet kisses along his length, relishing in his moans. When his fingers tight-ened in her hair, she took him in her mouth, surprised by the texture and taste. It was not at all what she expected.

She moaned and got busy, up and down, enjoying the hard length inside her mouth. After a while, he pushed her head and led the rhythm, resulting in a throbbing sensation between her legs.

She was so focused on her work that she didn't hear it at first, but Maros stopped her and moved her back up, concern on his face.

"Wha... what?" She panted.

Then she heard it. Screams.

"We're under attack," Maros said. He pulled his pants back up and caught her face between his hands.

"Shift and hide. Do not come anywhere near there. I will lose my mind."

And in a whoosh of wind, he was gone.

Angeline remained, feet fixed in the snow, already missing his warmth against her. She woke up, aware of the danger, and quickly undressed. Golden sparkles flew through the air.

Help! Help! They need help! The wolf shrieked, begging her to run.

Maros told us to stay safe, so that is what we will do.

After all, it's not as if she could be useful in a battle.

Then, she heard the screams—screams she knew too well, having spent five years listening to similar ones. Without any other thought, but grumbling inside, she pounced on her back paws and ran toward the battle. Not many girls were left besides Annabella and her. Some had been repatriated by their parents, but some were still there. They would be the last to get protection, but the first to be attacked.

There was no way she would let her new friend die. It was not every day she could brag about having an actual friend, and she would make sure that this one survived.

After all, she was a wolf; she could do some damage, and even if it meant getting hurt in return, she could handle a bit of pain.

Angeline's wolf went straight into the battle. Annabella shoved her hands into the face of a... wolf? A man? He was a mix of both, as if he had tried to shift but failed midway. His long nose resembled a wolf's, but he stood on his hind legs.

Something was deeply wrong with those attackers.

Angeline jumped on the duo, fighting in the mud as Annabella's horror flooded her mind.

I have known worse monsters than you, Angeline thought.

Angeline propelled herself and jumped onto his neck. His body was not fast or agile, like other werewolves. Any other wolves would have kicked her, but this one was unnaturally slow.

Blood filled her mouth, her sharp teeth digging into the furry neck, resulting in an agonizing half-human, half-wolf howl of pain from the strange wolf. The wolfman pulled her away, throwing her up in the air, but she fell onto her paws, landing in the snow as elegantly as a cat.

Angeline raised her head, waiting for the pain that was doomed to come—*damn this Magical Virgin business!*—but there was no pain. Instead, her wolf's eyes were wide open, witnessing the horror she created.

Monstrous screams erupted from the wolfman. He held his neck with both hands, scratching at it as if something stopped him from breathing. Black flowed in his veins, taking over his body, bursting into blood vessels. The wolfman combusted, imploding on himself.

Bloody organs and skin flew around, leaving a pool of blood in a neat circle around the man. Angeline shrieked and tried to shield her eyes with her paws.

What in the Goddess's name was that? She wondered, asking her wolf. She sure wished she had known sooner that her wolf could hurt someone without getting hurt in return.

We strong! We powerful! We never get hurt again!

Angeline pushed her back paws into the ground, bent her head, and howled like she had heard her friends do so many times. She stood there, tongue lolled.

Maros stood before her, looking at the bloody mess on the floor. He frowned, exchanging a look with his sister Blanda.

Turning to Angeline, he said, "You can't follow a simple order, White Wolf, can you?"

She shifted back from her wolf and stood before him, naked, wiping blood from her mouth. "Guess not." She retorted, a smirk showing on her face. "What are you going to do about it?"

CHAPTER 19

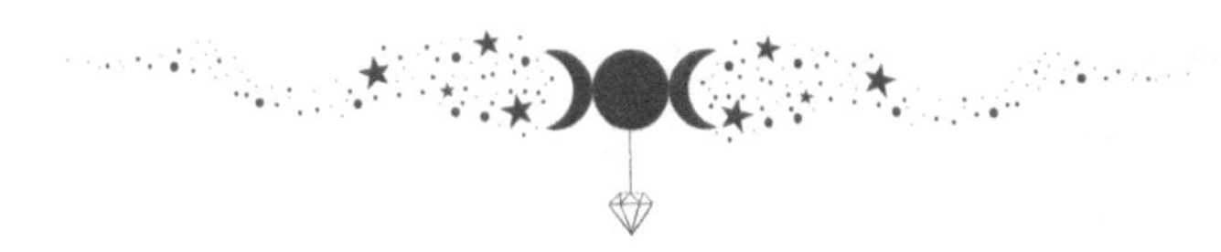

ANGELINE

H E DID NOTHING ABOUT it. And he did nothing about it, because he left her.

It had been one week since she had seen Maros, and to her immense displeasure, she missed him. She missed his body; she missed his devouring eyes; she even missed their banter. Most of all, she missed his presence against her body at night and their daily talks.

Today also marked her two-week anniversary of being a free prisoner, and she was losing her mind. Doubt crept in. Angeline wasn't sure she would get out of Maros's clutch. To be fair, she was not sure she *wanted* to. As Annabella said, they had it pretty good with the army, but not having him for so many days was driving her insane.

What if he changed his mind about her? Could he be bored with her already? Is that why he left? If Maros won, who knew if he would keep his promise to let her go? She thought he was enjoying her condition a bit too much. She could not blame him, as she happily gave herself to him every night, except for the past week.

After the wolfmen's attack, what was left of the girls was released once the First Family communicated about the attack. Their parents came to their senses and realized the lack of humanity they had shown their offspring.

Angeline and Annabella were the only ones left, the ones nobody wanted except the First brothers. Angeline was pretty sure that if Annabella's father had asked for her back, she would have laughed in his face and refused.

When they finally arrived in the new place, an old mansion that provided a roof and some beds for the exhausted army, Maros took Angeline aside. He told her that he and Manus were leaving for a few days to deal with some political matters.

He hadn't said a word since the attack, running and holding her hand during the last few kilometers. She could tell from his frowning face that something disturbed him; he was worried more than usual. She wanted to ask why he was leaving and to where, but a passionate kiss stopped her, engulfing her before he swiftly departed.

She had no time to yell and insult him; they had work to do in the mansion. The wolfmen bit many vampires, and the reaction from their bite differed from anything she had witnessed. She and Blanda agreed to work together, thinking their accumulated knowledge of magic would help find a remedy, but the solution was right there.

Without Maros around to disturb her, Angeline could focus on her magic, listening to the moon's singing and the trees whispering. She knew what she had to do.

Bite.

They lost twelve of their people to the wolfmen's venom before she could help one. They would have survived, but who knows under which form? They asked the First sisters to end their lives. The others survived, and they survived thanks to *her*. There was no hiding her wolf now. The White Wolf's bite seemed to have healing properties, and soldiers around her were thankful.

Angeline grumbled as she walked along the corridor, tripping over her new dress. Another treasure she found; it was made of white silk with pearls hanging on the shoulders and the back. She loved the dress; it was incredible to wear and touch, but more of a nightgown than a day dress. It was *not* warm enough to survive in Ukraine, even if spring was coming, and it was too flowy and long to be convenient. Her only other dress needed a wash.

A new dress and being the receiver of smiles, bowed heads, and sometimes even a slight curtsy, had made her time agreeable. She may not be a true princess, but she still enjoyed the attention.

Angeline opened the door leading to what had been her bedroom for the past week—a beautiful, large bedroom, with a bed the size of five of her convent beds. On the first night, she loved being able to roll and turn again, alone, pulling all the covers to herself. But as the days went by, she found herself missing this stupid vampire.

This stupid vampire who was now standing in her room.

Angeline gasped, but held back her smile, not wanting to give him the satisfaction of seeing her relieved by his return. She longed to run and hug him, to grind her body on his and keep him in bed for the entire night.

"Princess," he said, his eyes moving over her.

She hoped he enjoyed her rested features and brushed hair—a brush she found in this bedroom was her brightest victory.

MAROS

Maros's thoughts ran wild. She was in front of him, fabulous, exactly as he remembered her from their first meeting. Her features were at peace. Her dress looked as soft as a feather, and her fiery hair contrasted with the snow-colored fabric. Her large hips and the curve of her back drove him crazy. He had to control himself for the week, not to think about when he would finally rage against those. Their intimate moments every night led him close to madness. Her screams and the way she squirmed when he barely touched her.

Maros had been patient enough. A week away from her had been torture, and he was glad to be back. He could hear her heartbeat racing like a hummingbird, and her breath was scattered. He was proud of her, of how she had behaved without him here. Rumors were that she didn't even try to run away, and that made him hate himself more for what was coming.

They stared at each other, her blue eyes glistening with defiance. Angeline crossed her arms, pouting. She hadn't spoken yet. He moved closer and could not resist the urge to touch her long hair, so soft, shining under the soft glow in the room.

Angeline quivered but did not move away from his touch. She was like a little kitten who needed to be tamed, always screeching and getting their claws out at anyone bigger than them.

"Are you angry at me for leaving?" He asked.

She nodded and said nothing else.

"I'm sorry. I had... things to deal with..." He hesitated and leaned in, his face so close to hers that she had no escape. In a raspy voice, he added, "I want to be gentle with you. I know it has been one week since I touched you, and every minute spent away from you has been like torture. And now... your wolf, she is calling me..."

Her eyes filled with tears. "I know. She is mad at you," Angeline confessed, adding with a slightly constrained air, "she always whines like crazy when she feels you around."

"My wolf is crazy about you, too. Why does that make you cry, my White Wolf?" He brushed away a tear.

She took a deep breath, holding back her sniffles.

"I missed you, and I don't think I should. I'm scared for what comes next." She whimpered, turning away, trying to hide behind a curtain of hair.

Maros swallowed. "How about I promise you something?" He asked, pulling her chin so he could see her watery eyes. Her blue pearls sparkled with tears. "I told you before, and I am telling you again. I promise you, as soon as all of this is finished, I will make sure you can start a new life. Safe, free, wherever you choose to be. Even if it's not with me."

Those last words cost him, but he knew he had to say them. He moved closer, softly massaging her arms, then bringing her thin fingers to his mouth to kiss them. She jumped at the touch.

"Thank you," she murmured, placing a shaking hand on his chest. "Can you promise me something, Maros?"

Maros took her hand, kissing it. "Anything that I can do." He leaned in, unable to think of what she could ask him.

"When you are king, I want you to promise me that you will make sure that women and children are protected."

Maros tilted his head, waiting for more.

She continued. "I know you have a Promise parchment... I... I..." She struggled to say the next words.

Maros gave her another kiss, holding her fingers in his. "Tell me, Pet. Anything."

Angeline took a deep breath and squeezed his hand. "I just want to be sure nobody else goes through what I did. Nobody is thinking about us. We are just pretty things, sold for the best offer, or tortured in a convent until we give up on life. That's what being a Daughter of Europe is about." She let go of his hand to swipe a fallen tear, but Maros instantly caught her hand, kissing it softly.

"I was not planning to let the Lords of Europe repeat the same mistakes they have been making for hundreds of years. You are safe. I'll make sure of it. If you want it written, I will."

Angeline inhaled, and Maros got lost in her eyes, blue as the sky. She swallowed with difficulty and whispered, "I'm ready for you now."

Maros needed to hear no more.

She jumped when Maros took both of the pearl stripes of her dress in his hands and slid them down, letting her white dress follow the movement, the silk perfectly falling along her body. She was naked, trembling, and watched him with intention as he kneeled and ran his lips along her legs, kissing every part of her body he could reach.

Her legs shook. She was naked and beautiful, all his to take. He picked her up and stood, laughing at the light scream she let out, and placed her fair legs around his body. Maros brought her to the bed and softly dropped her there.

He took in the view of his brand new possession with a satisfied smile. Angeline blushed and moved her hands over her breast, certainly in an attempt to hide from him, but he kneeled above her and moved her hands.

"You are beautiful. Don't hide from me, because I could never get enough of you."

"They're too small," she mumbled.

Maros scoffed, then said, "Those two little mounts of yours are absolute perfection". He bent over her and kissed her skin, taking one of her nipples between his lips. "They are soft"—kiss—"beautiful"—pull—"delicious." *Bite*.

She whimpered, arching her back, shaking her hands, fisting the sheets.

He moved to rest behind her legs, facing her blushed cheeks, and with a naughty smile, he said, "I can't wait to see them bouncing as I thrust inside of you." He laughed with the earthiest sound when she gasped at his words.

Maros stepped away and removed his shirt and pants. Her body was still shaking, and he could see she was trying not to hide herself. Maros moved the blanket over her body; he forgot the temperature was too low for her.

He joined her under the warm covers and slowly brought his face closer to hers, brushing her pink lips with his before fully taking her mouth. She tasted of lavender, her breath was fresh, and it turned his senses on. She answered as she always did, with passion. Breathing into his mouth, pushing her tongue, playing with his, rolling her hips into him.

He held her face and kissed her deeply, only stopping to say, "Give me your mouth, My Wolf." His voice was dry and raspy. Desire took over his body, and she answered by opening her mouth and placing her soft hands around his face.

Maros could not hold back anymore. He left a path of wet kisses on her creamy skin to reach his destination. He moved his fingers around her intimacy and felt her tighten at the contact. He knew he had to be careful, but he could not wait any longer. He inserted one finger, bringing his head closer to hers, attentive to her reaction. She watched him, mouth half-opened, her pussy so wet that he knew he could take her right there, and she would be fine.

"I will go slow for now,"—he added, a second finger—"but you are so wet. This is driving me crazy."

Angeline answered with a moan. He thrust his fingers in and out, and her insides loosened. Maros moved his second hand to her throbbing clit. She arched her back when his fingers started their favorite dance on the small button.

It was time. Without letting go of her nub, he brought his erection closer to her warm body, feeling her slick juice against his tip.

"It will only hurt for a while, My Love," he whispered, unsure she heard him. Then, finally, he penetrated his princess. Her body tensed, and he had to stop, making his wolf howl with desire inside his mind. His eyes flashed red, showing his lust.

Her lips parted, and her fearful eyes widened, which made him lose all control.

With a firm push, while playing with her clit, he deflowered her, feeling the barrier of her hymen holding him back, and then falling under his power. She whined, trying to push him away, but he stayed inside. His wolf begged him to take her roughly. He had never had to resist such an urge before; she was leading him to insanity.

"Almost there, Love. Almost there. Just breathe." He spoke in a deep voice, as he pushed in and out, growling, still moving his fingers on her sensitive clit. She loosened a bit, and the whining stopped to leave space for a slight moan, which became a grunt when he pulled out.

She looked at him, a displeased and uncertain look on her face. He smiled and roughly thrust back into her soft, warm pussy, savoring the scream that came from her. Her back arched against the bed, and her hands reached for the headboard, as if desperately looking for something to hold onto. Maros groaned and pushed harder. She was perfectly open to him, and his cock could not get enough of the tight pussy around it.

"Against me... come... against me," she begged.

Both Maros and his wolf let out a long, raspy moan. He placed his hand under her back, bringing her closer to his skin. His other hand caught hers in a wild move and pinned them down above her head. He pulled out again, which made her whisper, "Please."

Her begging him to take her was the last step for him to lose the very little control he had over his wolf. He let a guttural growl out and penetrated her rougher than before, in a raging back-and-forth movement. Growling, groaning, moaning, not getting enough of her screams, which grew louder and louder, resonating in the entire bedroom.

ANGELINE

Angeline let out a last exhale when his fangs forced into her neck. She took in the waves crossing through her body that came then, trying to control her breath while Maros gently pulled out of her.

She turned onto her side, trying to hide her face in her pillow, ashamed of her screams and naughtiness.

Maros stroked her messy hair. After enjoying the caress for a few seconds, she turned toward him, and their eyes met in shock. His warmth and worried look made her feel better; she let him hold her hand and watched him kiss it softly.

"I am sorry I hurt you, Pet... don't be angry at me. I have no excuse but my lust for you."

"I am not angry. I am not sure how I feel."

"There is nothing bad about what we did." He moved closer, bringing her naked body against his. "You wanted it, I wanted it even more, and you don't have to follow your father's rules anymore. A new dawn is coming." He rubbed her back, following the contour of her body.

She pouted and stretched her sore body; she could already see the bruises where he squeezed her too hard. There was no actual pain in those, but she felt some ache in her neck where he bit her. She blushed at the thought of his fangs in her neck. Angeline forgot how quickly that could make her climax. That, and his body moving back and forth inside her.

She *did* like it; it was unpleasant at first, but she had reached his mind easily for once, and she could feel his desire for her. His wish to give her a good time was quickly overridden by his vampire and wolf lust. She wished he were always this way, instead of alternating between the monster and the lover.

Angeline knew a bit about what to expect from intercourse, thanks to people's memories. She remembered that for wolves, it was always quite passionate. She had been dreading this moment since destiny threw Maros on her path, with both fear and impatience, the latter brought by her annoying She-Wolf. If her hymen had no value, then she was better off making sure the future king enjoyed her company, and with his renewed promise, she had hope — too much hope.

A bit later, she left the bathroom, her skin reddened from the cold outside. Her hair was curlier than ever. Maros lay in bed and gave her body an appreciative look. She shuddered.

Angeline saw him looking at the bruises and bite marks on her smooth skin. She giggled when he let out a guttural growl, as if he were trying to hold the sound back.

Maros opened the blanket, inviting her to join him. She moved closer and let her fingers run along his torso, following his scars. Without looking away from him, she snuggled inside his burning arms. She sighed with relief as she lay down against him, enjoying his warmth and strong body.

In her place.

CHAPTER 20

ANGELINE

THE WINTER SUN CARESSED her cheek, pulling her away from her deep slumber. This was, with no doubt, the best sleep she'd had in years. Angeline blinked, but was forced to close her eyes straight away. A searing headache crashed into her like a tidal wave.

She always had headaches. But this was different; this was a raw pain, a pulsing ache that came from inside her and radiated around her brain.

Angeline winced, keeping her eyes shut and taking a deep breath. The pain was still there. She opened her eyes, blinking in the light from the windows.

That's when she felt it.

It wasn't just her head; it was *everything*. Every nerve in her body seemed to be possessed by something new, as if she were dead and brought back to life. After a few quiet breaths, the pain shifted into something else, a hum that ran through her cells and gave her new energy. She was new, incredible, and unbreakable.

The sensation of her Spirit magic had always been peculiar—a shadow that hid in the corner. But this was so different, so wholesome. Tears welled in her eyes, and not only because of the headache. The fierce, electric energy surged through her veins; every movement was laced with a newfound power. She looked around the room and felt at peace. In pain, yes, but at peace.

Her senses were sharper, too. If she didn't know better, she would have feared that Maros had converted her into a vampire, but she knew that was not the case.

What is this? Golden particles flew around her. She placed a hand over her chest, feeling her heartbeat.

There was one world, and she was one with it. Golden magic flowed through her veins, the voices in her head spoke louder than ever, and the beauty of nature overwhelmed her. She could sense everything from the bird singing outside the window to the golden particles floating in front of her. She could feel the man lying behind her and tensed at the warm presence.

Her heartbeat quickened when Maros began to wake and moved closer to her, her damn mortal heart sounding as if it would explode. He stroked her messy hair, caressing her, and she calmed down, enjoying the touch and the silence it brought.

It was true, then. When a Magical Virgin gave herself to a man, the magic changed. She could not help but smile at the thought of it, hoping there might be some badass consequences.

Maros caressed her bare shoulders, her back, then roamed everywhere and nowhere at the same time. She felt his desire awakening, his hard cock pushing against her lower back. His hands became insistent.

Was she ready for another session of passionate sex? She turned over, face-to-face with him. His eyes were red, his fangs were already out, and his cock acted like an uncomfortable barrier between them. Angeline didn't say a word, but she placed her hands against his bare chest, stroking his scars. Through her power, she felt the traces of dark magic inside him, caused by the blade that was used to hurt him.

He was quite charming despite his ravaged face, and his body had nothing to envy from any other man. Not that she had seen many naked men before. He was missing a nipple, and it looked like it had been torn off. Angeline ran her fingers over the huge scar on his torso. She had seen it before, but she was too shy to look. Now, she did not hide her curiosity.

She knew her uncles had tortured him for months, with a dark magic tool called the Blade of Misery. They invited all their friends to the show.

When his family retrieved him, they went on a killing spree in Europe and found all the men who had hurt Maros. They made a statement: if you went after the First Family, that was what you would get. She had learned all that at the convent, listening to gossip from more informed women. Annabella had completed the missing points during their two weeks together, Manus having explained in more detail what happened.

"How come you kept the scars?" She asked, facing him.

She knew a bit about the blade, including that it had been forged by the Spirits 1500 years ago, to make a weapon able to destroy any magical creatures. One cut from it, and you were dead, through agonizing pain. Maros was alive, though.

A bitter smile answered her. "The Blade didn't work as expected on me. It hurt, though. The most excruciating pain I have felt in my long life."

Angeline raised her eyes to meet his. She heard about the pain the Blade was supposed to bring. Nanabrok told her all about it.

"We don't know why I survived. We don't know if it's because I am one of the First or because I am a hybrid. And we'd much rather not know. The blade is safe now."

"You didn't destroy it?"

"No. Blanda told us about a powerful witch who tried to destroy other blades long ago, and it didn't end well."

Now, *that* was a story Angeline knew well. The witch was Nanabrok.

"Nanabrok was the witch. That's why she looks the way she does now."

His brows furrowed.

She continued, her hands moving around his torso as she spoke. "700 years ago, she decided to look for and destroy all the blades she could find. She found eleven of them, but never found the last one, which was said to be lost in the deep sea. She reunited her entire coven on the most powerful night of the year, and they began the spell. Everything went wrong. Her younger witches started to immolate, and the darkness from the Blade spread among all of them. So, Nanabrok decided to take the darkness on herself, so her coven could survive. You saw her. It melted her; her skin fell off, and some of her bones melted as well. It's a miracle that she survived… but at least she thought the blades were gone. She was quite upset when we heard rumors that the last blade had been used on one of the First."

Maros chuckled. "Not as upset as me."

He seemed to think her touch was an invitation, moving his hands around Angeline's body insistently. His hands were as warm as she remembered and softer than one would have thought. She opened her lips to speak, but her mouth was crushed with his lips, which moved in a burning ballet. Angeline tried to resist, but the sensation of his breath, associated with his strong hands caressing, pinching, pressing, was too much to handle so early in the morning.

She hesitantly moved her hands to circle his face, answering to the ardent kiss, and her hips instinctively moved toward his body, the usual fire in her groin. This seemed to please Maros, as he groaned and moved her under his naked body.

She wanted him, but she could feel the soreness in her lower body, and the pounding headache she needed to sort. Maros positioned himself between her legs, brushing her clitoris with his wet tip. When he pushed inside, Angeline tensed and stopped kissing him. She pushed his chest, whining. Maros growled and hovered above her, red eyes and erect sex. Incomprehension showed on his face.

Angeline stammered, "I... would prefer to wait a bit more... I am sore from yesterday." Not to mention the awful headache.

He didn't have to say yes; she was still his prisoner. Or was she?

Maros sighed and pouted. "Fine." He kissed her softly on her lips. "Let me make it up to you."

"Um... okay?" Angeline had no idea what he meant. She hoped for some gifts or cake. A new dress would be nice. She was so busy imagining all the pretty things she would be able to have once freed from the war.

Maros was moving toward her intimacy, leaving a trail of warm kisses all over her body. That was not what she expected.

She hesitated, close to asking him what the hell he was planning on doing down there, when she felt a new sensation.

"Oh, gosh!" She exclaimed, arching her back and clinging to the sheets. She glanced at the busy vampire and let herself be submerged by the waves of pleasure that drove through her.

It was much later when they finally got out of bed. The sun was high in the sky, and Angeline could not help but feel bad about being a lazy ass. Some of the vampires in their army were still on the mend from the nasty wolfmen's bite, after all. She had to push Maros away when he was threatening to give her a fourth orgasm. She didn't forget her part, and to his satisfaction, she finished what she started in the forest, obtaining a long howl of pleasure from her lover.

Angeline adjusted her blue velvet dress, still shaking from what he had done to her with only his fingers and tongue. She adjusted her outfit and glanced at Maros, still naked in bed, staring intensely. He obviously enjoyed the view of his lover getting dressed, a smile on his face showing how proud of her he was.

He lifted a brow and opened the blanket as an invitation, but received only a scoff.

A knock on the door interrupted their feeling of bliss.

Angeline jumped. She was usually good at hearing bystanders coming, but her mind was not yet adjusted to her new magic, and Maros's tongue didn't help the mush of a brain she had.

Maros chuckled, getting a grumpy look from Angeline. He did not let his eyes wander from her. "Come in," he called.

Manus appeared, a contrite look on his face, which was quite unusual. He nodded at Angeline, then sniffed the air. He looked at the bed, and with a sigh, death-stared at Maros, who snickered. Angeline's heart raced, her instincts telling her something was wrong. Manus had never commented on their foreplay.

"Princess," Manus said, "when you are ready, the witches of France are here to pick you up."

Angeline's blood froze, and a feeling of emptiness invaded her chest, while her headache grew stronger. Her wolf wallowed, rage and despair.

"W-what?" She stammered, looking at Maros for an answer.

Maros pulled a funny face and rose from bed, his naked body revealed without a pinch of shyness. "Right. Sorry. Forgot to mention. Nanabrok finally realized you were here, and she offered her coven's full support in the war if you were returned safely to her. Today."

Angeline stepped toward the vampire, fists clenched by her side, wishing she could read his mind.

"And when was this decided?" She whispered, her words slow, already knowing the answer. Crumbling under her wolf's whining, she tried not to pay attention to the pain and betrayal her sensitive She-Wolf felt.

Maros had the decency to stay silent for five seconds, stoic under Manus's judgmental look and Angeline's teary eyes. Knowing someone like Manus agreed with her on the whole

Maros-is-an-asshole thing made her feel better. Angeline knew little about relationships, but she knew this was not okay.

"You didn't think it might have been a great idea, or at least a *respectful* one, to inform me before we..." She interrupted herself. He deserved nothing more than getting an earful in front of his brother, but she was classier than that.

Her She-Wolf raged inside, screaming that they had both been played. An inside rage she had never felt before, accompanied by this awareness of betrayal she had already felt too many times, always caused by men.

She took a deep breath and turned to Manus. "I am ready. Just one thing."

Angeline stepped toward Maros, who did not move an inch, certainly knowing what was coming. She slapped him as hard as she could. Maros recoiled, taking a step back, and his eyes widened. He stared at her with a look of incomprehension.

"Thank you for making me stronger," Angeline spat at him, then calmly joined Manus, who had an imperceptible smile.

"Angeline!" Maros called.

Too late. She was already gone.

Angeline descended the stairs behind Manus. She wished she could throw Maros down the stairs and that he would break a leg. That would probably never happen. She needed to get out of there, fast.

A tragic, melted face was waiting for her outside. Angeline blinked, her heart racing with relief and disbelief. The terrific

Witch Nanabrok, head of the French Coven, stood there, so short and bent over that she was barely poking out of the snow.

"Nana..." Angeline's voice trembled, on the edge of tears. Memories of the last few days, weeks, and years came in waves. She wanted to be angry at the witch; she wanted to hate her for leaving her to rot, for not saving her, but her anger toward the witches was swiftly forgotten. She knew it was not their fault.

They're here, they're here for me, I still matter. Her shame swallowed her joy, and all the eyes upon her who could certainly smell her decadence.

Her headache finally lifted as she saw one of her favorite faces, one she had not seen in years.

"Jack."

He looked rougher than usual, and she could perceive in his mind how relieved he was to see her alive, looking at her as if he could not believe it. Knowing that Maros didn't lie about one thing was a little comfort. Louis really told everyone she was dead.

Jack's eyes scanned her as if to find any injuries on her body, even though the only pain she felt could not be perceived by the eyes. She took one step, and Jack finished the rest, lifting her and holding her tight as if she would fly away. A quick intrusion into his mind confirmed that, indeed, that's what he thought; he was holding a ghost. He inhaled deeply, right in her neck, and he grew stiff. Jack pushed her back to look at her with inquisitive eyes.

He knew. This damn smell of hers. She hoped it would not change after her decadence, but here it was.

Anger came from him in waves, which was strange for Jack.

She whimpered and got him to take her back against him. "Please. Don't say a thing. Not now." He looked like he was ready to kill.

"The deal was for her to be untouched," Nanabrok said, shooting an accusing look at Maros, who had finally arrived.

"No. You asked for her not to be hurt. I didn't hurt her," Maros said, back to his stoic self. Neither his eyes nor his face showed any feelings. Where was the man who, she thought, made love to her yesterday?

Angeline cried, hiding her face against Jack's shoulder; she just wanted to leave. The shame was unbearable. How could she be so stupid? She was so close, so close to being sent home intact, and she had to listen to her horny self.

Waves of doubt and fear crushed her. There was no doubt Maros would never keep his promise to keep her safe, not when he just toyed with her like a woman of little virtue. She thought he cared for her—she *heard* him care for her—but where had that gone? Her only hope now was Jack and her old friends.

Angeline dried her tears when she sensed Nanabrok's anger rising to a dangerous level. Nanabrok considered burning the vampire, her fingertips sparking with ice-blue energy, barely containing the deadly spell ready to escape.

"Nana," Angeline said. "No." She turned and looked at Maros. "He is not worth our time anymore. Let him have his crown."

Angeline listened to the old witch's thought process with fascination. Nanabrok was deciding the best course of action. Finally, Nanabrok started moving around, grumbling some incomprehensible words while rummaging in her gigantic purse, certainly for one of those lavender sweets she always had on her. At least Angeline hoped that was what she was doing, and that there was no weird spell hidden in her purse.

Nanabrok finally retrieved a purple sweet from her bag, a victorious smile on her lips, and gave it to Angeline. She smiled encouragingly and ambled to the waiting car, her short legs advancing with difficulty.

Maros sped to open the car door, trying to catch Angeline's eye. She ignored him completely while stepping into the warm and comfortable cubicle.

Nanabrok, on the other hand, stopped at Maros's height, who was at least two heads above her, and said without a pinch of fear, "If you touch her again, First vampire or not, I will make you think about your time with the Blade of Misery as the best days of your life."

Maros smiled sarcastically, but Angeline didn't need to read his mind to know he believed the witch. He would be a fool to get on Nanabrok's bad side.

Part 3

CHAPTER 21

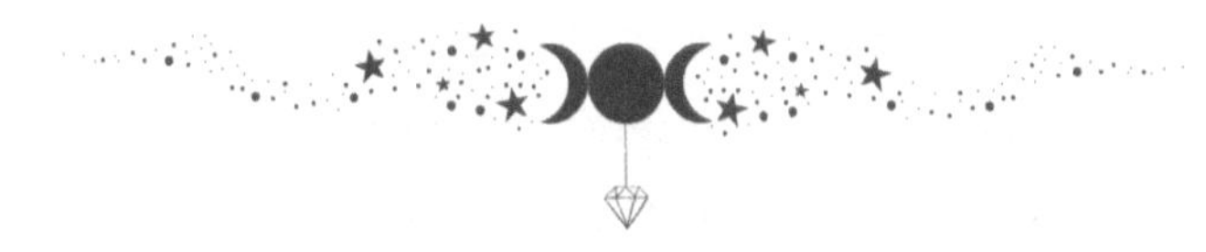

ANGELINE

LINOSA ISLAND WAS A different life from what she had known in the past five years. Warmth, blinding sun, and seagulls' screams had replaced the frozen walls and girls' cries.

The island had been fortunate enough to be spared from the ravages of war thanks to the strong coven in charge of this tiny piece of land. They set themselves up as neutral from the beginning; their view about the war was the simplest. It was a vampire problem.

Nina, the coven leader, was an older woman with dirty blonde hair. She was powerful and unafraid of bloodsuckers. In 200 years, she always managed to beat down anyone trying to enslave or kill her people. It had been fifty-four years since someone tried. The location of the island, lost at sea between Italy and Tunisia, also helped. One would be a fool to attack Water Witches on an island.

Angeline recalled her conversation with Nanabrok on the day of her return. The ancient witch had confirmed that the French Coven had decided to stop fighting in exchange for Angeline's safe return once they learned of her condition. So did all of the covens of Europe. Nanabrok was well respected among her peers, and they agreed for her sake, but that was not all. When they learned of Angeline's magic, there was no pushing the matter further.

A Magical Virgin was too rare to be left to her death in the hands of Maros the Terrible. Little did they know that three days prior, Angeline would have been more than glad to be left in his hands. Besides the witches, the werewolves had also stopped fighting, leaving Paul with only an army of vampires and a few witches. Misa and Quentin shared with their pack friends about Angeline's gift, and it didn't take long for rumors of the White Wolf to spread. After all, shapeshifters were rare and respected.

Angeline could already imagine her father knocking down furniture to express his anger about the situation. Not only did he lose his best fighters—both the French Coven and the pack were among the most dangerous creatures in the war—but his daughter was a damn beast. All she hoped was that this would end the conflict. Without them by his side, Paul's death was to be expected. Finally.

Feeling the anger bubbling inside of Angeline, Nana explained that everyone was convinced she was dead. They had been told that five years ago, she jumped into the Falls of Mischief following her decadence with Maros. Angeline laughed out loud at the story; her father sure was resourceful. Paul and Louis had lied to entire nations, and when the war came a few years later, it was the norm to hate Maros, who led the princess to kill herself.

"I am done with all of this," Nanabrok said. "I should have known better. I should have trusted you better. You're no weak little girl. You don't go and kill yourself because some man carried you butt-naked on his shoulders! So, instead, I will let the Spirits decide. After all, this kind of war, all those lives lost of magical creatures, this should not be our doing. The balance. The balance is everything, Angeline."

Angeline was given another lavender sweet.

Now, Maros was on the brink of becoming king, but tensions were still high on both sides. Paul did not give up despite losing his strongest allies.

Nanabrok told her that the First came to negotiate with the French Kingdom following their attack from the wolfmen and asked for a break in the war while he and his siblings assessed the situation. Louis was on the point of refusing, but Maros smartly took Angeline's argument out. That shook Louis's confidence and revealed his lie to the witches and werewolves. Angeline wished she could have been there to see it.

Angeline sighed and got up from bed, glad Jack finally gave her some alone time. He hadn't left her side for a few days, and despite her love for him, she was begging to have some space. As relieved as she was to be alive, all she wanted was peace—to be done with the magical world. She guessed Maros wouldn't hold his promise—that freaking asshole—but Jack already convinced her to put their Caribbean plan into execution. He spent days telling her of ships bigger than a building and promises of riches while drinking mocktails on a beach.

Only Jack knew what Paul had done; she couldn't hide it from her best friend any longer. Angeline hadn't said a word to Nanabrok or anyone about it, and it seemed like Louis didn't either. Of course, as Louis still believed his compulsion worked. She wondered if Paul knew about her fake death. Angeline had blamed him and her father for the torture at the convent, but she started to consider that it was only her father's doing.

She would keep her secret until it was time to use it or retaliate, but there was no point in creating more of a mess. Who knew how the covens would react? Angeline was not selfish enough to risk a new civil war in the Kingdom of France as soon as a king was elected. Her father and Nanabrok had a long history of fighting each other for any reason they could find.

She changed quickly into her outfit, a white dress edged with gold and turquoise patterns, the typical outfit from the Linosa coven. Her magic had developed so much since her intimate night with the First. Truthfully, even if it came to it, she wasn't sure she would need any help to deal with her father or Paul. She felt stronger. She felt powerful. And she could finally fight back.

Well, she sure wished she had known years ago that her She-Wolf could hurt without being hurt, but there was no point in crying over the past. She had always dreamt of being stronger, and now she was. She didn't know how to use it or what to do with it, but she did not doubt that the Spirits would guide her when the time came. Magical Virgins were supposed to be created for balance, nurturing, and love. All she wanted to do was burn her enemies and bury them in their blood.

At the thought of love, she held back a whine, her She-Wolf clenching inside of her. Angeline couldn't help but reminisce about the time spent with Maros.

"It's okay, My Love, we're stronger than that," she whispered, closing her eyes and reaching for her twin inside her mind.

Since her magic changed, her link with her wolf was stronger. Before, it was always a shock and annoyance to hear the wolf inside her. Now it was not. They were as one, and Angeline was ready to fight to ensure her She-Wolf would never leave her again.

One thing she and the She-Wolf disagreed on was that Maros cheated them. Angeline felt uncertain about what had happened and why the man decided she was worth being hurt and toyed with. Her wolf, after a few days of peace and reflection, seemed to think his wolf could not handle the link they had, and she only remembered the good moments.

One more night. She could have been stronger for just one more night, and she would not be hurting so much. Angeline knew deep inside that what she was scared of was other peo-ple's reactions, and she hated it. She thought she was above this; she *should* be above it.

Angeline groaned and reached for her amethyst pendant and tiny charm bracelet—Maros's gifts. Jack had given them back to her. He found them in her bedroom at their house years ago and held onto them. She hated herself for this, but she needed to feel the small diamond wolf against her skin, as a reminder.

"*Angeline.*"

Now that was a voice she hadn't heard in a while. Her father interrupted her thoughts and entered her room without knocking.

"Louis?" Stupor showed on her face.

Nanabrok stood by his side, and the old witch raised an eyebrow.

"Ahem... I..." her father started.

"Don't."

Her father straightened, pulling his shoulders back. She spotted the familiar way he clenched his fists, something he did when vexed. Before he could add anything, she continued speaking.

"Don't even try to find a good excuse. You have none." Her mouth twisted in disgust, and her golden magic tumbled inside, ready to burn him.

Burn him. Burn him. We want him burned. Her damn She-Wolf agreed with her on one thing.

It was the sight of her brother, peeking behind the two guests, that stopped her. She smiled when she saw him pulling a funny face behind Louis's back.

"No need to rehash," Nanabrok said, cutting in. She stood in front of Louis. "What is done is done, and I have already expressed to Louis my displeasure about his lies."

"Why is he still alive then?" Angeline asked, eyebrows raised, placing all the fake innocence she could into her voice.

While Louis was ready to jump at her, Nanabrok laughed heartily, as did Jack.

"I like the new you," Nanabrok said, looking at the young woman above her purple glasses.

"You have Louis to thank for that." Angeline retorted, walking away from them to finish getting ready. She grabbed a hairbrush and pulled on her hair with angry motions.

And Paul, and Maros, and all the freaking nuns and their torture.

"I have called for this meeting," Louis said. "We need to discuss the... latest news from the front."

"Do you mean that your best friend, Paul, lost his only hope of winning?" Angeline couldn't help but smile.

Louis sighed and threw a look at Nanabrok, who nodded gently. Angeline rolled her eyes. This would be much faster if she were sneaking into their minds. People were so slow.

"I have taken a step back from the conflict, for various reasons." Louis waited for a salty repartee from his daughter, but she didn't bother. "We have another danger coming our way; one bigger, I'm afraid, than who will be king."

Angeline remained silent, but she doubted there could be a worse danger than Paul with a damn crown on his head. Louis cleared his throat, and his eyes met Angeline's. She knew she might be wrong at the moment when Louis, for once, didn't know what to say to her.

"We may have made a mistake years ago," he said. "The Alpha."

Angeline's heart stopped. Even though many could be referred to as The Alpha, only one could make her father tremble.

"The Russian?" She asked, incredulity showing in her voice. "Is he still alive?" Her tone was not the kindest, but come on, they had *five years*.

The wolfman attack. Was that his army? Is that why Maros was worried?

"There is a lot to do." Louis was not going to give her any time. She knew he wanted to speak now before she reminded him again of his failures as a father and leader. "While we were busy with the War of Kings, the Russians built an army stronger than ever. He has thousands of wolves like him, and he's coming for us now, after negotiations with Paul failed." Louis stopped, observing his daughter with a sharp look. "He wants the crown, too."

Angeline scoffed, ready to tell him what she thought about how he handled the situation, but Louis turned to Jack.

"Contact everyone we know," Louis said, "every coven, pack, or nest. We want to be sure that every magical creature knows what's coming for them, so they can take precautions. We can't afford the Alpha to convert anymore werewolves."

"I already ordered for every pack to retract. Didn't wait for you to ask Paul's permission." Nanabrok snickered.

Louis didn't show any reaction, but he stopped Jack from leaving. "Are you in... any kind of contact with Maros? Or Manus?"

Angeline snapped out of her stupor, in disbelief at what she read in Louis's mind.

Jack pursed his lips, but nodded. Angeline let her branches reach her brother, and she couldn't believe what was right under her nose. Jack had been working double with Paul and Maros.

Damn this pirate!

She *would* have to talk with him, and she hoped for his sake that he was not aware of her presence in Maros's hands. She needed an explanation.

Jack looked at Angeline, and without a word, he left the room. One of his thoughts reached her.

I'll tell you everything.

Angeline huffed. Perhaps she should just get rid of her amethyst; she was surrounded by lies and needed a clear head to hear all of them.

Angeline was left with Louis and Nanabrok. Nanabrok was quiet, but anger and sadness rolled off her in waves. There was no point in trying to control her gift anymore. She was like a ghost, taking in all the information from both minds around her.

"Why was nothing done five years ago?" Angeline asked bluntly. "When they attacked the pack—my friends, my godson. *Why?*"

Louis avoided looking at her. "Paul was to deal with the Alpha, which... he did... but apparently the man survived."

Angeline almost choked on her laugh. "And... you trusted Paul? Cowardly Paul? To deal with a psychopathic werewolf?"

Louis was so dumb sometimes.

"I do not doubt that Paul did what he could. He was saddened by your... loss, too."

This time, Angeline lost it, laughing hysterically. Disgust gnawed at her. If Louis thought for a second she would forgive him, he was wrong.

"Why did you send Jack to the First?" She asked, knowing she would not love the answer.

Nanabrok answered for Louis. "We need everyone who is not turned into a crazy psychopathic werewolf to join us. Paul has already accepted, probably to compensate for the fact that he failed years ago, and we were hoping Maros would accept a truce for the time being. After all, if this Alpha gets more people, he could very well win the crown."

Angeline closed her eyes. Right. Maybe there were worse people than Paul after all. Her blue pearls reopened at the next words.

"We would like you to be present at the strategy meeting," Nanabrok said. "We are hoping for the day after tomorrow."

Angeline scoffed. "No."

"Don't be a—" Louis started, but Nanabrok's glare swiftly silenced him.

"Angeline," Nanabrok said, "I know the last few weeks have not been easy, but we could use everyone's help, and as far as knowledge of magic and territories go, you are one of the best."

Angeline grunted, pacing, arms crossed, and her mind going wild.

"I'm not even sure if I would rather see Maros or Paul," she spat, glaring at Louis, who had the decency to look away.

That's when it hit her. Her father was not as scary as she once thought he was. All of her childhood, she had walked the straight line, fearing not only an eventual punishment, but the lack of love from her parents. It didn't matter anymore. She was not a child, and she was not afraid. Louis had better learn that fast if he hoped to survive the war.

CHAPTER 22

3 days later

ANGELINE

S HE TRIED TO ESCAPE it, but Nanabrok was dead set on her being there. It took only a few more words and compliments for Angeline to agree to participate, on the condition that she would be listened to. Louis dared to protest against the idea, but thankfully, Nanabrok shut him down. Louis didn't know it yet, but Angeline was counting the days he had left.

My time to shine.

Angeline was done being a victim or a pretty little idiot. She was supposed to be one of the smartest beings in the world, and she was not planning to let the Alpha win the war or the crown. Nor was she planning for Paul to survive the war, and Louis was a fool if he thought otherwise. She hadn't mentioned to him yet that his poor attempt at compulsion five years ago had failed. Her time would come, and she could not wait to see his face when it did.

The Magical Kingdom of Europe was reunited in the Great Hall of the Castle of Estrella, on Linosa Island. Angeline stood between Jack and Nanabrok, and she couldn't help but shake at the thought of what would come. With so many enemies in such a tiny space, tensions could rise in an instant. Thankfully, her neighbors alternated snarky comments and gossip, keeping her entertained. She suspected they did so to get her to relax.

"OMG, look at Astronella. I'm telling you, she's older than she claims," Jack said.

Nanabrok could not resist answering. "Did you know that fifty years ago, she slept with the Count of Marikeb? She made him eat her boogers."

"Nana!" Angeline gasped, outraged by her words. "What does OMG even mean?" She asked Jack in a whisper, ignoring her friend's laughter.

Angeline was delighted to see so many people attending their meeting from every side.

Vampires, werewolves, witches, everyone was there. Anyone involved in the War of Kings was busy throwing glances and threatening looks at each other, only to be immediately called back to order by the French and Linosa witches, who were in charge of the event's security.

Hopefully, they were ready to fight. This time, they would fight together, against a common enemy, as they all agreed the Alpha should not get the damn crown. She spotted many of her acquaintances in the crowd. Nana and her coven were all there, of course, leading the way; the French Pack was in a corner, watching all the blood suckers closely. Being in an alliance didn't mean they had to be friends with everyone.

She could feel that the war had an impact on her friends. Quentin and Misa yearned for their children and the grassy smell of their home. Angeline waved at them quickly. It felt better to know her friends were there. She talked to them briefly the day before, and her wolf had yapped with excitement to see them again. She thought they had given up on her.

Misa almost cried, which was an incredible event. They were furious at Louis for lying to them, but Angeline had begged them not to interfere, that she would deal with it. One of her biggest fears, after all, was that her country would be brought back to a bloody civil war; her friends didn't deserve that.

Any new coven or pack that entered the room could see her, and without hesitation, they went to bow before her. Witches, respecting her Spirit-Gift, and werewolves respecting the shapeshifter in her.

It was strange, being bowed to not because of her last name but because of who she was. Vampires still behaved as usual, and she perceived their astonishment at the new-comers honoring her. They were surprised not only by her being alive, but by her unfamiliar scent.

Oh, come on. Just leave my freaking smell alone.

Jack had confirmed that she still smelled like an angel, but different, maybe even stronger than before, which did not make her happy.

Nanabrok waved people away, grunting. "Move along, move along. Nothing to smell here!"

Nobody deserved any explanations. Angeline was done with the perfection club her father raised her to be in. She was strong and took great pleasure in holding back the look all of her acquaintances were giving her. She raised an eyebrow disdainfully, provoking them to dare say a word.

Jack laughed as discreetly as he could while watching his sister show off what he had called her 'resting bitch face.' Angeline was outraged at the name, but thought it was a rather cool thing to be called.

Crowds of newcomers penetrated the magical barrier built by the witches. Angeline felt little pricks of pride anytime she could spot a new cover or pack. They all joined, thanks to her and her magic. Irish witches, Scottish werewolves, most of Britain's magical creatures, and even the witches of Iceland were there, which was quite reassuring, as the Icelandic witches were terrifying in a battle.

She tensed when she spotted Paul in the crowd, surrounded by other German Vampires. Vampires were the only magical kind left in the country, seeing that Paul made a mission to exterminate all other species two centuries ago. Jack moved closer, placing a comforting arm on her shoulder and bringing her to his side.

"Don't you worry. I am not letting you out of my sight. His time will come," he whispered the last words, and flashes of a very dead Paul crossed his mind. Jack had been overprotective for the last three days. Angeline could feel the guilt inside him, even though he had confirmed that Maros didn't tell him of her presence. He thought she was gone, for five freaking years.

Men are men, after all. That's what he thought, but didn't dare tell her to her face. Jack was hurt that Maros didn't inform him of her presence as soon as he found her, and he added things together when he discovered his sister was heartbroken.

Angeline didn't push the topic. Jack thought she was hurt because of Maros, but all she could think of was Paul and Louis's betrayal. She tried not to revert to the weak person she was five years prior, but it was an arduous task. Her shame and anger mixed into a confusing feeling.

She glanced at her brother while he was waving at an old friend. Her brother, her best friend, had put on one of his favorite outfits: black leather pants and a white floaty shirt that revealed his hairy chest. His long, raven colored hair was let down freely along his face. That was what he called his 'gonna get laid tonight' outfit. She could not believe he expected to have fun despite the new war coming their way.

Angeline was not sure what she was supposed to wear for events like these, so in order to contradict her father, she wore the Linosa Coven's war outfit, which Nina had proudly agreed for her to wear. The dress was shiny turquoise, shimmering under the light. Two triangles of fabric surrounded her breasts, linked between her neck by an owl brooch, the witch's em-blem. She was showing more skin than she was used to. The dress fell elegantly around her hips, displaying her entire back. Both sides had a slit up to the leg, to allow for horseback riding, according to Nina.

Angeline laughed at Jack's thought: *"Or to get men riding."*

According to him, the witches of Linosa were known to have many lovers on their isolated island.

Angeline didn't mind that. She loved the dress and being free from a corset or an ugly, heavy nun's dress. Surrounding her were people who lived in the modern world and had been at war for months. There was no point in being overdressed.

Angeline knew deep inside she was craving Maros's atten-tion, and hated herself for spending more time than necessary in front of her mirror. Tiny purple bruises were still scattered over her neck from Maros's fangs, and at the thought of the canines penetrating her skin, she felt an old desire awakening. Her heart raced.

Maros was an ass. A total, complete ass who played her. He didn't deserve an ounce of her attention, desire, or feelings. Louis and even Nanabrok suggested hiding the marks, but she decided she should proudly display them. Her fingers brushed the two dark marks, and she inhaled, trying to slow her heart-beat.

She turned back to glance at her parents. At least Isabeau was attracting all the attention with her large 18th-century dress. Louis was, as usual, by her side, and anger rushed through

Angeline's body. Her father was like all other vampires, a lying prick. He lied to everyone, and until Maros offered her in exchange, he didn't think about mentioning to Paul that she was still alive.

Paul had only forgiven Louis because the French Army was impressive enough to forget about a lie. Sure, Louis had decided to stop following Paul for the time being, but in his mind, there was still the possibility of a wedding, once Paul became king. After all, now that Louis knew how devoted to his daughter the witches and wolves were, there was no doubt Paul could win the war with her by his side.

Angeline scoffed when she heard this. Too bad she was not planning for Paul to survive long enough to see the crown. Her lips twisted as she watched him gloat with his friends on the other side of the room. He threw looks of disdain at anyone who was not a part of his army. She could not wait to see his lifeless body, and if Louis didn't back down, he would suffer the same fate.

The crowd was too large to fit in the hall, so only the leaders of the various packs, covens, and families were allowed, while their people were in the gardens. She went to her spot at the table, to the right of Nina, who sat beside Nanabrok. Angeline could not help but smile proudly when looking at the magical map on the table. She was the one who had contributed to it, already planning their attack against the Alpha. Despite Louis raging by her side, this was the strategy they would go with. Her foolish father wanted to place the Irish Witches on a field, with no river to support their incredible water magic. Angeline was glad she pushed back.

A familiar sensation prickled up the back of her neck.

Angeline's breathing stopped, and she tried to control her heartbeat, but it was a lost cause. She could feel Maros's burning look on her when she walked past without addressing him. From the corner of her eye, she watched the First Family move to the other side of the table with their usual grace. Maros kept his intense gaze on her.

She smoothed down her dress, biting her lower lip when she acknowledged her nipples pushing through the light fabric. Angeline was aroused by the man's mere presence. She stood upright, holding her head high. Maros's look still burned her. His jaw clenched when his emerald eyes lowered to her breasts, and he gripped the edge of the table. She knew that if they were alone, he would already be pounding her pussy with all his strength.

By the Goddess, calm down, girl.

She needed to stop the vision of her lying down on the table, legs spread, welcoming his hard dick.

She took a deep breath, controlling her desire, and looked at him. Being an extremely mature young woman, Angeline stuck out her tongue. Maros instantly showed surprise, trying to stifle a laugh. Manus bent down to him and whispered something in his ear whilst looking at her. Maros nodded and responded with a damn, annoying smirk. She turned her head and decided she would simply ignore him.

"Silence!" Louis ordered. And silence fell.

CHAPTER 23

ANGELINE

A TROUBLED SILENCE FELL over the room. Angeline knew she must look like a deer caught in headlights. She tried to silence Maros with her look, but he flashed a cocky smile and continued.

"She. Is. Mine." Maros turned to Louis. "Think about the powerful alliance it will bring us, Louis".

Angeline snorted. She was sure Maros couldn't care less about this kind of alliance; he didn't need it.

"Maros," Louis growled.

"Oh, please. When she was our prisoner, you didn't care. My poor White Wolf waited weeks before one of you finally decided she was worth getting back. Even though that would have been hard to do, considering you told everyone she was dead."

"What do you mean, 'you made sure of it?'" Paul asked, hands on the gigantic table, arms shaking with fury. His red eyes contrasted with his ghostly skin.

Did he just wake up? I'm so done with this shit.

Before Maros could say anything else, she spoke.

"Just to be clear for everyone," Angeline bellowed, her tone sharp and decisive. "There will be no Delacour-First alliances, as I am not a Delacour anymore. I'm a Loublanc." She made the name up; she would need to work out the details later.

Louis made a sound of disagreement, but she gave him a sharp look and, with a movement of her hand, magically compelled him to stay quiet. Whispers in the room didn't stop her. Louis clutched at his throat, and Angeline's smile was full of satisfaction when she looked away.

She placed both hands on the table in front of her. "Not that it concerns any of you, but I gave myself to him." Her crystalline voice cut the whispers and giggles, resulting in disturbing silence. "After all, I was not planning to return to this latent hypocrisy." She glanced at Maros, holding his heavy look. She knew that if she could touch him, she would feel his desire, and he probably could smell hers.

Angeline smirked and said, "He asked nicely."

Maros chuckled.

Paul screamed in German and threw a chair against the wall, shattering the wood into pieces.

Carata spoke loud enough for everyone to hear. "Well done. I'm guessing she hates him more than she hates you."

Did she make a terrible decision based on her hate for Paul? Yes, she did. The damn She-Wolf made her do it.

But he virgin-shamed her. How was it a thing?

Paul said all of it aloud. Vampires had no decency whatsoever. The blood ran to her face, and she knew she looked like a tomato, which was certainly enhanced by her fiery hair.

She heard Paul's thoughts. Angeline tried to avoid them since he arrived, but now it was all there: he was gloating with arrogance, convinced he would be the one to finally put his hands on her. An alliance with Germany, especially now, was still interesting to Louis despite what he called his 'daughter's misadventure.' Paul knew Louis would return to him with the right leverage.

Maros's burning eyes undressed her, and she was not sure it had been the smartest decision. She wanted to make him pay for how he played with her, but she knew it was nearly impossible. Her heart melted just looking at him, but she hated herself for it.

"Also," Maros said, "and I am telling you this as a bad guy myself: the Alpha won't stop slaughtering innocents just because you give him the girl. Come on, what are we? Children who believe in cute little fairies? The next person who mentions that we should give the princess to him, I swear to you, I will rip out one of your organs and eat it right in front of you."

The room went quiet.

Maros stepped back to his place, scoffing while whispers of 'cannibals' rose in the room. Angeline didn't want to laugh out loud, but during their conversations, Maros assured her the rumors about him being a cannibal—on other vampires, which was disgusting and forbidden—were spread by Carata for fun during the 12th century. Angeline had thought that was hilarious.

Maros brought his attention to Angeline, catching the laughter in her eyes, and the look they exchanged was filled with promises, passion, and care.

"After all," Maros added, "we *are* talking about my future queen."

Well, that's new.

They were locked on each other, her lips only a thin line, not wanting to back down despite how her She-Wolf begged her to cross the room and undress him.

Their fiery exchange was interrupted by Louis, who had finally taken back the usage of his voice. "I sent her there for her protection."

How dare he lie to her, to all of them?

Angeline scoffed. "Is that right?"

"Five years ago," Louis said, "when I received the news about our friends from the Ukraine pack, it was the Alpha who informed me of it. He offered me the same exchange as today." Louis tortured his silk tie, pulling it, and Angeline, after a quick breach inside his mind, realized he was telling the truth.

Angeline should have sneaked into his mind on that day. Speechless, she looked at him, then at Paul, trying to grasp whatever the hell had happened that day.

"Things didn't happen as planned," Louis added. "I thought it would be safer for you to be considered dead while we dealt with the Alpha." At those words, he glared at Paul, who had the decency to stay silent.

Angeline breathed deeply, ignoring the whispers and the anger rising from many of her friends around her. She spoke the next words carefully, feeling her magic bubbling inside her and begging to explode.

"Let me summarize. You announced my wedding with Paul, then you received a letter from the Alpha, telling you that he knows about me and wants a wedding also, then I got violated by Paul."

Her father tried to interject.

"Do not interrupt me!" Angeline roared. "Then, I ran to you, my father, begging you for help and care... and instead... You compelled me to forget the rape and decided to send me to a convent for... protection? From what? Paul? Or Igor?"

"From your magic. And I didn't know you could not be compel—"

"I do not need protection from my magic!"

"Your magic is what makes those men obsessed with you. After what happened with Paul, I thought it was for the best. Who knows what would happen if a wolf were to marry you?"

"Of all the places you could have sent me"—her voice rose—"of *all* the places, Louis... you sent me to the Convent of Lamursa to be tortured by your rules, to be forgotten! How did that protect me?"

Everyone was silent, too focused on the exchange and gossip.

"Well, you misbehaved. I thought you could use some straightening." Louis pronounced those words as if it was evidence. He looked around the table, probably searching for some support from other Lords.

Her hands shook, and she gripped the table.

"Misbehaved," Angeline muttered.

"You know," Louis said, "first Maros, then Paul—who, by the way, was your fiancé and was allowed light touching. With your passion for wolves, who knows what you would have done with the Alpha? I'm not an idiot; I knew your magic was something else."

"Not sure about the idiot part..." Nanabrok mumbled.

"Are you fucking kidding me?" Angeline screamed and threw her water goblet, hitting Louis right on the forehead. It struck him with such strength that Louis stumbled backward.

There it is, that strength again.

Golden sparkles flew, but before she could shift, a warm embrace wrapped around her. Angeline and her She-Wolf fought back, trying to kick Maros and Jack.

"I'm going to rip his head off!" She growled.

Maros laughed out loud. "You're so adorable when you're angry," He whispered in her ear, tightening his hold on her. "Shush, Pet." He closed his arms around her and added, whispering so low she could barely hear him: "I promise you, My Wolf, his time will come."

Angeline inhaled his scent, trying not to linger in it. An icy breeze sent goose bumps all over her naked arms. She looked around, searching for the open window, but there was none.

Maros looked at her, a light of worry behind his gaze. The winds howled, and everybody stopped screaming at each other.

That's when she felt it.

She held her breath and turned to look at what everyone in the crowd was staring at. Incomprehension showed on their faces.

No.

There was a hole in the space, surrounded by lightning, and getting bigger by the second. She felt fear invading her. This was shadow magic, a dark portal, created to pull a specific name into it. It was commonly used in the 1400s, when witches were at war with vampires. Some of them decided to practice dark magic to survive, and kidnapping vampire children was the best solution they found at the time.

She felt it. The pull.

The portal was here for her.

"Jack!" She screamed.

Jack held onto the table, his feet anchored in the ground, trying to resist the strong pushing of the black hole. He held out his hand, but he flew away, unable to resist the magic.

Angeline threw her arms around a foot table, hoping the huge wooden table would resist the portal. She knew that even if the table would hold, her arms would not. There was no resisting the pull. She had read enough and heard enough from Nanabrok.

She screamed and held on stronger. The First Family were the only ones able to fight the push. Manus held Blanda, and the witch desperately tried to sing a spell against the portal. The wind was so powerful that she was unable to finish.

"Princess!" Maros succeeded in staying close, holding the table, digging his claws in so he would not fly away.

"Maros!" She cried. Her arms were giving up.

He let go of one hand and jumped behind her while planting his claws on the table, using his body to protect her. There was nothing that could be done, and she knew it. The pull was getting stronger, and Maros must have used his full strength to hold for so long.

She let go of the foot table, too weak to hold on any longer.

CHAPTER 24

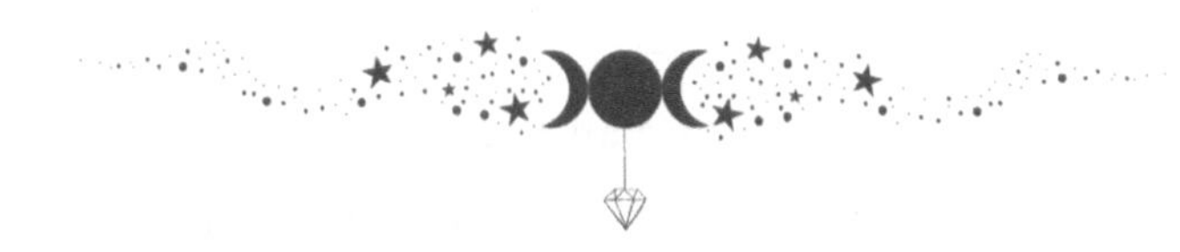

MAROS

Maros growled. Staying on her side of the table had been a real pain in the neck. He had never felt such a powerful force before. His claws were bleeding, some ripped out by the force of the current, and he knew he couldn't hold on much longer. When his princess lost her grip, he had to make a decision, and he knew he would regret it no matter what.

He threw a look at Blanda, who was grimacing from pain. She, Nina, and Nanabrok were trying some kind of spell to stop the black hole from swallowing the princess, but it was impossible. Angeline raised her eyes to meet his, and she spoke so softly that he had to strain to understand: "Let me go."

Maros let out a desperate yell and released his claws, surrounding her body. He held her tight and pushed into the portal.

They crashed in a snowy landscape, their bodies entangled. Head turning and sparkly stars behind his lids, Maros only realized he was lying down when he noticed the green treetops above, floating in the freezing wind. They were not in Linosa anymore.

Maros leapt up, his claws and fangs out, ready to fight whoever was out there. Angeline stumbled upright in the deep snow, already shivering. She peered over her shoulder with a terrified look on her face. He turned and saw a tall and broad man, but what attracted Maros's attention was his surroundings—his army. Hundreds and hundreds of... men? Wolves? They looked the same as the ones they met in the forest.

What the hell are those things?

The wolfmen stood on their hind legs, but they were bent like animals. Their faces looked like they were halfway through a shapeshifting, but had stopped in the middle of it. They were all some ugly motherfuckers. Maros had to hold a disgusted grunt at the view of their bloodied and naked selves, and their hanging dicks.

Angeline whined and moved closer, trying to steal some of his warmth. Her skin was as pale as the snow, and her extremities had already turned blue.

What seemed to be the leader of the monster army stepped closer. Maros stood in front of Angeline, hiding her body from the hunger in the Alpha's gaze.

"Well, looks like we have an uninvited guest," Igor, the Alpha, said. "I knew the spell couldn't be perfect. Too bad we can't send you back, Scarface. My witch had an accident."

Maros spotted the dead body lying not far away, its intestines out. The view of one of her legs marked with multiple magic marks told him she used to be a witch.

Igor did not hide the perverted look he gave Angeline, bending his head sideways as if trying to see behind Maros. She tried to move closer to Maros, shoving her face into his back. Maros wrapped an arm around her thin waist as if he could protect her from the army, and growled at Igor. That's when he heard her, but as he looked at her lips, they were not moving. Her voice resonated in his mind.

Run!

Maros's eyes widened, and he tried to catch her eye, to confirm he was not dreaming.

Run. You're faster than them. Run. Leave me. People need you.

Angeline's heartbeat was erratic, and Maros tightened his grip on her.

Igor huffed and puffed, his Alpha senses exacerbated by the eye contact with Maros. A disgusting smile appeared on his face.

"It seems someone here is trying to steal my fiancée," he said in a raspy voice. "The question is: do we kill him now, or... do we make him watch me take her on our wedding night?"

He surveyed his army, as if expecting an answer from the speechless monsters.

Maros bent over Angeline, whispering so low he hoped she could hear him. "Whatever you do, do not show any of your gifts. They won't make a difference against thousands of monsters."

Angeline winced but nodded.

If Igor knew all of her talents, there was no saying what he would use her for.

"I am not your usual vampire," Maros said, looking at Igor.

"Whatever,"

Igor pulled Angeline away from Maros, and at least thirty wolfmen jumped on him. His knees buckled under the weight.

ANGELINE

Angeline was helpless. Despite fighting back as hard as he could, Maros didn't stand a chance against the hundreds of men attacking him. He collapsed, and she let out a cry, making a movement toward the raging fight. Igor drew her closer.

"Please!" She wept.

He struck her across the face, and Angeline landed in the blood-covered snow. She raised her head and wiped blood out of her nose.

Not her blood. Not Maros's. It was the wolf-men's—Maros was still fighting back, kicking, biting, and ripping out their hearts.

Angeline perceived Igor's doubtful thoughts as he commanded the rest of his men to join the battle. They couldn't all get to Maros at once, but the flood of bodies overtook Maros, dragging him down to his knees. Angeline threw a sorry look at the vampire. His clothes were torn to shreds, and bleeding claw marks covered his body and face.

The marks were healing before her eyes. Angeline held back a sigh of relief. At least the wolfmen's bites didn't have the same impact on him as they did on other vampires.

Angeline didn't need to read his mind to know he was giving up the fight, and she did not blame him for it.

"Well, you're a tough one." Igor laughed out loud. "Enough play. We have a wedding to prepare, and I promised my boys here they would have the right to have some fun with the lady."

Maros's growl resounded with despair, but he didn't resist when they picked him up from the ground and pushed him forward, barely holding onto his legs. Igor dug his claws into Angeline's arm and made her walk by his side. Maros walked in front of them, surrounded by wolfmen.

"You're still a virgin, right?" Igor asked, sticking his claws deeper in her frail arm. "I was promised a virgin."

Angeline whined and tried to twist out of his reach, but the pain was too deep.

"Of course, you are," he murmured, moving his hands from her arm to her hips, digging into her back. One of his hands moved to her hair. "You smell like an angel. I wonder how you will smell once my men try you one by one".

Angeline's legs shook. Was he stupid? For a Magical Wedding to work, she was not supposed to be touched by another man, or else her powers wouldn't spread to the husband. Ever. He might even die.

Igor came to an abrupt stop, catching her chin between his cold fingers, and placed his nose against her neck. He groaned and moved onto his knees, sniffing her lower parts.

His scream was that of a demon. His eyes glowed purple, and his claws popped out. "You fucking slut!"

Igor slapped her harder than before, his claws breaking her tender skin. The strength propelled her onto the frozen ground, her blood splattering onto the snow.

The army stood around, a mass of brainless bodies. She raised her head to look for Maros and realized with relief that he had listened to her. Tears rolled down her cheeks.

Igor must have understood the same thing. His fists clenched, and Angeline knew she could not hope for a quick death when he reached for her, forcing her to stand on her wobbly feet. To her surprise, he laughed.

"Looks like your little friend didn't think you were worth risking his life," Igor spat. "I don't blame him."

His words pierced her cold chest.

He turned toward the three who were guarding Maros and ripped their heads off, not minding the few grumbles rising from his army.

"Oh, well," he said. "Moving on."

Igor pouted and continued. "Sorry, darling. I was planning to be the only one to touch your sweet little cunt and ass because of the silly rule." He looked around, as if judging his army, and with a nod of his head, he made five of them step forward. "I guess it does not matter now. Let's see how many dicks you can take before our wedding."

Angeline was not sure what that meant. She reached Igor's mind one more time and stopped breathing when she understood what he was going to allow his men to do. Hundreds of them.

"I won't survive." Her lower lip trembled. "If you have hundreds raping me, I won't survive, and you will lose everything."

"Don't you worry, silly." He pinched one of her nipples so hard she screamed and bent in half, trying to escape his grip. "For now, we will spread them over the days leading up to our wedding. When they're being good boys, their little reward will be to taste any part of you they want. Once we are married, of course, that will need to change. I'm afraid only your ass will be available for them. But I am thinking, let's start slowly, and have only those five tonight."

Angeline cried. She never thought there would be a loophole with her magic. She tried to fight back, but he picked her up and threw her over his shoulder.

They reached a camp with many tents set up in the snow. A disgusting smell of death mixed with strong male scents reached her sensitive nose, and she felt nauseous. They entered one of the white tents, and Igor dropped her indelicately on a camp bed.

Angeline wanted to pinch her nose. His powerful scent was everywhere, and the thin mattress was covered with stains. She sat up and shuddered. The wolfmen were getting agitated. Igor caressed her, his dry fingers on her cheek, pushing along the claw marks he had made earlier.

She winced, trying to pull away from his touch, but he immediately dragged her closer. Igor was large, a bit taller than Maros, and had more muscles. His T-shirt was bursting under his oversized body.

He didn't say a word but gave a nod to the surrounding werewolves. They growled and prowled toward her. Igor sat on a rusty chair, legs spread, ready to watch.

Salt licked her wounds, tears rolling down her cheeks, sobs falling from her lips. She held her knees and tried to hide her face behind them.

Anywhere but here. I want to be anywhere but here.

The wolfmen jumped on her, fighting each other to be the first to reach her frozen skin. It was the race to see who would catch a leg or an arm; she struggled but knew she could do nothing.

Her screams got louder when they turned her over and, with claws digging into her flesh, forced her to spread her legs. They fought about who would have her first while Angeline waited, trying to move away from the firm grip and turn onto her back. She kicked and fought despite the little chance she had to escape them.

Igor sighed. "Come on, boys. Just talk about it and d—"

A wolfman entered the tent, grumbling something in Russian that Angeline could not catch. Igor's brows furrowed, and he stood up and barked an order while he walked toward the exit.

"Go for it, boys. It seems her little friend is still out there. I'm going to bring him back and make him watch." He received only groans as an answer.

Maros should have run and looked for help, looked for their army, even though their army was back in sunny Linosa. She hated him for staying here, risking his life when her friends and family would need him soon.

She felt a hard block against her butthole. The first wolf had finally convinced the others to let him go first, but his awkward body and her slippery ways did not help. She was not planning to make it easy for them, and despite hands and claws holding her, and blood running from many wounds, she was still fighting.

She was bravely kicking when she heard a clunk behind them; the wolves heard it too as they turned their half-shifted faces toward the provenance, only to show stupor displaying on their ugly features.

It was too late. Maros was there, and with a rage and speed she had never seen in any other vampire, he ripped out everybody's heart.

He came back.

CHAPTER 25

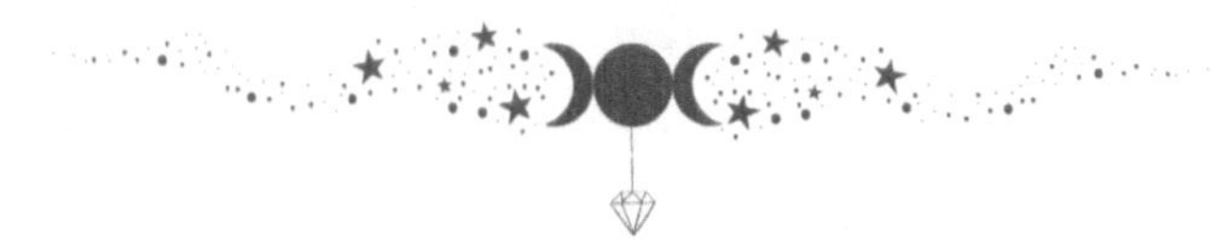

MAROS

A NGELINE CRIED, HER BODY trembling uncontrollably. She tried to speak, her voice breaking into a strangled noise, but before she could utter a word, Maros placed a blood-covered hand over her mouth.

"Shhh, My Love, now is not the time to be noisy."

Her wide, tear-filled eyes met his, a light of despair in them. Her tears ran over his fingers, and he wanted nothing more than to comfort her—but there was no time. Maros pulled her from the bed without a word. Angeline shook from head to toe.

"We need to run, and we need to run fast," he whispered, his voice strained. Maros cupped her face and stole a soft kiss from her trembling lips. Her frozen fingers brushed against his skin, and she nodded.

Angeline could barely stand. Her legs shook, and her feet were bare. How was he supposed to get her to freedom?

Maros asked, "Can you be anything smaller than your wolf?"

Angeline was a shapeshifter, after all, even if she hadn't explored the full nature of her abilities.

She shook her head, but then she lifted her head as if hearing an unknown voice. A gasp fell from her blue-tinged lips.

Maros tilted his head as Angeline ripped off what was left of her dress. He should have turned away, but he was not that kind of gentleman, and he was fascinated by her gift.

Golden sparkles flew around her. Before he knew what was happening, a tiny White Wolf stood at his feet, howling so faintly she sounded like a kitten. Maros chuckled despite the gravity of the situation, and he picked her up, stuffing her in his jacket's inside pocket. He sprinted out of the rancid tent, running like never before.

He ran in the opposite direction from the pack. Before they realized they escaped, he and the wolf would hopefully be far enough away. Maros still had no idea where they were. He ran through the snowy forest, jumping above dead trunks and through a river, to hopefully cover their tracks. Her scent was so strong that the pack might still pick her up, but he could run for hours before being tired.

Looking at the surrounding landscapes, he tried to recognize where they could be. Nothing looked familiar. It was only snowy forests and wide plains, with a few farmhouses here and there. His best guess was an Eastern European country.

The pack was in Ukraine the last time they heard of them, moving west for the other armies.

Maros stopped at the cliff's edge and patted his pocket, feeling a tiny wolf under his fingers. A weak whine answered him, followed by a purr. Not very wolf-like.

A noise far away pulled him from his thinking.

"A train?" He murmured.

Angeline must have heard him because he felt her claws pushing through the fabric.

The steady, metallic clatter in the distance gave him some hope. A train would keep Angeline warm, and with so many smells in a small place, the wolves would not find them. He ran again, following the edge of the cliff, listening to the rhythmic sound that was still too far away to see with his own eyes.

He grunted and jumped from the cliff, chuckling at the whine escaping from his pocket. Maros climbed down, grabbing rocks and trees, until he was close enough to the ground to jump. With agility, he weaved through the forest, focused only on catching the train. Hopefully, it was heading west.

When he reached a small cliff, he got his answer, spotting one of his favorite travel memories in the gorge below. It was the Orient Express, without a doubt, only such a fancy train would travel in such places.

Could they be somewhere around Hungary? Maybe Romania, if they were less lucky. The further west, the better.

Snow crunched behind him.

"Fuck," Maros grumbled, dodging the wolfman who tried to sneak up on him. The howling monster tumbled off the cliff.

One was gone, but they were not safe. A dozen wolfmen encircled them, wearing menacing stares and emitting hungry growls.

"Princess?" Maros whispered. "I am going to put you down for a few seconds."

Without listening to her complaints, he lowered her to the ground. She looked around, likely terrified. Her fur was covered in ice despite her being in the warmth of his jacket.

Maros waited no more. He jumped onto the group, to their surprise. The wolfmen were slow and clumsy—and this time with fewer numbers—they were overthrown.

A whimper came from behind him. He turned on his heel, and his body froze. The wolf who fell down the cliff must have climbed back up, and he held a white fur ball in his hands, dangerously crushing the frail body.

If Maros had a beating heart, it would explode to see his princess at the mercy of those enormous hands. Maros raised his hands, hoping to negotiate or at least turn the wolfman's attention on him, but Angeline didn't need help anymore.

Inhuman screams erupted from the wolf, who howled at the sky. His skin grew darker, burning by the second. His veins were purple and bursting. The White Wolf sat on her butt, licking blood from her mouth.

Maros could not hold back a sigh of relief. He ran back to the wolf, picked her up again, and placed her against his chest. "Well done, bitey."

He sped, monitoring the train, ready to jump the twenty meters separating him from it. Hopefully, this would get the wolfmen off their trail. He needed somewhere warm to place the princess, unless she told him she could shift into a heater.

As he propelled himself from the cliff, pushing on his legs while keeping a hand on the small shape against him, he didn't feel what was coming straight for him.

More wolfmen appeared, slamming into him, making him miss the train's roof and roll over in the snow.

"Damn it!" Maros leapt onto his feet and prepared to welcome the other wolfmen. "Stay put, Princess. We're not there yet."

He dodged the attack and ran, following the train, hoping to catch at least the tail to get Angeline to safety. Catching the train was easy; he jumped onto the rail, took the little wolf out of his jacket, and dropped her behind the guardrail. Angeline looked at him in her wolf form, her eyes too expressive for such a small thing. He jumped back in the snow without listening to her whimpers, catching two wolves running and stumbling with them on the rail track.

He could hear the small, sad howl coming from the train, but at least she was safe. Maros gracefully landed in the snow. He tried not to get overwhelmed by the growing distance between him and Angeline. A pure growl came out of his throat, his fists clenching as a dozen wolfmen encircled him, like a pack of starving wolves would do to a hurt deer.

Well, Maros was no deer.

One of the beasts made the mistake of stepping forward first. Smoke escaped from his nose, but he did not expect to be jumped on by his prey. Maros sped to him in a blur and dove his hand into the hairy chest of the wolfman, encountering a wide rib cage. With a satisfied growl, he pulled the beating heart out. It was covered in a dark goo he would rather not touch.

Evil magic.

Maros smirked, his fangs descending. "Who's next?"

The werewolves lunged at once, but Maros had learned his lesson. Without Angeline to worry about, he moved like he was used to. He was a shadow, slicing throats and Achilles heels, opening fountains of dark blood that tainted the snow. A claw slashed across his chest, shredding skin and fabric. Pain burned, but it was nothing compared to what he had been through. He ducked under the fist that came at him and dove to his knees, grabbing the testicles hanging in front of his nose. He twisted them until only flesh and blood were left in his hand.

"Should have worn pants, asshole."

The three remaining werewolves didn't look dismayed by the loss of their companions, but they hesitated, closing the gap between them and the vampire.

Maros rolled his shoulders, cracking his neck. "Come on. I don't have all day. I've got a princess to warm up. Ideally naked."

They howled and charged at him, but Maros met them head-on, slashing their bellies open and spilling their guts onto the train tracks.

He turned to peer at the distant train and ran toward it.

"For fuck's sake, bitey!" He yelled.

She was right where he left her, her fur frozen, her eyes closed, and her paws crossed over her nose. The damn wolf didn't think it would be smart to get warm and comfortable on the train. Maros picked her up, worry rushing through him, but he could hear her heartbeat. She nipped at his fingers, and he sighed in relief.

"You should have gone inside, princess. What if I didn't come back?"

Five minutes later, they were in one of the fantastic first-class cabins. He was unsure what they were calling those now, but this one must be worth at least 10K for the trip. Maros had to compel both the train controller and the honeymoon couple who had booked the room, but he didn't care. He had a princess to take care of.

Reaching into his pocket, he took out the tiny wolf. She whined weakly, and droplets of ice water ran down her fur. Maros dropped her onto the bed and turned on the heater to its full power. He took off his jacket and shirt, and lay on the bed, placing her against his bare chest, which had already healed from any wounds. He threw a blanket over them and waited for her whimpers to stop.

Golden sparkles glowed under the blanket, and she appeared in her human form. Angeline placed her frozen fingers against his skin, intertwining her legs around his. His heart shattered when she looked at him from under her eyelashes.

"You always come back," she whispered.

CHAPTER 26

MAROS

MAROS DIDN'T DARE TO move. Angeline was sleeping against him, and after some arguing, he even convinced her to stay naked, for 'survival.' She had rolled her eyes, probably not believing him, but still lay happily against him for an hour before finally falling into a well-deserved sleep.

She fit perfectly against his body, and Maros knew he had the stupidest smile on his face. Her head nestled against his shoulder, the same way she always slept on him, and she possessively spread her right leg and arm across his body, which he did not complain about.

He extended his arm to caress her back, enjoying her soft skin and warmth. Maros didn't stop the gentle brush when she started moving, waking up with a yawn. She groaned and adjusted herself, keeping her eyes closed.

ANGELINE

Maros held her on her back and moved his other hand to her face. Angeline blushed and begged for her heartbeat to slow down when he caressed her burning cheeks. She hated that she enjoyed this, but most of all, she hated that she missed it.

You are pitiful, lady.

She lifted her head to look at Maros, unsure what to expect, but she certainly did not anticipate the coveted look he watched her with. His eyes were filled with affection and determination.

"I will take care of you, Love," he whispered, featherlight fingers caressing her face.

She scoffed. "Or maybe I will take care of you. I have a Magic Bite, you know."

He laughed.

Angeline intertwined her fingers with his, jumping at the touch.

He squinted, as if he were curious.

"I always expect touch to feel like ice, but you are burning," she murmured, answering his silent question. "I should be used to it."

"Werewolf warmth beats Vampire cold," Maros said. "I don't think you were complaining an hour ago. Or during our time in the forest."

Angeline flushed and cleared her throat. "Well, where will we go next?"

"The train is taking us to Vienna, the next stop. We should arrive there in four or five hours. Our families know and will be there. At least your kidnapping finally convinced everyone to move ahead together."

Angeline groaned in agreement. That *was* good news.

She jerked away, remembering she was supposed to hate him. At the sad and quick shadow on his face, she realized that she didn't care anymore. She wanted to feel safe, and Maros felt like home. She sat, exhaling loudly while pulling the covers up to hide her breasts.

"I'm still angry at you, you know." She threw a pillow at his face, chuckling as he groaned.

He moved the pillow away and fixed his gaze on her. "I... have no excuse. I wanted you so much, and you were going to leave me. If you were offered freedom, I had no doubt you were going to go."

Angeline stayed silent for a few seconds, holding back the childish pout she knew was threatening to appear on her lips. "Maybe you should have asked." Her voice was drier than she wanted it to be, but she had been mucked around long enough. "Maybe you could have asked what I thought of it. Do you think I have such little value that I have no opinion?"

"That is not what was happening, and you know it." He caught her chin between his fingers. "You know very well how much I care for you. I would have come back to you; I would have conquered you all over again after the war if I needed to. But this. Those wolfmen? They're too dangerous."

She tried to remain steely, even though his words tugged at her heartstrings. "That's a good excuse."

The lump in his throat bobbed. "After their attack, I was terrified. That was one of the few times in my life that I felt true terror, Angeline. I couldn't stop thinking about those wolfmen hurting you."

Angeline moved her chin away from him, trying to get some distance from the intense stare. He stuttered, struggling to find his next words, and she couldn't help but look.

"You have no idea how it feels," he whispered. "I have been powerful and strong, my entire life. Even as a mortal, I was the best warrior of our tribe, better than Manus. I didn't know fear; our mother raised us never to feel fear again. When I was made immortal, it was worse. I didn't *have* to fear anything. I was not even worried about my siblings. They were all so powerful. Carata was always a bitch, she was fine."

Angeline chuckled. She could perfectly imagine Carata being a badass Gaul woman, not letting anyone dictate her destiny.

Maros brushed her skin. "When I met you, that changed. I knew how it felt to lose someone. For five years, I longed for someone I didn't know existed two weeks before, and I blamed myself. After the damn wolfmen's attack, there you were, taking fucking risks with your life. Keeping you against your will with the risk of getting you killed was just…" Angeline interrupted him by capturing his hand.

"I don't understand why you're so... into me," she murmured, clenching the blanket between her fingers. "Other men tend to follow the smell. I attract them, my magic screams at them. But you? Is it different?"

"Are you doubting my feelings, my Wolf?"

"Well... you did break my heart. And before that, you kidnapped me. Twice." She threw another cushion at his face.

Maros dodged it and caught her by the neck, pulling her closer and growling. "If you need to break my dead heart to forgive me, do it, my Princess. But you're mine. I don't care if it's your magic. I don't care if it's your She-Wolf. *You. Are. Mine.* You have been mine since I met you, and I'm not letting you go anymore. If you can't acknowledge that you are smart, beautiful, kind, with a somewhat skeptical sense of humor, then let me show you. Let me worship you. The way you always deserved to be worshipped." His eyes reddened. "And if you're gonna show me those tits of yours, I hope you're ready to have a taste of my worship now."

Angeline flushed. While he spoke, her fingers traced the longest scar on his body, along his entire midsection. The covers dropped. Her lower body was the only part hidden. She gasped, feeling the cool air on her skin, but didn't move to cover herself. Instead, she pushed her small breasts up to tempt the vampire.

It was with satisfaction that she saw Maros's jaw clench, his lips twitching, his eyes wandering over her body, not daring yet to touch her.

He grunted when she placed her legs on both sides of him, moving the covers away. Angeline knew her pussy was fully displayed, and she could feel how wet she was at the thought of Maros's hands on her again. She wiggled her hips against his hardened length and smirked when Maros closed his eyes under the pressure, a light growl escaping his throat. She placed her hands on his torso, as if she could push him and hold him in place, and bent over the vampire, kissing his scars one by one and joining her hands in a soft caress, knowing she was driving him crazy.

Angeline raised her head and brought it closer to his, their lips almost joining.

"Touch me, Maros," she whispered.

Only a groan answered her. Powerful lips caught hers while he raised himself, holding back her head with one hand, forcing the kiss. With the other hand, he gripped her back, trying to hold her closer.

The kiss was nothing like their previous ones. Angeline could feel their despair and desires. She was not an innocent, sad virgin anymore, and she was going to make sure he knew that. She was the one to push her tongue inside his mouth, asking for passage, which he gladly gave. Maros grunted and lowered his hands to hold her ass, seeming to enjoy her curves. He was still massaging them when Angeline tried to push him back against the bed.

"I don't think so, Pet." He laughed, catching one of her nipples between his teeth and pulling on it so lightly it didn't hurt. He released a growl of approval as she moaned under his touch. Angeline rubbed her lower parts hard against his bulge, and she gasped when his hands reached her drenched folds, following the curves of her pussy. She pouted at him, and he dared to laugh, even more when she continued to push him. Angeline was stubborn, but it was like trying to move a statue.

"Ask me nicely," he whispered, inserting one finger inside. Angeline moaned under the intrusion and threw her head back while grinding against his finger. She pushed her face closer to his while raising her cunt to escape his hungry hands. "Let me fuck you, Maros."

He scoffed, surprise showing in his eyes, but this time he let her push him onto the mattress. She knew he was giving up when she moved her hand to his dick, stroking him, before she teased his length along her wet folds and slipped it inside.

Angeline winced; the pain was present, but her desire overtook all else. She impaled herself on him, moaning, not letting go of his gaze as she descended onto his sex, whining under the painful stretch and the burning sensation she had been craving. A hungry grunt answered her whines. Maros caught her hips, guiding her up and down, leading the rhythm of her dance.

"Very well, White Wolf." He gasped when she managed to fit him entirely. "But after this, you're getting on your knees for me."

CHAPTER 27

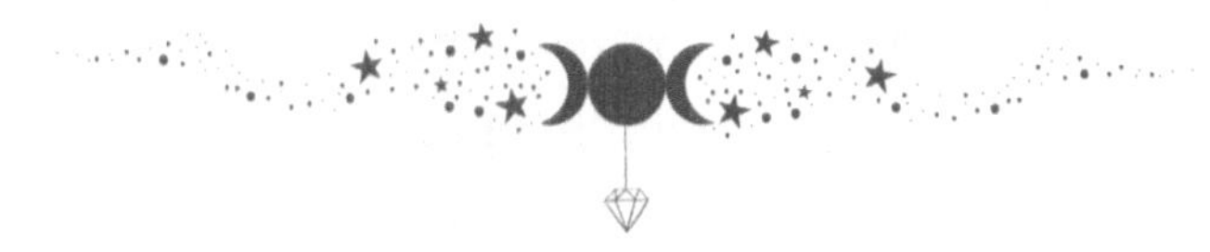

ANGELINE

I F THERE WERE SUCH a thing as a perfect world, it would be in Maros's arms, embraced by his warmth, smothered by his musky smell.

Angeline was unsure what time it was, but her lover interrupted her peace of mind by mentioning they should start getting ready to leave soon. She sighed and pulled away from him, and under his amused expression, she stretched her sore body.

So, that's how it feels to fuck all night.

She glanced at Maros from the corner of her eye, giggling when she saw he was quite focused on what was between her legs.

Maros laughed. "You little minx"—he caught Angeline and rolled over her— "you can't display that pussy of yours and hope I'll leave it alone now, can you?" Maros pinned her arms above her head, tickling her with his nose, until he caught her lips in a kiss. When he deepened the kiss, Angeline wriggled and tried to speak.

"Maros... we need to take a shower... and get dressed." Her speech was cut off by her gasps, according to which part of her body Maros's tongue tasted while she talked.

He groaned and brought his head back to her face. "How about we don't take a shower, and I use those fifteen minutes of free time to make you mine one more time?"

Angeline's eyes widened. "Don't tell me you want me to get out and meet people while I'm all sticky, sweaty, and covered in... stuff." She blushed. The things he did to her. By the Goddess.

Maros laughed and stole another kiss, forcing his tongue into the minty mouth of his lover. She could not help but wriggle under him, bringing her sore pussy closer to his dick, already grinding into him.

"No," he said, "I want you to scream my name one more time. And I want everyone out there to know you belong to me, White Wolf."

Angeline scoffed, outraged. "I do *not* belong to you!" She stopped talking when Maros moved onto his knees, desire burning in his eyes, and stroked his sex, beads of cum already shining on the tip.

She pouted, feeling her arousal between her legs. When he flipped her over, she waited without saying a word, her ass in the air as an offering. When she felt the familiar intrusion, spreading her folds, gliding inside of her as if it was nothing, she knew she would, indeed, scream his name one more time. Angeline could not hold back her screams or body, banging against Maros, asking for more. More strength, more power, more depth.

Maros's strong pounding drove her insane, hitting her in the right spot. She could barely stay up on her knees. She whined when he pulled away from her, and to her shame, she shoved her ass closer, as if she could catch his dick to put it back inside.

"Your head on the mattress, Princess." He ordered her around, pushing her head. "Give me your hands."

Angeline whined but moved her arms behind her back, hands open, waiting for him to do whatever he had in mind.

She scoffed when she felt the tight touch of his belt encircling her wrists and moved her head away from the bed to look at him. He wore a naughty smirk, tightening the belt with expert fingers. With a pull, he finished the job.

"Head on the mattress, Love," he said again, crimson eyes full of desire. "And bend your back a bit more." Angeline felt like she had no control over herself, and she happily obliged, arching her lower back. She pushed her hips up in the air, wide open for her lover.

Angeline screamed when he penetrated her with force. He held her butt and spread her cheeks. She felt offered, with no shame, only pure desire, which turned her on more than she expected. Her thoughts quickly became mush as he pounded her brutally from behind. She didn't hold back her screams, which joined Maros's animalistic grunts. Tears pooled at the corner of her eyes, her body reaching the limits of its pleasure. She was close to giving up, not holding back anymore, her face crushed against the mattress when he retracted from her pussy. Angeline knew he was listening to her panting. She took a deep breath and moaned when something soft caressed her, one of his hands playing with her pussy, softly brushing her clit, which still throbbed with excitement.

Her moans got louder when he slowly inserted his fingers, and she spread her legs as much as she could, welcoming the soft intrusion after the brutal sex he gave her.

"Keep this ass of yours up, my princess," Maros whispered, his voice so raspy he sounded as if he had screamed all night. And she knew he was trying something new when she felt a wet touch on her tight hole. Angeline gasped and jumped, triggering a genuine laugh from her lover.

"Maros!" She exclaimed, looking at him and his dirty expression.

"If you don't like it, I will stop."

Angeline blushed, but nodded after a few seconds, and she grabbed a pillow to bury her head in as she offered her bottom to the vampire. Moans quickly took over her fear. He obviously knew what the hell to do with her butthole. He moved his wet tongue in and out, turning around, poking it. Angeline had no idea what he was doing, but it worked well for her. With Maros's fingers playing with her little nub, she was soon drenched in cum and sweat, moving her hips around, begging for more, moaning her pleasure into the pillow. A last push of Maros's fingers against her clit finally helped her release her climax. She screamed like she had never screamed before, tense with desire as she felt the welcoming wave rush through her body.

CHAPTER 28

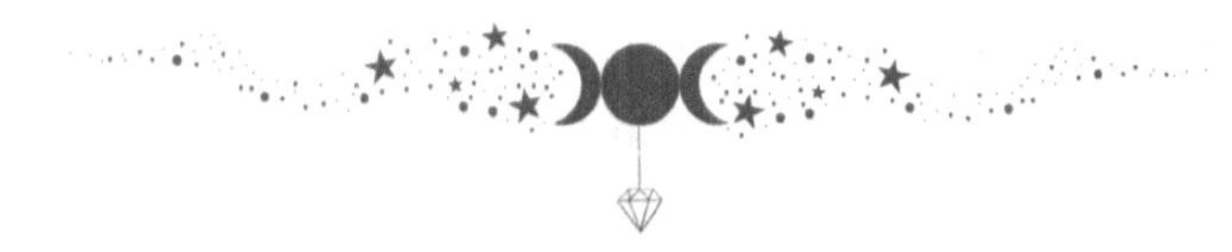

ANGELINE

THEY FINALLY ROUSED WHEN the train speaker announced their arrival in Vienna. Angeline had a brief moment of excitement at the name before remembering she was not there on holiday. She certainly wouldn't be able to have a nice, warm hot chocolate in one of Vienna's best eateries while thinking about which gown she could wear at a ball.

At least Maros had left the cabin earlier to 'borrow' some warm clothes from other passengers for both of them, and they got dressed, despite him trying to convince her they could add one more orgasm to the day.

He found her a warm ribbed emerald dress, which clung to 'all the right places' according to him. She had to run away from his exploring hands to stop him from taking her again. It was not her usual style, but she still appreciated her image in the mirror when Maros dropped a furry white cape on her shoulders to complete the outfit.

Angeline shuddered when he moved her braided hair out of the white cape. He would need to stop being so touchy when they returned to their family, and she pouted at the thought.

She smiled in satisfaction and turned away from the mirror, glancing at his outfit. All black, of course. Her heart raced, and she stepped closer, pressing her hands against his chest. His scarred hands covered hers with his warmth, and a soft light danced in his eyes.

"I don't think I want to leave this train," she whispered.

Maros smiled at her, a more natural smile than she had ever seen on him. "I can assure you, my Princess, my White Wolf... I don't either." Maros reached for a curl that escaped her braid and brought the strand to his nose, closing his eyes as he smelled it.

Angeline laughed. "You're so weird."

A low growl was his answer as he kept his eyes closed, rubbing the strand of red hair between his fingers.

"You know, I forgot about it, but I think we met someone like you... a long time ago..." He didn't mind Angeline's stiffness and continued. "We arrived too late; she was gone, but her smell lingered in the air. Powerful, raw. Virginal."

"What happened to her?" Angeline asked.

Maros opened his eyes, as if memories were flooding him. "Young vampires found her."

Angeline didn't speak. She was unsure how much she should say, even though she did not doubt that he would ask his sister if he wanted information. Maros cradled her face in his hands with such tenderness.

"You are rare. You are precious." He smiled. "But I already knew that. I knew it since the first day I met you."

Angeline scoffed but fell into his embrace, wrapping her arms around his waist. "You and I remember that day quite differently, I believe."

After a final kiss, they left the train.

The first person she saw was Jack, worry showing on his face, which was becoming more common. She ran to him and jumped into his comforting arms, full of love and relief. She pulled her head out of the embrace to have a look around. The only other people in attendance were the First Family, and she was thankful for that, especially with Maros's smell all around her. She didn't have time to take a shower.

Maros caught up with the little group. Both his sisters jumped on him, smothering him, but Manus was as cold as ever, giving a nod to his brother.

"Maros," Manus said, "next time you plan to jump into a magical, dark, scary hellhole, could you *please* inform us beforehand?"

Maros snickered lightly while kissing Blanda on her forehead, then something that Angeline didn't think was possible happened: the two brothers hugged. Quickly, but still.

"Let's go, people. We have a wedding to stop, may I remind you?" Jack said with enthusiasm.

Everyone around him tensed. Angeline became light-headed, and she knew she might be at her palest. Apparently, they missed some events while away.

Maros was the first one to speak. "Which wedding?" His eyes darkened, his fists clenched, and Angeline was glad to see that he was a tad enraged.

Blanda put an appeasing hand on his shoulder. "Paul and Louis have agreed on an alliance between their families. They want to go ahead with Angeline's wedding to Paul... despite her... disagreement during the meeting, thinking it would avoid more trouble if she ever fell into the Russians' hands. Paul is ready to let you be king, if you..." She stopped, glancing at Angeline.

Manus interrupted. "Nothing is set in stone. They still need our help against the Alpha, and I hope your report will convince them they can't do much without our help. If a wedding is being forced, they can forget about us."

Angeline wanted to go back on the train and hide under the warm blanket, against Maros's body again, ideally for a few weeks. The exhaustion of the past twenty-four hours finally caught up with her, and she did not feel like the strong, independent woman she wanted to be. She hated herself when warm tears flowed down her cheeks, and she could not hold back her sobs.

Jack moved toward his sister, but she felt a pull from a stronger hand, and the next second she was in Maros's arms.

"I'm not leaving your side, White Wolf," Maros whispered. "Don't worry."

Angeline was lighter after his words, but still. A crown or a woman? She would not blame him if he picked the former. After her previous exchanges with Louis, she could not believe her father was still trying to control her life, even if many, including her, expressed their disagreement. She thought laying all of his lies in front of the entire Magical World would shut the man up a bit. Well, she was wrong.

They led Angeline to a warm car. Blanda left a blanket on Angeline's knees, and they waited for Manus and Maros, who were still whispering outside. She wished she could hear what they were saying. Maros, despite seeming upset, listened carefully to his brother.

Finally, they joined the others in the car and drove to the rendezvous point.

Angeline took a deep breath. She needed to know now, so she could get ready to shift and run. Run as fast as she could, as far as she could.

"What happened?" She asked. "Last time we were there, it was clear that Paul would not be considered my husband. I didn't agree to it. I still don't agree to it. That one,"—she nodded at Maros—" made it clear that... I was taken." She grimaced, glancing at her lover, who could not hold back a laugh.

"Not funny, Maros," Angeline said. Gosh, he was infuriating sometimes.

"Silence, Maros," Manus ordered. "Paul and Louis seem to think we were born yesterday."

Angeline widened her eyes. That didn't sound good.

Manus continued. "They agreed behind our backs to renew their alliance as soon as the Russian problem was dealt with. This time, Paul offered us a proposition: he would let Maros have the crown, under the condition of allowing the wedding, and also something about putting Paul in charge of a part of Europe."

Manus stopped, interrupted by Blanda. "Which, technically speaking, is not a bad idea."

Maros glared.

"Do not look at me like that," Blanda said. "It is *not* a bad idea. I didn't say we had to pick Paul as a potential... what? Minister? Sheriff?" She looked at Angeline. "Your father agreed to it; in their minds, it seems they would be more than happy to share Europe."

Angeline scoffed, while her She-Wolf laughed hysterically inside her mind. Of course they would—but not on her watch.

Not being able to hear Maros's thoughts did not help her. She would like to know what he was thinking about the situation. After all, he messed with her mind and heart once before; nothing would stop him from doing it again. And again. And again. Until she finally stopped forgiving him. Were his promises and beautiful words on the train only dreams? He wanted the crown so badly, she knew that.

Angeline caressed her charm bracelet, which still hung from her wrist despite the recent misadventures. She extended her golden branches to Blanda, the only one she could hear among the First Family.

Blanda had doubts about her before. She knew Angeline was *something*, but now she had talked to Nanabrok and confirmed what Maros had guessed earlier. There was no doubt in her mind that whoever married Angeline would get an advantage in the war, but also as a leader. Blanda was worried that the White Wolf would be powerful enough to kill her immortal siblings if she were to marry a man like Paul, who would then have control over her through the Magical Wedding link. Angeline was glad to hear that Blanda also hated Paul with all her guts, and she would not wish the wedding on Angeline, ever.

Angeline thought fast. An alliance with the First Family would mean the French Pack and witches would be safe. Nobody would ever go against them, and it could turn the tables in Europe. Not to mention that she always wanted to marry a werewolf, and not a vampire, as Louis and Isabeau wanted. Well, Maros was kind of both...

Her heart raced as she thought about their time on the train. Her wolf inside was running in circles and yapping excitedly at the idea of Maros's wolf against her. Angeline had to be careful, because she could not trust her She-Wolf to make smart decisions when it came to him.

"No", she said, pulling herself away from Maros, who gave her a worried look.

"No, what, Pet?" he asked.

"No to everything. There will be no arranged wedding, no alliances, and certainly no Paul and Louis as the head of anything but their own asses. Paul is going to tragically pass away on the battlefield."

Jack's laugh took them all by surprise. "My sister, I swear, I love the new you."

Angeline rolled her eyes.

"Is he now?" Maros chuckled, placing his finger under Angeline's chin.

"You bet he is." Angeline was on a roll. "And if you"—she tapped her finger on his chest a few times, supporting her words—"ever want to be on a train naked with me again—"

Maros's eyes darkened.

"—You will do as I say, or else I will steal your crown." Angeline paused, looking around. "I'm the one with the nasty bite that can kill weird wolfmen. I'm the one who can read all of your minds. I'm the one who can shift without breaking my freaking bones. I'm the one who has allegiance from witches and werewolves." She rolled her eyes at her brother, who was pointing at his chest. "And the pirates, yes. The point is, I am done being bossed around. There will be no Russian Alpha, no Paul in charge of anything, and certainly no Louis in charge of anything. He can consider himself lucky if I decide to let him live."

She pushed her chin forward, looking at the terrifying creatures around her. Jack was still laughing while Carata and Blanda showed proud smiles.

Angeline turned to Maros and lifted a brow. "I swear to you. I will steal this crown and place it on my head before I let any of this happen. The Spirits never said it needed to be a man in charge after all." She poked his chest harder. "And you, no more play. You want me? You will marry me, Monsieur!"

Maros took her hand, placing his full lips against her fair skin. "What My Queen wants, My Queen shall have."

CHAPTER 29

ANGELINE

Two hours later, they had reached an old, condemned hotel building in the backcountry, located right at the edge of a cliff. It overlooked an immense field, where the battle was supposed to occur the next day. Information about the werewolves' army moving in that direction had been received, and everyone was ready for war, eager to end the madness.

Angeline exited the car.

She could not hold back a yawn, and already regretted the little sleep she had had. The nap she took in the car didn't help at all—mostly because she could not fall asleep easily with Maros's hand stroking her back, while her head lay across his thighs.

Angeline's feet pressed into the snow-covered ground.

Great. More snow. Images of her traumatizing misadventure with the Alpha rushed to her mind.

Tears pricked her eyes, and she clenched her fists, trying to contain them. Now was not the time to show weakness.

Maros pulled her against his chest, and she sighed in relief, pressing her wet cheeks against his torso. Despite the turmoil of thoughts she could hear from everyone watching them, she surrounded his waist with her arms, making a statement about the situation. Bending her head back, she looked at him and let out a giggle and a sniffle.

"What is making you laugh now?" He whispered to her, his eyes flashing red.

"Your eyes are always red. Are you just always horny or something?" She whispered back.

"Only when you are wriggling against me. Or touching me. Or looking at me. Or just existing, really."

Angeline scoffed, and her cheeks burned. Her She-Wolf was spinning around in her mind, content. She pushed onto her tiptoes to reach his lips and murmured, "If you behave yourself today, I might let you do that thing that makes my eyes water."

Maros laughed out loud and slung an arm around her waist as he walked toward the entrance. "Don't act as if you are doing me a favor, White Wolf. I know you enjoyed it the bestial way."

She tapped his arm, but didn't add anything as they approached Louis, with Nanabrok by his side.

Nanabrok pushed her glasses up her nose to watch them closely. She had a smile on her wrinkly face, already pulling some lavender sweets from her bag to place in Angeline's hand. As for Louis, he was displaying the opposite.

"Louis!" Maros exclaimed. "Good to see you!"

Louis groaned, but was interrupted by the witch.

"No time for fiddles. Everyone in, now. We have a battle coming our way." Nanabrok scurried inside the building without looking back.

Louis made a noise of disapproval but followed her, not without whispering to the couple, a finger pointing at them. "This is *not* happening."

Angeline had to place a hand on Maros's chest to stop him from jumping on her father, but it was Manus's iron grip that interrupted the potential slaughter.

"Not now, brother," Manus said.

Angeline knew her decision was made. Louis should never have tried to stick his nose into her business again. She didn't know if it was the last five years, her time with Maros, or the assault she had endured from too many men, but she was burning now—furious, finished with their games. Or maybe it was simply his poor, tentative excuse for why she had been sent to the worst place on Earth.

She carefully opened the candy and stuffed it in her mouth as they entered what used to be a ballroom. The windows were dirty, and the rays of sunshine hit the dirt spots and cracks. At least there was enough space to host hundreds of magical creatures.

Angeline felt all eyes on them. Maros offered her his arm, and she accepted, holding her head high and moving forward. She could hear every thought: the surprise, the fear of the war to come, and the exhaustion of the past few months.

Like her, they all had one wish: to end the war. Both wars.

They reached the east side of the room, where a magical map was displayed, showing the field for the battle with glowing points that represented the various armies. At least they had worked while Maros and Angeline were busy escaping death.

She spotted her father advancing toward Paul, and her rage spiked. She was unsure if it was the She-Wolf or herself, but she made a note to add Louis to her list of battlefield 'accidents.' Maros followed her look over to Louis, who was by Paul's side, both displaying fury and disgust. Maros growled lowly.

"*Angeline!*" Louis yelled.

MAROS

Maros glanced at Angeline, whose eyebrows were raised provocatively. She still had her hand resting on his arm, and if it weren't for her furious heartbeat, nobody would guess how upset she was.

Louis continued. The fool.

"You are engaged to Paul, and you will honor that engagement!" Louis tried to look fierce, pointing a finger at his daughter.

Angeline didn't appear impressed. Maros found that fascinating. It was like she became a different person. He wondered if her misadventure in the woods might have helped that. He turned his attention to Louis, who tried to show his reasoning.

"Paul gladly accepted the loss of the crown in favor of Maros, proving his professionalism and showing who the bigger man is."

Maros scoffed and hid his laugh, turning his head away. Angeline threw him one of her unimpressed looks.

"Paul lost the right to wed me when he forced himself on me," she announced, "and *tonight*, I will marry another man. Tomorrow, I will pray to the Spirits that Paul dies on the battlefield. The next day, I will place the crown on Maros's head myself."

She sat down after her announcement, not paying attention to the rage coming from Louis and Paul. She ignored Maros's victorious smile, too. Murmurs and protests rose from every side and forced Nanabrok to ask for silence.

"A wedding? Angeline?" Nanabrok looked over Angeline, probably trying to detect if she was under a spell.

"Yes, Nana. A wedding. The problem is that the Russian could get his hands on my magic if he were to marry me, right? So, I'll get married tonight. Problem solved." Angeline smiled and looked at Paul. For one second, Maros hoped he would do something stupid, giving him a reason to kill him right there. Angeline interrupted his wishful thoughts.

ANGELINE

"Sorry... do you agree, my King?" She muttered, giving him the sluttiest look she could muster, the one she knew he loved.

Maros gave her a smirk. "Who am I to refuse?" He kissed her hand, seeming not to care about the whispers around the room. She knew he was keeping an eye on Paul, ready to jump, his face ravaged by anger. He would do the same for Louis.

"Excellent, then!" Nanabrok interrupted, cutting off Louis's protest. "As for the king, I propose that this time we do this properly. With a vote. With no killing. There has been enough slaughter. Magical creatures must bind together, the same way we are uniting against the Russian threat."

Magical beings around the room applauded cheerfully. Angeline rolled her eyes. How hard would it have been to hold a vote before all of this?

She waited for the cheers to diminish. Carata gave her a slight nod of approval.

"I believe the Spirits made a Promise Parchment available," Angeline said. "Maros agreed to consult with all the leaders, to inform them about his plan as king and mark down the promises on it, which he will have to follow through with. There will be no surprises; you will know what you will get. Be forewarned, some places will burn down."

She did it, and she was proud. Angeline planned to destroy any convent that did not fit her idea of a proper place. Education for ladies? Sure. Humiliation and torture? Never again, not on her watch. Rape? Genocide? Pedophilia? Not on her watch. She would love for Annabella to witness their victory, but Manus had sent her back to Chicago for her safety.

Lords of Europe looked worried—as they should—but American vampires were cheerful.

At least now, the biggest topic was tomorrow's battle, and it was with a disconcerted movement that the crowd returned to talking about serious matters. While everyone was organizing themselves, Angeline reflected on her decision. She didn't think that going against her father would be so delightful.

She knew now that Maros could not be worse than Paul, or any other suitors her father had thought of giving her hand to. Her time alone with him had already proved it to her. He did not have to care for her, or jump in the portal—even if that was stupid. He could have run from the wolfmen. Instead, he took a beating and risked his immortal life for her.

Plus, he smelled good and knew how to use every part of his body the exact way it should be used. He didn't even seem disturbed by her little speech in the car.

An influx of excited sounds came from the crowd. It was time for everyone to relax, and she heard the dreadful word 'wedding' said by a few. She glanced at Maros, and he was standing up, in a victorious position, gazing at her with the lustful look he always had when with her.

Her legs shook. Her vision went blurry. Buzzing replaced the cheers; all she could hear was her heartbeat. The world around her faded.

Angeline woke up from her slumber, opening her eyes with difficulty and moaning while changing positions on the bed, one of the few 'working beds' in the hotel. The poor bed may once have been quite comfortable, but now springs poked into her back. The poster bed was made of oak, with vines twirling around the columns, as if the bedroom were in a jungle instead of a luxury room. Nature took back its right over the abandoned place.

Thankfully, they were now away from the crowd.

She spotted Nanabrok once her vision adjusted and watched the old witch shuffle around. Nanabrok grumbled some incomprehensible words while rummaging in her gigantic purse. As usual, she pulled out a purple sweet. That was when the door opened, and a hesitant Maros appeared.

Angeline's heart raced. She forced herself to give him a timid smile; this was likely as hard for him as for her. Not that she knew how he felt, but he had been single for thousands of years. She didn't give him a choice but to change that.

Maros moved closer to the bed. He acknowledged the old witch's presence with a quick nod. "Nanabrok. Thank you for taking care of my fiancée."

Angeline shuddered. Right. Fiancée. Marriage. Tonight. While she was panicking inside, she listened with a wandering ear to the conversation. Or the lack of conversation.

Nana grumbled again, watching the man from above her glasses, while placing a few treats for Angeline on the bedside table. Nanabrok smiled encouragingly and ambled to the door, her short legs slowly advancing. She stopped by Maros, who was at least two heads above her, and spoke without a hint of fear. "My words still matter. Hurt her one more time, and I will make sure the queen becomes a widow."

Maros smiled sarcastically.

Angeline gasped. "Nana!"

Nanabrok left without a word; her soft limping sound could be heard until she finally went through the door. Maros sighed and walked to the bed, kneeling on it, still too close to Angeline. She could smell his wolf under his skin, and her She-Wolf was running laps in her mind.

He stroked Angeline's arm, and she felt at ease. Her eyes closed, savoring the moment, but Maros stopped the caress, to Angeline's disapproval. He adjusted beside her, lying on the bed, but above the covers. Angeline's heart galloped again, and her wolf settled down, curling into a ball.

"So... we're getting married, huh?" Maros said, with a naughty look on his face. "You were serious about it."

Angeline's eyes flung open. She was still freaking out about the idea of marrying him—unlike her wolf, who was quite satisfied with the situation. She blushed; she knew she had forced his hand, but she was done being played with. Being queen would assure her protection and that of every young woman and girl. She was surprised at Maros's next words.

"I had a talk with the witches. They said an engagement would be enough to assure the protection of your magic... if you wanted to plan for an actual wedding."

"Are you trying to escape me already?" Angeline joked, moving one of her hands to rest on his chest.

Maros laughed and softly brushed his lips against hers. "Never. I'm yours, as you're mine. I'm just giving you a choice; the most important thing right now is to protect your magic."

Maros stroked her hair, and his warmth grew closer. He playfully snuggled his nose into her neck. His breath gave her goose bumps. "Don't worry, my White Wolf. I would still be eager to consummate our engagement if you pick that for tonight."

Angeline's crystalline laugh answered him, and she gave him a slight tap.

"I have been obsessed with you since the day I met you, my White Wolf," Maros whispered, grabbing her face in the palm of his hand to make her look at him. "When I thought you were dead, at first, I had no idea how to react. I was lost. I wanted to burn the world and find the culprit. Then, I learned I was the one responsible for your suicide."

Angeline sighed; Louis had done quite a number on everyone. She didn't answer, but moved closer, encircling him with her legs and looking straight into his eyes while he spoke.

"When I saw you at the convent... I... I had no words. You were a ghost, coming back to haunt me, and you were... so different."

She swallowed, holding back her tears, digging her face against his chest.

"I'm sorry I hurt you. I really am." He pulled her face back to look at her. "I know that's the worst, most pitiful excuse ever. I know I'm repeating myself, but I was truly trying to protect you from the wolfmen."

"Why did you lie with me, right before you knew I would leave you?" He already told her why, but she wanted to hear it again.

Maros scoffed. "Well... as I told you, I have no valid excuses for that, except that I desired you and I was not sure I would ever get you back close enough to finally taste your sweet pussy."

Angeline gasped, then giggled when he reached under her dress.

"You're so naughty." She tangled her fingers in his hair. "You're lucky you're cute."

"I made myself a bath." Maros nodded at the steaming tub behind him; indeed, he could use a bath. "I was hoping this time you would join me." He winked.

Angeline could not help but laugh. She had been resting for hours, enjoying the torture of Maros finger-fucking her, and she was ready for some tension release before the war. She dropped her dress onto the floor, letting the fabric follow the curve of her body, and stood in front of him, appreciating the desire awakening between his legs. She caressed his arms with the tip of her fingers. When he tried to kiss her, she giggled and stepped over the bath to immerse herself in the warm water, sighing with pleasure.

"Little tease," he murmured.

She could only try to protest until his strong body finally joined her in the bath. He pulled her against his torso and imprisoned her in his arms, digging his face into her neck.

"Remember on the train, when my tongue played with your tight little hole?" Maros whispered, breathing against her skin.

She gasped and tried to glance at him, but his head was still hiding in her neck. "Yes?"

"Trust me. Just relax."

Angeline sighed, but let her body relax, feeling the luke-warm water taking over her senses. Her desire for Maros was always so strong that it terrified her and excited her simultaneously. A finger pushed at her butthole, setting off a jump, followed by a shy giggle.

"This... this..." She gasped, closing her eyes, trying to appreciate the intrusion. It was so different from the talented tongue he had used on the train.

"Trust me, my Wolf, trust me," Maros whispered, pushing further inside of her, growling at her whining and catching her face to kiss her with passion. Releasing her mouth, he accelerated the pace, keeping both his hands busy. One on her pussy, torturing her clit while fingering her, and the other slowly going in and out of her tight hole, driving her insane.

After a few seconds, he asked, "Is this enjoyable, or do you want me to stop?" He pushed harder on her clit, almost resulting in a wave.

"Don't stop... both of your hands..." She begged, closing her eyes, and she let herself get taken over by the wave.

CHAPTER 30

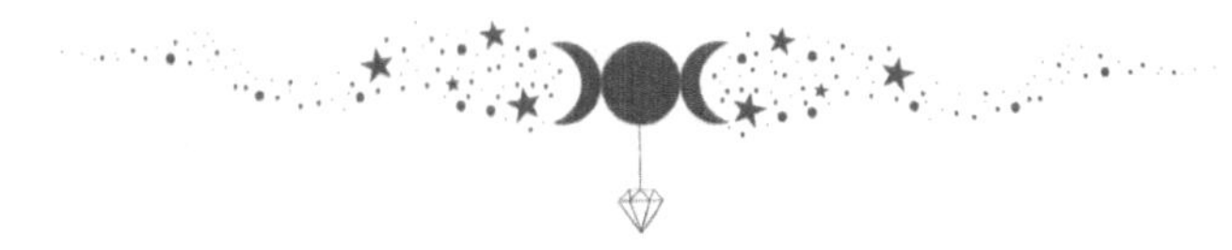

ANGELINE

H ER LEGS WERE STILL shaking when she and Maros finally joined the rest of the troops, who were all waiting for them. Angeline could not hold back a smirk when she heard people's thoughts. They all thought Maros had broken and asked for an engagement instead of a wedding.

The truth was, Blanda and Nanabrok confirmed to her that Angeline's magic would still spread to her fiancé, without the need for a rushed ceremony. It was their little secret. A safety net for Angeline and her future, and a potential source of power for Maros on the battlefield, even though both witches advised him not to try anything new.

"You don't need to hear people's thoughts," Blanda had said. "Don't even try. Those will drive you insane." She turned to Angeline, a begging look on her face. "Please, don't give him your telepathic gift; he will be out of control."

"And a pain in our ass," Carata added, her arms crossed.

"Whatever the Spirits allow me to share, I will listen to them," Angeline had said. Deep inside, she also hoped there would be no sharing of her telepathy. Having Maros hear all of her thoughts was not the best plan.

Now, she stood in front of Maros. His eyes devoured her, and his smile was already promising new pleasures. They held hands while making their engagement vows. Angeline's heart raced as she stood before the vampire, holding his gaze. Nanabrok took a purple ribbon picked with daisies—who knew where those had even come from?—wrapped it around their joined hands, and declared them bound by the Spirits.

"The wedding shall be consecrated in the next thirty days," Nanabrok said.

Cheers and applause welcomed her and intensified when Maros caught his future wife's face in his hands, kissing her like there was no tomorrow. Paul and his German army were absent, as was Louis, who still disapproved of the alliance. To Angeline's pleasure, Louis could not stop thinking about how long he had left before Maros, or even her, killed him.

Good, let him fear me.

We are fierce! We are strong! We bite! Her She-Wolf agreed.

After the fast ceremony, there was no time to mess around, and to the couple's sadness, certainly not to celebrate in bed. The army was outside, spreading to their allocated space on the battlefield.

Angeline knew Paul was not to be trusted and begged Maros to be careful. After all, Paul didn't survive all those centuries without being a sneaky son of a bitch. The only answer her soon-to-be husband gave her was a loud laugh and a passionate kiss. She pouted, disappointed that he didn't take her seriously. Or perhaps he was arrogant and didn't think Paul could be dangerous.

She sighed and had a quick look around. The crowd was composed of every magical creature, which was a funny mix. Angeline was still wearing the same dress as the day before, not that she had a choice. Her white fur was a lifesaver. Maros had given her some gloves he had found as well, so she was quite ready to confront the frozen temperature of Eastern Europe.

Maros tightened his arm on hers. "You look beautiful, my Love. You are glowing." He winked.

Angeline's face burned, but she moved closer to her lover, trying not to look at those lips she loved so much. *Especially when they are down your crotch, you naughty girl!*

She perceived a familiar mind in the crowd, moving toward the far east—her brother. She turned her head to spot Jack among the masses. As if he could feel her watching, Jack turned and threw her one of those winks like he had a secret. Angeline stuck out her tongue.

Angeline was focused on not falling down the icy entrance stairs, and a lord could not help but comment on her bruises.

"Looks like someone had a good time," he said, triggering some snickers from the vampires around him.

Maros moved to jump on the vampire, but Manus stopped him, expecting such a reaction from his brother. Angeline blushed but transferred her hand into his, trying to keep a good hold on her jumpy vampire. He was still growling in the lord's direction, but at least he was not jumping on him anymore. Instead, he brought Angeline's hand to his lips and kissed it tenderly.

Angeline blushed and turned her head back toward the lord. "My Lord. I don't think we have met... is that an Italian accent I hear?"

"Your Highness, I am Signore Arregazzoni. We haven't had the pleasure of meeting yet."

"Oh, right." She paused, locking her eyes with his. "We've met plenty. I am a good friend of your daughter Annabella." Ice crept into her voice. Annabella's memories were filled with images of her father. Her father, with a whip in his hand, making her bleed. Her father, with his dick out, stroking himself in front of a young Annabella. That father.

The man scoffed and kept his face straight but didn't answer.

"Good luck on the battlefield," Angeline said, returning her attention to Maros, who was holding back a smile.

Manus now had his eyes dead set on the Italian Lord, and the look he gave was terrifying.

"My work here is done," she whispered to Maros, who laughed and picked her up from the ground, setting off a giggle from Angeline.

He lifted his brows as if confused.

"No tiny wolf or potato bag this time!" She exclaimed. "You're carrying me like a princess."

Maros smiled warmly. "Maybe because you are *my princess*, Princess."

Angeline blushed and wrapped her arms around his neck to get a better hold while he sped to the end of the cliff, where they had decided the night before would be a safe place for her. He dropped her onto the frozen ground, but she kept her arms around Maros's neck, not wanting to lose his warmth.

Despite the others preparing for battle below her, Angeline was the happiest she had been in a long time. She felt complete and at peace for the first time in her life. Angeline pressed against Maros, wanting his lips on hers. He held her face in both hands and kissed her passionately.

She stopped the kiss with a giggle and blushed, burying her face in his shoulder while moving her hand down his torso, sneaking under his shirt. The urge to touch him was uncontrollable. Skin-to-skin contact seemed to be an efficient way to read his mind, and she felt his desire awaken. A now familiar fire roused in her when she caught a glimpse of the bulge in his pants. She lifted her head to gaze into his red eyes. Maros looked at her as if she were the next delicacy on the menu. Her eyes widened, and she pulled herself away, standing more ladylike. He didn't seem to be on the same page, bringing Angeline's hands back and placing them onto his flat belly, while encircling her shoulders with his left arm.

"Don't you dare go away from me, Love," he whispered into her ear, bringing her goose bumps to a new level.

"You're going to battle soon," she said. "You may have to let me go."

Maros answered with a snort and kissed her one last time before jumping from the cliff, landing as elegantly as a cat.

The army spread across the snow-covered battlefield, streaks of mud and patches of grass poking through in places as spring fought to take over winter. Angeline and Blanda stood rigid on the edge of the cliff overlooking the field below, all traces of merriment forgotten. Angeline tightened her jaw, trying to ignore Blanda's worries taking over her mind; she was worried enough as it was.

The Russians had numbers, true, but they lacked experience and strategy. Angeline's side had the witches, who were not to be messed with. Every member of the First Family was spread strategically around the field, each more lethal than the last and ready to fight.

According to Maros, the plan was easy: get in, kill everyone, get out.

Angeline had rolled her eyes when he said that during the strategy planning, and while he laughed, she quietly took the leadership job, blossoming in the role. Battle strategy was easy when you knew everyone's strengths, weaknesses, and fears.

The plan itself was almost as easy as what Maros said. The First, as the oldest and most powerful beings, led the way, showing their predominance in battle. After all, they had fought wars, mortal and immortal, for thousands of years. They were scattered strategically around the battlefield to give everyone a similar chance to have a stronger power by their side if needed. Nanabrok and her Earth witches were in the back, a bit further on the left from Angeline and Blanda. Thanks to their powerful Spirit magic, anchored through the ground, it was the perfect battle space, giving them enough speed and reflex to fight against wolves—or vampires, though the Alpha had none of those by his side. They were there as healers, if worse came to worst. By their side and surrounding the field were the Wind witches, whose job would be to carry any wounded with their air magic.

Angeline's last sneaky plan? Blanda, standing away from the center of the battle, used a subtle enchantment to give their troops an advantage in the snow-deep field. Only their enemies would feel the crushing weight of the snow beneath them. Angeline was proud of the idea; she had remembered the memoirs of a Russian general who fought against Napoleon during Waterloo. Why do you think Napoleon lost against the Russians? Napoleon didn't have witches with him—duh.

It was fascinating to watch Blanda work. Angeline had witnessed many spells in her short life, and even for powerful witches, it always took a toll on them. Not for Blanda. She wielded her spell craft with deadly precision and looked like she could do it all day.

Angeline knew the wolfmen were coming long before any vampire could sense them. It was her time to shine. She inhaled, arms stretching outward, eyes closed, and let her golden branches seek out the assigned leaders. Her magic was sharp and insistent as it entered their minds. Without hesitation, she let her magic take over—without a struggle, without an ache in her body. She was one, and her magic was part of her. She knew her engagement to Maros was to thank for her strength, but she would make sure *not* to tell him, or else he would brag about it for decades. She hoped he could feel it too—not that he needed to be stronger.

"They're coming. Biggest in the front, through the forest. Both sides have about a hundred."

She swallowed and reopened her eyes. Something disturbed her, but she could not put her finger on what.

Blanda glanced at Angeline, asking a silent question.

"Something feels wrong," Angeline whispered, stepping forward. She searched the field, eyes scanning the lines below for any sign of what was freezing her heart. It did not look like the plan she had shown everyone the day before.

"ANGELINE!"

Jack's voice slammed into her mind, and Angeline gasped, jerking her head eastward. She reached out telepathically, searching, calling for Jack as his voice echoed louder in her thoughts.

"PAUL IS MISSING. ALL OF THEM."

"Stop screaming, you idiot!" She said aloud. She really didn't need a headache because her brother didn't know how to communicate telepathically. She turned to Blanda and blurted out, "Jack says Paul's forces are missing."

Blanda rolled her eyes and muttered something sharp under her breath. "It's okay. We don't need him. Maybe he found out you put a price on his head." She laughed, and as if it was not important enough, she returned to her exhausting spell, her fingers crackling with energy as she poured her protection magic into their allies below.

Angeline nodded. Knowing Paul, it would be unsurprising if he decided to run away and let them deal with the war; he had always been a coward.

She tried not to think further about it when she saw it. Her eyes widened as her gaze returned to the field's far side. A deep, dark mass moved through the forest edge, spreading like a wave. Her heart stopped, and a cry escaped her.

Thousands.

She could barely see the edge of the Russian army. Bodies merged into a solid black shape that surged forward as they charged relentlessly to the frontline. Manus—obviously the vampire refused to leave the front row—and the American vampires stood their ground, ready for the fight.

Angeline shook with fear. She was relieved the leaders listened to her and left their werewolves in the back lines to protect the witches. Angeline had begged everyone not to throw the werewolves in the first line, which is what vampires used to do in previous wars. With those wolfmen, that was not a solution. It was too risky as a bite from their Alpha could transform them into one of them, and the last thing they needed was more wolfmen.

She caught Blanda's hand in hers, squeezing with her ice-cold fingers.

CHAPTER 31

ANGELINE

Ngeline and Blanda stood atop the cliff, staring
down at the battlefield. The sight was nothing short
of a nightmare. The two armies collided with a deafening
roar that echoed in their ears. As screams filled the air,
Blanda remained focused, her jaw clenched tight as she
continued casting the ancient spell to protect their army,
calling all elements to support her.

Angeline felt useless, more than she had felt in her life,
and that was saying a lot. She paced back and forth along
the cliff, not intending to disturb the witch but yearning
to yell into the void. If only she could contribute in some
way. Angeline may not be a fighter, but she had her snarky
She-Wolf bite. Perhaps she could pop in, bite, and pop out.

Blanda continued producing glowing blue symbols from
her fingertips. Her eyes narrowed. "Do not even think about

it. You will only disturb Maros and others who want to protect you."

Of course, the witch could tell what she was planning to do. "But I am so useless here!"

Blanda's face softened. "You're not a fighter, Angeline. It's okay to stand by and let others do the work for once. So, unless you tell me you can kill people without trying to grab their skin with your teeth, you're staying here." She waved her hands, focusing on the magic, before adding, "Seriously, Maros would go mad, which would make him lose focus. He's doing well." She smiled, proud and vile at the same time, her eyes reflecting a dangerous light.

"Psycho family," Angeline muttered.

Blanda laughed. "Welcome to your new family!"

Her feet steady on the cliff, Angeline moved her branches to reach those near Maros. Her magic propelled along the cliff, heading straight to where she knew she would find her lover.

Her heart rate sped up when her branches brushed him; she read the soldiers around him to get a glimpse. Handsome and already covered in blood, Maros was incredible to watch. His speed and precision showed he had been fighting for a long time, and worse, that he enjoyed it. There were no survivors on his path, only destruction and bloodshed, all while laughing.

"He just decapitated someone and laughed," Angeline grumbled to Blanda, who snickered, likely unsurprised.

Angeline focused back on Maros, trying to obtain a global image of him by mixing the different points of view. Now that was something new—reading more than two or three people at the same time was not something she usually enjoyed. But now? Nothing could stop her; it was as easy as breathing.

Maros came to a halt, his feet planted in the bloody ground, and sniffed the air. A low, rumbling growl rose from his chest.

MAROS

He turned on his heel to locate the disturbance.

The man who hurt his White Wolf. The Alpha.

Igor stood five feet away, shirtless and covered in even more blood than Maros. His fists clenched, and icy smoke flew around his head from his rapid breathing. He saw Maros, too. The tension in the air increased, nearly suffocating. His eyes flashed purple, and he knew it was due to shadow magic. Now surrounded by death, the darkness of the forbidden branch was obvious.

Well, that would explain why this motherfucker can create wolves.

"Scarface," Igor said, his voice a low rumble. He didn't move closer—he didn't need to, as the other fighters moved away from them. "I finally know who you are. Do you think you can beat me as a wolf, bastard?" Igor sneered, his lips curling back to reveal sharp teeth, longer than the average werewolf. "I'm the true Alpha. My bite creates more wolves and kills your species. What are you?"

A few members of his pack who were standing behind him, at a safe distance, rumbled with approval.

Maros smirked. "Old. I'm old."

With an infuriating calm, Maros's eyes locked onto the Alpha's, and he unfastened the buttons of his shirt.

ANGELINE

Angeline left the witness's mind, back to her position, and exhaled loudly. She turned to Blanda. "Your brother, who is 'doing good'"—she added air quotes to the comment — "is now shifting into a werewolf because the Russian dared him to."

Blanda's eyes widened. "Are you freaking kidding me? Men are just incredible, aren't they?"

"It's kind of hot," Angeline said, sneaking again into a soldier's mind to watch Maros.

"It won't be hot when the Alpha bites him. We don't know what happens then, Angeline. Who knows what that could do to my brother, or you, now that you are linked?" Blanda spat. "It's the full moon; Igor's bite can link wolves to him."

Angeline's heart sped up. Blanda was right; this was stupid. He was stupid. Her future husband was an idiot. But then, one does not survive 2,000 years while being an absolute dumbass, right?

It was too late to do a thing about it. Both men were on edge, ready to shift. The Alpha was the first to go while Maros continued his slow, deliberate striptease. He didn't even flinch at Igor's gruesome change. Angeline winced, disgusted. This is worse than any other werewolf shift, as if his body were unnaturally changing. She could almost hear the bones breaking and see the skin shredding into black smoke, revealing his fur. His nose elongated until reaching this wolf shape. Unlike other werewolves, he stood on his hind legs.

Then, it hit her. Something new sang to her, vibrating across her skin and raising her hair. Her magic. It could help. She inhaled and stepped forward, propelling her golden branches out, calling on all of nature's power. She reached Maros and pulsed her magic into him; he groaned under the new sensation. She wished he could see her. Instead of brushing the skin as she usually did, her golden branches were deep inside him, reaching his veins, his muscles, and his dead heart.

Maros turned toward her briefly, as if he were aware that something had happened. She could not see it with her eyes, but her mind still branched into soldiers around him. He smirked. A dangerous, powerful, gonna-make-a-mess smirk.

Without wasting another moment, Maros jumped, pushing toward the Alpha, who did not seem to know what to do with the naked man jumping on him. Maros started shifting during the flight, golden sparkles flying all around. His gigantic black furry wolf landed on Igor, pushing him into the snow. They rolled around, and Maros snapped at him.

Angeline giggled. The feeling inside of her was incredible; her magic combined with Maros's strength. He was unstoppable. *They* were unstoppable.

"Angeline, that was amazing!" Blanda exclaimed, nearly jumping with excitement.

Blanda's happiness was short-lived as she had to turn her attention back to the fight.

The battlefield erupted into chaos.

Screams. Growls. The clash of claws mixed with the slashing of bodies. Both armies battled around the Alphas. Above the cacophony, it was impossible not to get distracted by the roar of the two men, reverberating around the entire land, drawing every eye.

Igor, the so-called 'True Alpha,' was massive. His grey fur was so sparse it showed patches of skin. Unlike the fake wolves he created, he was fast, almost as fast as Maros. After the initial surprise at Maros's shift, he fought like a bull, jumping at Maros with his fangs aimed for his throat.

Maros met him mid-leap. His darker, stronger wolf did not show any signs of backing down. The two collided, a storm of claws and fangs that sent snow, blood, and dirt spraying in every direction. Their fight was brutal, primal, and unforgiving. Igor's strikes were powerful and precise, each swipe of his claws capable of drawing blood—if Maros were slow enough to let him catch up. His vampire blood mixed with his wolf was the reason why thousands feared him.

Angeline could not watch her lover anymore. She inhaled and looked for someone else to spy on. Vampires and wolfmen clashed in violent skirmishes, their roars and cries creating a macabre symphony. Despite their advantageous position on the battlefield, the ally werewolves were caught up in the fight, and some of their wounded were in too much pain to continue. Quentin and Misa were in the middle of the battle. Quentin howled and turned to Angeline, staring from afar as he spoke into her mind.

They need to leave. Call them. His instructions were simple; the urgency in his voice incited Angeline to act fast. She nodded, even though he probably could not see it, and used her magic to reach the mind of every wolf.

Wounded, fall back! Get to the witches! The command was blunter than necessary, but Angeline knew werewolves were a damn stubborn species. She saw why Quentin was in such a hurry to get the packs to safety. The flesh of the wounded was already blackening, the poison from the wolfmen's bites working through their veins. Only Igor could create, but his army? They could kill.

Thankfully, they listened and began retreating under the protection of other members of various packs. Icelandic witches transported the ones who were too shattered to walk.

Angeline's heart pounded in her chest; she recognized most of the wolves. Many were her friends. The witches welcomed them under their protection, but for how long? The wolfmen just had to breach the few rows of vampires standing between them and the wounded, and they would lose hundreds of ally wolves, not to mention the witches.

That's it. I'm not standing around. Magic Bite, here we come!

"Should I go as a wolf?" Angeline asked.

"You cannot be serious!" Blanda glared.

"I have to," Angeline pressed. "There are no other options."

"I don't know. Maros said your wolf was a bit useless."

"Yes, he did, and that was plain rude! My wolf's bite is the only thing that can save the wolves. How is *that* useless?"

"Healing is different from fighting. I just don't want to see you get hurt." Her voice faded at the end—it was clear her magic was taking a toll on her.

With a new determination, Angeline left, not giving Blanda a chance to stop her.

"I'm going with the witches!" Angeline yelled. "We can't lose so many werewolves. They need my magic."

"For fuck's sake—" The rest of Blanda's words were lost in the icy wind.

Angeline's feet barely touched the snow as she ran down the hill, with Blanda's magic propelling and protecting her. Her outfit was not the best for battle, but what she needed was her She-Wolf's nasty bite. She ran toward the witches and kicked off her boots, flinging her fur cape and dress out of the way. Angeline shivered, but it was not long before her She-Wolf took over, warming her and landing with grace.

CHAPTER 32

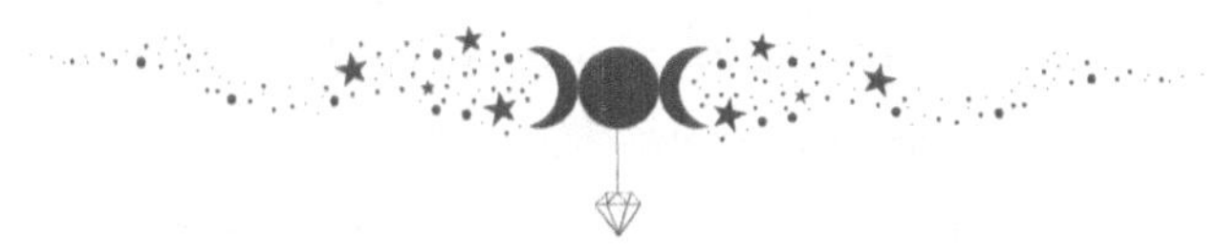

MAROS

The Alphas were locked in a vicious grip. Maros's teeth sank deep into Igor's shoulder. Blood laced with dark magic filled his mouth. A guttural growl erupted from Igor as he twisted, reaching Maros's flank with his claws, forcing him to release his grip.

Maros snarled when Igor stepped back, trying to hide behind dozens of his men.

Coward.

Maros knew he could win against Igor alone, but the wolfman was already trying to shield himself, using his monsters to protect him. Maros dug his back paws in the red snow and unleashed his fury, howling to the wind to grab everyone's attention.

ANGELINE

Angeline froze. She was busy giving soft bites to their wounded, immediately taking away the dark magic that flowed inside of them, and sending most straight back into the battle. Now, she couldn't move. She couldn't breathe. Her She-Wolf was immobile, searching for Maros, their Alpha. Her instincts screamed at her to run to him.

As a wolf, she never answered to an Alpha. Sure, Quentin was an Alpha and her friend, but he was not *her* Alpha. He swore allegiance to her, not the opposite. She finally spotted Maros in the battle, jumping, running, and slashing through the pack of wolfmen standing between him and Igor. Watching him, it was obvious he knew better than all of them how to fight, and his wolf was twice the size of any Russian wolf.

There was no returning to her work, despite Angeline's whispers to her damn fur ball. Her mouth was wide open when, from the corner of her eye, she saw Luna, one of Nanabrok's daughters, stop her incantation and turn. Luna gestured widely and sent a group of their enemies flying into the trees.

For fuck's sake, girl, focus! She yelled to her wolf.

Angeline was furious with the wolf for being distracted and taking over whatever they had left of common sense.

But most importantly, she was furious with herself for not spotting the enemies surrounding them. Her gift was useless since her mind was taken over by the thoughts of Maros and his hands on her body. Thankfully, the wolf was back to herself, and she growled, her fur erect.

Paul.

Paul's presence was a bad omen. He faced the witches, exhausted by their powerful healing spells.

It was too bad for Paul; Carata was also there. The ancient vampire must know something about hitting first because she didn't beg before slaughtering five of Paul's.

Angeline took a leaf from Carata's book—she did not want to talk to Paul. Instead, she crept into his mind, retrieving his memories, full of anger, shadows, and deals he made with Igor.

Traitor. Why am I even surprised?

She begged the wolf to hold back from jumping on him. It was one thing to attack a slow wolf who would die from your bite; it's an entirely other thing to take down a 500-year-old vampire. They weren't strong enough.

A scream resonated. Angeline shifted back to herself, shaking in the snow, and listened again, all her senses open.

"Blanda," she murmured.

Carata stopped her happy slaughtering, her eyes wide. She still held two vampires by their intestines.

"She's under attack. Go!" Angeline ordered.

Carata glanced around to judge the state of the witches fighting against Paul's men.

"Go, Carata!" Angeline yelled. "We'll be fine." Without waiting a second more, Angeline returned to her wolf form.

"Dammit all," Carata grumbled. "I'll be back." Carata ran away, leaving a trail of blood in the snow.

Paul's men laughed as they faced the White Wolf, towering over her like she was a puppy ready for a fight.

And she was ready.

CHAPTER 33

ANGELINE

A NGELINE DIDN'T SPARE ANOTHER thought for
Blanda. With her crazy vampire sister to protect her,
she had no doubt their enemies would have some regrets.

She had other concerns—the ones she considered her
people. Her witches, her werewolves. Some were healed
from the nasty bite, but they could barely stand on their
feet due to other wounds from the battle, added to the
darkness of the magic that had left their bodies.

Nanabrok reached her side, standing a few meters to
Angeline's right. Despite not being physically impressive,
the old witch was not to be messed with. Even Paul would
know that. Right? Nanabrok wore her usual purple coat,
glasses, and gigantic purple handbag. One would agree it
was not the best war outfit, but Angeline didn't judge; she
had seen what treasures the handbag could hide. Besides the
candies.

Angeline spotted close to thirty witches advancing in a half circle, surrounding them, and she knew her plan had failed.

He has witches. She spoke to Nanabrok, her telepathic voice cutting into her mind.

"Yes, he does," this one replied, not moving an inch, giving an unimpressed look to the Shadow Coven. Nanabrok paused to look at the witches, watching from above her glasses, as if daring them to try.

Angeline recognized a few faces. She had met some or had seen them in various memories. Most were witches denied by their coven following their practice of dark, forbidden magic. The purple eyes showed their link to shadow magic. They were all bound together, and worst of all, bound to Paul. Angeline could easily reach into their minds and see that some were nuns from various convents, all places of perdition.

I bet they knew Sister Agatha, she said to her She-Wolf, who growled, ready to slash throats.

It was with a slight strike of fear that she perceived something else. More wolfmen were coming their way. They broke away from the thick of the battle, where numerous enemies still surrounded the First brothers.

"Angeline," Nanabrok said. "I think it's time for you to show why Magical Virgins are to be protected and feared."

Nanabrok raised her arms to the sky and sang unknown incantations. One by one, she was joined by her coven, pulling themselves from any spell they were casting. They all linked hands.

The witches were calling the Spirits. Angeline felt it, and the call was impossible to resist. The beginning of the Earth, the magic flying through the wind, surrounding them. The most beautiful and intense feeling took over her, bringing tears to her eyes. Her Spirits.

Bowing her head, Angeline tried to take it all in. She anchored her paws in the ground, claws digging in as the power of nature, of her Gods, flowed through her. When she raised her head back up, snarling, her bright blue eyes glowed a vivid, otherworldly green, pulsating with a new energy.

She looked at her friends—the wolves—fighting valiantly against Paul's men. They strove to keep the enemy from breaching the protective barrier around her and the witches.

But Angeline didn't need protection anymore.

Big! Big! Big! We can be big! Her She-Wolf chanted inside her mind.

A snarl ripped from her throat, reverberating like a battle cry. The ground beneath her trembled, nature and Spirits answering the call of the witches. Her wolf stepped forward, power radiating from her in waves. Whatever Paul thought he had planned, whatever trick he'd thought to pull—she would end it.

Her transformation began as a tremor beneath the ground, shaking under the magic. Without a thought or an effort, her body started to change, shifting, her limbs elongating, a golden shine surrounding her in the purest form of magic. The

She-Wolf opened her eyes, towering above others as a gigantic White Wolf. The vampires barely reached the top of her leg.

Paul froze. He stopped laughing a while ago, when his witches failed to stop Nanabrok's coven. His usually smug face cracked as he took in the monster before him. His witches faltered, running—smart move—toward the trees, but Angeline didn't care about them. With a gesture of her head, she instructed the wolves left alive to chase them.

No, what she wanted was Paul's head.

She had heard enough tales of battles to know to take the victory when it was presented to her. She let out a thunderous growl and lunged forward, her gigantic claws breaching the first line of enemies as if slicing cheese. Vampires scattered, unable to match her strength; it was not every day that a giant wolf decided to take you down. Paul screamed orders, but it was too late.

Angeline's massive jaws caught him, clamping around his torso. Her fangs sank into his flesh slowly, deliberately. Paul howled in agony as she shook him like her dogs used to shake a toy, and she tossed him into the air. In a dexterous jump, she caught him before he hit the ground and shook him again, snarling at the taste of the blood in her mouth. Angeline knew he was gone when his body snapped in half. There was only so much someone could take, even when they were a vampire.

Nanabrok watched the carnage without saying a word, gnawing on some of her sweets. At Paul's snapping body in half, she let out a cackling laugh. "Serves him right."

The White Wolf let out a snicker mixed with a snarl. She didn't take time to appreciate Paul's death, her nose lifting into the air. Carata arrived, carrying Blanda, who was bleeding but well. Both had to bend their heads back to look at the giant wolf.

Carata chuckled. "Go tell them that size doesn't matter now."

Blanda rolled her eyes at her sister and advanced toward Angeline. "We're good here, Angeline. Go to my brother now. It's time to finish this war."

Angeline knew exactly what to do. It was as if the sun had finally cleared the darkness. There was no doubt anymore, no fear.

The She-Wolf bowed her head, closing her eyes, focusing. Her form shifted once more. Great wings sprouted from her back, white feathers that matched her fur. She stretched them, flickering them a bit to test them. With a victorious howl, she spread her wings out, casting a shadow over the snow.

"Was that necessary?" Carata yelled as Angeline leaped into the sky effortlessly.

Angeline glided with a natural elegance toward Maros. Her gigantic form shadowed everyone on the battlefield, receiving mixed reactions. Most were astonished. It was not every day that one saw a flying wolf. Angeline went straight for Igor, grabbing him in her jaw before flying in circles, ready to play again, before Maros quickly shifted back to himself, interrupting her.

"My Love, he's mine. Come on!" Maros protested.

Angeline circled, nagging him, still holding Igor between her teeth.

"Be a good bitey. Give the mean guy to me." Maros laughed when she threw the body at him. Igor landed on the snow with a sickening noise. Before Igor could get back on his knees, Maros stood behind him and ripped his head off. Dark blood and goo splashed onto the ground and Maros's hands.

Angeline landed in the middle of the battlefield, beside Maros, who was putting his pants on. When she hit the ground, she was back to her naked human self. Angeline walked the last few meters with confidence. Blood covered every inch of Maros's body. He saw her coming and let out a choking snarl, observing her. His eyes widened at the view of the wings sprouting from her back.

All armies had watched the previous scene silently. Vampires, werewolves, and wolfmen forgot about their fight. She took in the soldiers, spotting the friends and foes. Without saying a word, she stretched her hands, pushing her power into the enemies. They froze, immobilized, their expressions vacant, mouths hanging open in a silent scream.

The silence was absolute until Maros spoke. "My Love?" His eyes devoured Angeline.

In a strong voice, Angeline said, "What are you waiting for? Kill."

She watched with joy as her order was executed by all allies. Chaos returned to the battlefield, but it was not a fair fight for the enemies. She welcomed Maros's body against her.

"Do you think that's cheating?" Angeline whispered.

Maros laughed, squeezing her against him. "It definitely is, my Love."

Screams of victory echoed through the battlefield, and friends surrounded Angeline. To her relief, she spotted Jack trying to reach her, but the crowds around her and Maros were too thick for Jack to cut through. Maros was still holding her, arms wrapped around her waist possessively as if he had just realized how naked she was. All eyes were on her. Maros leaned over, brushing her lips, cold and tasting of blood. She could hear his desire; he was trying to refrain from taking her right there.

"I'm so proud of you, my White Wolf, my bitey," he murmured into her ear.

Angeline snorted, her cheeks flushing. Her body warmed itself in Maros's warmth. Before she could respond, a searing pain ripped through her mind. She gasped, breaking away from Maros and clutching her head.

"No!" she screamed, collapsing to her knees in the snow, not feeling the burn of the ice. The agony was unlike anything she had ever known, as if her brain was going to explode. Maybe this was it. Maybe she had overused her gift, and the Spirits were punishing her.

"Angeline!" Maros grabbed her shoulders, his face twisted with worry, while the rest of his siblings rushed toward them in a panic.

She couldn't answer. Her vision blurred. As her sense of hearing faltered, the pain intensified, and then it came: a sensation of growth rippling through her body, *pushing* through her body.

It hurts. It hurts. Make it stop! Her She-Wolf howled, but there was nothing to do. Something was growing out of her skin, pushing the protective layer on her skull, a flickering golden light shining all around her.

That's it, I'm exploding.

But she didn't. She opened her eyes, carefully, as the pain faded.

Whispers from the crowd filled the air, but also other voices. Voices that were neither vampire, witches, nor wolves. Spirits. Her Gods. Her gift-maker. She lifted her head toward Maros, who had a stupefied look. After a few seconds of silence, he gave her his hand, helping her rise. That's when she felt it. She touched her skull, and there was something new. Surrounded by the blood was a crown.

Angeline gasped, eyes widening.

"The spirits made their choice," Maros said, loud enough for everyone to hear. His voice did not tremble, and his expression shifted from fear to an indescribable pride. His sister gave him a cloak that he placed on Angeline's bare shoulders to shield her exposed body, then he shouted, "Long live the Queen!"

Anyone still standing dropped to their knees, repeating Maros's words, except Nanabrok, who murmured, "I'm too old for that shit."

Louis, the fool, also stood. His clothes were covered in blood. He did his part in the fight, that was for sure, but now his face reflected disgust and anger. He stepped forward, waving his hands. Jack tried to make him hear reason, but it did not work.

"This is unacceptable!" Louis roared. "The crown was meant for a man, not a queen—especially not her!"

Maros's expression went from mocking to dark. "Watch your next words carefully, Louis."

Louis sneered. "What will you do, little boy? She doesn't need you any—"

Angeline raised a hand, stopping Maros from jumping on the vampire. Her eyes locked onto her father, and with a flick of her wrist, the snow at her feet formed one long, pointy icicle. It broke from the frozen floor, hovered for a heartbeat, and shot toward Louis. The icicle pierced right into his cold heart. Louis gasped, his eyes wandering to his daughter, then his body crumpled to the floor. Gone.

Angeline smirked and turned to Maros. "Oops." She giggled.

CHAPTER 34

ANGELINE

THE PINK BLOSSOMS ON the cherry trees were the only proof of the time of year. Their gorgeous shade of pink could only make one feel joyful. It was even more joyous because it was the crowning day.

Not to mention the wedding.

Angeline lifted onto her tiptoes to capture one of the blossoms. The trees were located in the south garden of the Delacour mansion, and they were more gorgeous than ever, now that nature had taken back its rights. When Maros asked where she wanted to get married, Angeline knew just the place. She wanted to close the previous chapter of her life once and for all. She asked for the wedding to be held at the Delacour estate, which she took ownership of after the *tragic* accident that happened to Louis.

Despite her rage and broken heart, Isabeau bent at the knee to her new future King and Queen. After all, having a daughter as queen could be useful.

Maros joked at the time and asked if Angeline wanted to get married at the falls where they met, but she shut him up, devouring his lips.

"I'll save the falls for the wedding night," she had whispered.

As Angeline prepared for the wedding, Carata stormed into her peaceful space, pulling on her arm with no pity. "Come on. It's time to go."

"Carata! It's okay. I'm not going to be late." Angeline laughed, not even trying to resist the pull of the vampire.

"I'm not scared that you are going to be late, girlfriend, I'm scared you're gonna change your mind, and I will have to pick up my brother's heart in little pieces." She winked.

Of all the sisters she could have, Angeline was glad to have Carata and Blanda. They accepted her without an ounce of hesitation, without a shred of fear, despite her being a flying wolf. So did Manus. They loved her as she was, a powerful being, but with the flaws of a twenty-five-year-old woman. Her new family finally made her understand the concept of 'family,' making her realize it was okay to choose your own.

They reached their destination — Angeline's bedroom, and an army of maids activated themselves around them, gasping at the beauty of the dress and the jewels, gifts from Maros. They whispered tales of battles and flying heads. Even poor old Rose was there, but she did not bother moving around. Instead, she sat in an armchair, barking orders at the younger ones.

Angeline laughed. She enjoyed how her people behaved since Louis had gone; she would not dare tell Isabeau, of course. Angeline had broken her heart enough as it was.

Annabella, repatriated from Chicago, jumped on Angeline, and they hugged tightly.

"I knew you were a hugger deep inside," Annabella joked, pulling away from Angeline.

"Yeah. Look what you make me do," she retorted.

Angeline stopped breathing when she spotted her dress. She designed and sewed it herself, so there was no surprise, but damn, she was proud.

The gown featured an off-the-shoulder neckline framed with delicate lace, creating a soft and ethereal appearance. She had added rhinestones and diamonds to the lace, so tiny and shiny it looked like she had the night sky on her skin. Angeline did not doubt that Maros was going to be a fan of the naked shoulders, and she could not wait to feel his lips on her collarbone. The bodice had a draped, structured design that highlighted her thin waist, and she had embroidered the First Family symbol, a silver Celtic circle, which now included a triple moon inside. Her symbol.

The sleeves, also crafted from sheer lace and diamonds, extended from the bodice and reached down to the wrists. Her only hope was for her dress to survive the wedding night.

With her maid's help, she slid into the gown, enjoying the soft touch of the skirt. Flowing silk fell to the floor with an elegant train. It was perfect.

Angeline turned on her heel, enjoying the view in the mirror. Carata complained as she brushed her hair, finally looking satisfied with her artwork of curls, a savant hairstyle pulling Angeline's hair high. Her mass of curls was pushed to the side, revealing her bare shoulders and neck.

"You'll be lucky if your dress survives the night," Carata said.

Rose hushed her while the maids and Annabella giggled.

Angeline laughed. She took a deep breath, nodding to her maids, and stepped out of the bedroom. They didn't have long; the full moon was drawing near.

Reaching the top of the stairs, she spotted Manus waiting for her. His eyes took in the bride, but he jumped to a point behind her shoulder, where Annabella stood. The brunette was more gorgeous than ever in the lilac flowy dress Angeline had picked for her bridesmaids, the purple color contrasting incredibly with her ivory skin and ebony hair.

Thankfully, Angeline was not in the way of the lovers for long, as Jack arrived. He would be the one 'giving her away.' Jack pulled out his favorite costume for the occasion, an authentic pirate black jacket, which he had worn since the 17th century. Angeline rolled her eyes at the view but didn't say a word.

Angeline grinned victoriously as she approached her brother. He didn't speak—just offered his arm with the brightest smile. She swallowed hard but slipped her hand onto his arm. Her legs trembled with nerves, and she welcomed the support.

The grand ballroom was like something out of a dream—a vast space bathed in shimmering golden light, with crystal chandeliers suspended from a ceiling so high it seemed to touch the heavens. Leonardo DaVinci had painted it in 1895—yes, Leonardo was a vampire. The moon's light was strong, but one could barely notice the darkness outside the walls. The walls were draped in luxurious, deep violet silk for the occasion, reflecting the candlelight and the shine from above.

A gentle hum filled the air, voices murmuring in awe and anticipation as they turned to watch Angeline enter. Taking a deep breath, she advanced slowly. Her steps were measured and graceful, but one could see how tightly she held onto Jack's arm. Her gown flowed around her like liquid, elegantly floating behind her with each step. She kept her gaze steady, but her heartbeat was another story. When she saw Maros at the end of the never-ending aisle, she imperceptibly accelerated, forgetting everything else.

Maros stared at her with an intensity that made her shiver. His dark coat was embroidered with subtle silver threads, proudly displaying the triple moon his wife had stitched into it.

Jack gave her hand a gentle squeeze and released her, stepping back. She took Maros's hand in place of Jack's. A slight smile curved at the corner of Maros's lips, and he quickly kissed her shaking hand. They turned together toward Nanabrok, who was wearing her special cloak and had marked her face with symbols of old magic. Her piercing eyes took in both of them.

The room fell silent as Nanabrok began the ritual, not bothering to ask for silence. Everyone knew it was time to shut up. "Under the eyes of the night and the witnesses here gathered, we join two hearts, two fates, and bind them as one in eternity."

With a nod from Nanabrok, Maros lifted Angeline's hand to his lips. There was a pause, filled with anticipation, before he bit down. His fangs pierced the skin of her wrist in the same intimate way he used to in their bedroom. Angeline felt the pulse of her blood flowing into him, and she was lost for a moment in the sensation—a mingling of pain and something deeper that bound them irrevocably. The spell was working.

Manus gave Maros a sapphire-encrusted dagger.

Maros sliced his wrist and offered it to Angeline. She tasted him for the first time, her tongue slipping out hesitantly before her mouth clamped down. She watched him from under her eyelashes; she could not help but give him *the* look. He smirked in return.

Nanabrok's eyes gleamed as she held out the rings—more of a decoration. Angeline liked the concept of it, but they didn't need it for the spell. She chose a sapphire surrounded by diamonds, and Maros picked a simple silver ring. Maros took Angeline's hand and slid the cold ring onto her finger, his hands steady as his gaze locked onto hers, reaching her mind with his voice.

"My White Wolf, My Queen. I make you mine."

Under the crowd's surprised look, Angeline chuckled. "And I make you mine, My King." Angeline took his hand, sliding the matching ring onto his finger to seal their bond.

At Nanabrok's signal, they knelt before her. The room held its breath as she reached out, holding the twin crowns above their heads. Crafted in silver for Angeline and black metal for Maros, they were simple, but one could feel their powerful magic. With a solemn gesture, Nanabrok placed the crown upon Angeline's head first, then turned to Maros, setting the second crown on his head.

Angeline and Maros's eyes locked. His expression softened, and they rose together, hands clasped, as the room erupted in applause.

THE END

Thank you for reading and I hope you have enjoyed this story :) If you did, please consider writing a review on Amazon or Goodreads, it really does make a difference.

You can also find me on Instagram:
https://www.instagram.com/paulinewaltersauthor/

Do you want to know what's coming next? Subscribe to my newsletter:
https://paulinewaltersauthor.com

In the mood for a (funny) dark romance? Discover Dangerous Double-Jeu

In the mood for a werewolf erotica short-story? 30 Nights with the Alpha is waiting for you!

www.ingramcontent.com/pod-product-compliance
Lightning Source LLC
Chambersburg PA
CBHW051603100726
47898CB00001B/205